Cassie felt surrounded...

Brendan's maleness overpowered her as his dark head bent closer and the warmth of his breath touched her cheek, her lips. *No,* she thought, but before she could shove him away, his lips touched hers....

The taste of him, the smell of him—all overwhelmed her. His kiss was everything she had fantasized and feared it would be. And still she couldn't stop herself. The tiny bit of her mind that was still rational justified the foolishness. He'd be gone tomorrow, she thought. Where was the harm in a kiss?

But my God, what a kiss! When—and where—would it stop?

ABOUT THE AUTHOR

Before writing her first romance, Anne McAllister wrote short stories for children and book reviews. She holds a bachelor's degree in Spanish and a master's in theology, and is now a full-time writer. Born in California, Anne now resides in the Midwest with her husband and four children.

Books by Anne McAllister

HARLEQUIN AMERICAN ROMANCE

89—STARSTRUCK
108—QUICKSILVER SEASON

These books may be available at your local bookseller.

Quicksilver Season

ANNE McALLISTER

Harlequin Books

TORONTO • NEW YORK • LONDON
AMSTERDAM • PARIS • SYDNEY • HAMBURG
STOCKHOLM • ATHENS • TOKYO • MILAN

I would like to thank Dr. James Pearson, M.D.,
Dan Foster, Curriculum Director
of the Athletic Training Education Program
at the University of Iowa,
and Paul Padilla, trainer of the Los Angeles Dodgers,
for their time and help.
The expertise is theirs; any errors are mine.

To Janet,
who understands

Published June 1985

First printing April 1985

ISBN 0-373-16108-5

Printed in Canada

Chapter One

Dr. Cassandra Hart, M.D., might not have realized immediately that Lefty Craig, star major league pitcher, was actually Brendan Peter Craig, the plague of her youth, if she hadn't suddenly noticed the faint ragged scars on his rear end as she was picking out the gravel.

Of course, she thought later, the steady stream of cursing should have tipped her off. Brendan had certainly never minced words. But she hadn't seen him in almost fifteen years, and at first she was so preoccupied with setting his very nasty fracture and trying to cope with his questions about the future of his arm that she scarcely noticed much about the man himself. It wasn't until she had finished wrapping the cast from his fingers to the shoulder of his left arm and had turned to scrubbing his hip and thigh and finally to picking out the most stubborn bits of Pacific Coast Highway with forceps that she noticed the old scars and her eyes widened. Her hand froze in midair, a piece of gravel still clutched in the tips of the forceps, as her eyes moved from his bare bottom to the back of his dark head and down again.

"Is something wrong, Dr. Hart?" the attending nurse asked anxiously, edging the sheet that wasn't covering Lefty Craig even farther up his back, as if Cassie didn't have a good-enough view already.

"N-no." Cassie dropped the gravel carefully into the small stainless-steel tray and moved back to probe for another piece. But first she peered closely once more at the black head lying above the sheet at the top of the hospital gurney, trying to glimpse the face that was barely visible even in profile due to the heavy thatch of dark hair across his forehead and a thick, equally dark mustache. The Brendan Craig she had known also had had black hair, a scraggly mop of it, rarely cut and so roguish looking that it always made him appear even fiercer and more intrepid than he was. And even as a teenager he had been quite fierce and intrepid enough, thank you, she recalled with a shiver. Surely this couldn't be! But she felt a prickling awareness all the way down her backbone that she hadn't experienced in years. Fifteen, to be exact.

It would be just like Brendan Craig to do something dangerous like bang himself up in a motorcycle accident in Malibu at 2:00 A.M. And those scars... She stared down at them again, and the forceps slipped.

"Cripes, what're you using, lady? A pitchfork?"

Cassie smiled ironically. Not "doctor," she thought. Never that. "Lady," in the most scathing tones possible, was the politest thing he had called her since she had been summoned to set his arm. And at first she didn't think he was even going to let her do that.

"Phillips," he had growled through teeth clenched with pain when he had seen her come through the emergency-room door. "Nobody touches my arm but Phillips." Navy-blue eyes, glazed with pain, glared at her. "I want Phillips."

Cassie did, too, at that point. Gene Phillips, her partner, was team physician for the Mustangs. He liked dealing with jocks; bone spurs and damaged knees enchanted him. They didn't do a thing for Cassie. She was a wrist and hand specialist, content to care for piano players with smashed hands and typists with arthritic fingers. Athletes didn't interest her, and for the most part they didn't sustain injuries that she had to deal with. But one look at Brendan's wrist and she knew that even if Gene had been in town that night, he would have called her in, anyway. With his baseball players he always called in the best available, and for wrists Cassie Hart was tops. All the same, she wished he had been there, too. A little professional moral support would have been nice.

"I'm a specialist," she told Lefty Craig firmly. "Dr. Phillips would have called me, anyway." She didn't wait to listen to any more of his protests, just finished scrubbing up and giving quick instructions to the nurses who would be helping her. "All right?" she asked him finally, not really looking at him other than as an arm in need. She tightened the elastic cuff on his upper arm and shot pain-killer in below it.

He winced, his face white with agony. "All right," he rasped. "Get on with it then, if you can," he added, with as much bad grace as he could muster.

Cassie had got on with it, but it had taken three nurses holding and steadying him and every ounce of strength she possessed before she was satisfied that his bones were properly realigned. She took another X ray to be sure. Not for the first time did she wish she had chosen dermatology or another less strenuous medical specialization. Well, she reflected now as the forceps glinted silver in the bright hospital light, tonight she had got dermatology, too. You couldn't get much more dermatological than scrubbing out the skin abrasions on someone's bare bottom.

What kind of idiot would ride a motorcycle in jogging shorts, Cassie wondered, then answered her own question immediately: Brendan Craig.

She finished the largest abrasion and moved alongside his thigh so that she would reach more easily the one closest to the ragged scar. "Dog bite?" she asked, carefully steadying her voice, though she felt her heart quicken as her gloved finger traced it lightly down his firmly muscled buttock. Of course, she thought, it might *not* be Brendan, but how many men named Craig were there with nicely stitched up teeth marks on their rear ends?

"How'd you guess?" he muttered through clenched

teeth, shifting under the probe of her unrelenting forceps.

"A course in med school." Now was not the time, she decided, to tell him that the competent Dr. Hart who had so ably set his fracture and was now engaged in impersonally removing grit from tender portions of his anatomy was the same Cassie Farrell whose Labrador retriever had sunk her teeth into his posterior at Leadbetter's Beach sixteen years before.

"Oh?" He shot her a skeptical look, flinching as her fingers grazed the scar again.

"They taught us how to recognize all kinds of skin tears," she went on lightly, just as if she weren't thinking, *My God, it is!* "Bottle gashes, dog bites, knife wounds." He'd probably had them all by now, judging from the way he'd been behaving when she knew him. She dabbed antiseptic on the two raw patches she had finished with, and Brendan jerked under her touch.

"Don't make jokes, lady," he growled into the pillow. "Just get on with it so I can go home."

Cassie looked up from his bloody abraded thigh and stared at the back of his head. "You're the one who's joking if you think you're going home today. Or even this week."

Brendan's head whipped around. A darkly mustached mouth scowled, and one blue eye glared at her over his tanned shoulder. "What the hell do you mean? You set my arm, didn't you? What's to keep me? I've got things to do."

"Unless you're a stand-up comedian as well as a pitcher, Mr. Craig," Cassie said bluntly, waving a piece of gravel in the forceps for effect, "you're not going to be doing anything for quite some time." She turned to the nurse hovering by the door staring at Cassie's patient with a mixture of sympathy and, as far as Cassie was concerned, wholly unnecessary awe. "Call admitting and get Mr. Craig a room in orthopedics," Cassie told her.

"No," Brendan snapped.

Cassie shrugged and began scrubbing another abrasion. "Pediatrics, then. Hold still." Obviously he hadn't changed a bit. Thank God he hadn't recognized her. Yet. Grimacing as she thought what he would say when he did, she scrubbed harder.

"That hurts, damn it!" Brendan snarled as though he hated to admit it. "What the hell do you think I am, a floor?"

"I'm convinced you're not a floor," Cassie assured him, scrubbing as though he were. "Floors don't talk back."

"You sure you're a doctor?" he demanded.

"Of course I'm a doctor," she snapped, nettled to think that he, like so many others, would think that women should only be nurses. "Why shouldn't I be?"

"You've got the bedside manner of a porcupine."

Cassie knew her face flushed. She ducked her head, continuing to pick at his wound, ostensibly looking for gravel but actually avoiding his probing stare. How humiliating that he was right! And how much worse to know that such prickly behavior was not usually her way at all. Of course, she rationalized, being dragged out of bed in the middle of the night hadn't improved her disposition, but she had been perfectly congenial to her previous patient, a drunk who had stumbled down the steps when he left the bar and broke his ankle. In fact, Cassie was usually the sweetness-and-light member of the team. It was Gene who habitually grumped and growled and slapped patients on the rear like a football coach sending them back into the game. But you'd never know it from the way she was reacting tonight! She shook her head, trying to escape a strand of gingery hair that had edged out from beneath her green surgical cap. Tonight she was behaving with all the savoir faire of a gauche schoolgirl—which was exactly what she had been in her previous encounters with Brendan Craig.

"Forgive me," she said, trying to keep her voice level and calm. "I'm not always at my best at three in the morning. There." She finished daubing antiseptic on the last of his abrasions and pulled the sheet over him, unable to resist taking one last peek at the dog-bite scar before she covered him up. "Ms. Traynor will take you upstairs and get you settled. I'll be up before I leave to check on you again." She lifted her eyes to meet his only long enough to give him her best professional smile. Then she darted out of the room, the stainless-steel tray still clutched in her hand.

Not a moment too soon, she thought as she set the tray on the equipment cart. Another few seconds and her trembling hand might have dropped it. She took a great gulp of air, as if that might settle her rattled emotions, and stared after the gurney as it disappeared down the hall carrying Brendan Craig.

Damn it, what was he doing back in her life? For thirteen years, from the time she was four until she was seventeen, Brendan had inspired a wider range of emotions in her than anyone else had. She didn't like it; she never had. He confused her, attracted her, set her on edge. He messed up her life. And judging from her trembling hands and racing heart, things hadn't changed a bit.

It was just like him to drop from the blue—gone one minute, there the next. But if he was as big a baseball star as all the hospital whispers and mutterings seemed to indicate, why hadn't she recognized who he was before then? Admittedly, she was not a baseball fan, but her late husband, Michael, had talked about the Mustangs sometimes, and her sons, Keith and Steven, went on about them endlessly. Surely she would have put things together. But no, she scarcely remembered hearing about anyone called Lefty Craig, and she had certainly never connected that name to the dark-haired nemesis of her childhood. She frowned. She couldn't remember Gene Phillips mentioning him, either. Perhaps he had never been injured before. A glance at his chart seemed to support that theory. It was new. The only things it told her were things she already knew—his name, his age, thirty-two, and his birthplace, Santa

Barbara—and an address in Marina del Rey. Not much at all.

"So where did he come from?" she wondered aloud.

"Philly," an emergency medical technician named Dave said.

Cassie looked up, startled. "What?"

Dave shrugged. "I thought you were askin' about Craig. He come from Philly. Mustangs got him in a trade this spring." He shook his head, dismayed. "Ain't gonna do 'em much good, is he? Not now."

Cassie shook her head. "Not for a while," she agreed. Philadelphia? Well, at least that explained why she hadn't heard of him. She couldn't even get excited about the local team. She was surely excused for not knowing of his success if he was achieving it a whole continent away. The very fact that a roughneck like Brendan, whose whole aim in life, as far as she could remember, had been to see how much hell he could raise, had become a success absolutely amazed her. It disconcerted her a bit, too, but she pushed that thought right out of her mind.

"Is he gonna be all right?" Dave asked, concern furrowing his brow. "He *will* pitch again?"

"I'm sure he'll be all right," Cassie hedged. She meant by that, that she was sure his bones would knit properly. Whether they would ever be able to sustain the pressure required to throw a baseball at nearly ninety miles per hour was beyond her power to guess. That was Gene's area of expertise. He could decide what Brendan's future would be far better than she could; and she wouldn't be doing anyone any favors to cause speculation and rumor at this point.

"You'll check on him?" Dave urged as she finished writing her notes and gave Brendan's chart back to the nurse.

"Yes." Because it was standard procedure, not because she wanted to see him again, that was for sure! Gene couldn't return from South Africa fast enough.

As soon as he did, Brendan was going to be his patient. From the sound of Brendan, she didn't imagine he would give her much argument.

"Make sure he gets lots of rest," a pretty young aide told her as she turned to go. "He's gorgeous, don't you think?"

Cassie just stared. The last thing she wanted to think about—or talk about—was Brendan Craig's looks or their effect on her. "He looks worn out," she said noncommittally. "Yes, I'll tell him to rest."

"Do that," the nurse said.

"You too, doc," Dave added. "You look pretty beat yourself."

Cassie's mouth turned into a tired smile. "Compliments. Compliments."

"I don't mean you look bad," he said hastily, and lifted a roguish eyebrow that Cassie frowned at. "Just that you look tired. You work too hard, doc."

Cassie sighed. "You may be right." It wasn't the first time someone had told her that or that she had thought it herself. But it went with the territory. She hadn't worked for years to become a doctor so she could play golf, for heaven's sake! She tugged off the surgical cap and loosing a riot of gingery curls, raked her fingers through them. "I'll see you all in the morning," she said. "Or should I say, 'In a couple of hours'?"

Dave glanced at the wall clock, grimacing at its reading of almost four in the morning. "Enjoy your catnap, doc," he said with a grin.

"I intend to," Cassie promised. "Just as soon as I check on our Mr. Craig."

What would he say, she wondered as she ducked into one of the doctors' dressing rooms to doff her lab coat and comb her hair, when he discovered who it was who had set his arm? She was certain that he had no idea that the former Cassie Farrell, whom he had baited and teased throughout childhood, was now the Dr. C. F. Hart whose name appeared on the office door below Gene's. Unless he had come for a physical, she doubted if he had even been to the office, so he might not have even seen her name at all. Of course, Brendan knew she was going to become a doctor. Lord, he had teased her about it often enough when they were growing up. "Dr. Cassie the Bandage Lassie," he used to chant mockingly until she thought she would scream. But he probably hadn't followed her career any more than she had followed his. In fact, after the incident of the dog bite, which could still make her grin even now—served him right for snatching her bathing-suit top and running!—they had had as little to do with each other as possible. With luck he wouldn't have thought of her in years.

She had on occasion thought of him and wondered what he was doing. She had certainly never guessed he would become a professional athlete. Her mouth curved into a grin at the thought of Brendan as a ballplayer. Who'd have ever guessed he would put all that rock throwing to such a productive end? Trust Brendan to make piles of money at a child's game. She could just imagine what his straitlaced theology-professor father must have said about that. All she could remember of Dr. Hamilton Craig from her childhood was his stern scowl as he implored Brendan again and again to "grow up." Obviously, Brendan never had, she thought as she finished brushing her hair and put the brush back into her purse. Pity. He would certainly have to now. And with that thought she zipped the purse shut and headed for the elevator to the orthopedic floor.

Once in the elevator, committed to seeing him again in scant moments, her emotional collywobbles returned. Why, she asked herself. What's he to you? A good question. There was absolutely no reason for Brendan Craig to have any effect on her life now whatsoever. Except, she acknowledged ruefully, that just seeing him again had reduced her to a gibbering idiot. And why is that, she asked herself just as severely.

Because, she thought, *I never know what he's going to do next.*

And?

She stared at the elevator doors, refusing to think about that.

And, her stubborn little inner voice prodded.

And, she thought sighing reluctantly, *he is still the most gorgeous guy I've ever met.*

Aha.

Aha, nothing, she thought, annoyed. No one knew better than she that looks weren't everything. So what if Brendan was as appealing as a triple-decker hot-fudge sundae; he was about as good for her, too. *Chin up,* she told herself, straightening against the functional metal wall of the elevator. *Feet on the ground. If you still think Brendan Craig is a hot-fudge sundae, chances are you're still a carrot in his mind, too.*

"Just remember that," she cautioned herself out loud as the elevator doors slid open to admit her to the orthopedic floor.

Brendan had been assigned the last room on the corridor, which allowed her plenty of time to practice keeping her chin up and her feet on the ground. But she felt her resolve fading, rapidly overcome by an influx of butterflies in her stomach, by the time she reached his room. There was no one else around, and the door was nearly shut. Cassie pushed it open gently, grateful for the single strip of indirect fluorescent lighting that gave her a dim view of the high hospital bed in the center of the room.

Brendan was lying on his side facing the door, his plastered arm held high on a pile of pillows, a thin sheet draped loosely over his hips and legs. He looked awkward and uncomfortable even in his sleep, and Cassie's professional demeanor crumbled further. She hovered in the doorway momentarily, mustering her courage. Then, scraping it together—what, after all, could he do to her now? she chided herself—she crept quietly over to the edge of his bed. The closer she got, the more his very presence drew her. As if she had no more will than a pin pulled by a magnet, she thought with dismay.

Still, her eyes feasted on the sight of him, seeking signs of the boy he had been in the man he had become. She found them. The line of his nose was still slightly crooked from the day he had broken it bodysurfing. His thick black eyelashes were still longer than any man's had a right to be. And in the hollows of his cheeks and the firm line of his mouth beneath the very adult mustache, she found hints of boyish innocence that she was sure were as deceptive now as they had been when he was a child. Her eyes left his face, following the line of white plastered arm to where the pillow rested against his chest. What she could see of it was strong, muscular, dusted liberally with dark hair in which nestled a tiny gold medal that glinted even in the dim light. Her fingers itched to touch it. She shook her head firmly.

Cassandra Farrell Hart, get a grip on yourself, she ordered. Daft adolescent infatuations ought to be left where they belonged. In adolescence. Besides, she reminded herself, her brief infatuation with Brendan Craig hadn't been very sensible even there. He hadn't been her type then, and she only had to look at him to know with certainty that he still wasn't now.

He groaned, shifting awkwardly, his arm slipping off the pillows to fall against the bed rail. Instantly, Cassie lifted it, edging it gently back onto its perch. Her knee clanked against the metal of the bed frame, and she pulled back hurriedly. Too late. Brendan opened his eyes.

"How are you feeling?" she asked awkwardly, her attempt at professionalism suddenly eclipsed by the pain and drugged confusion she saw in his dark eyes.

The eyes widened disbelievingly, then narrowed as he tried to focus on her with his drug-fogged brain. "Marigol'?" he croaked.

Cassie's heart lurched. It hadn't always been carrots he had compared her to, she remembered. "Some girls look like roses," he had once teased her. "And some like lilies. But you're the only marigold I've ever met."

And he had ruffled her gold-orange mop of hair. For once the memory didn't nettle her, and she smiled, just a tiny smile, almost a wistful one, enchanted with his irrepressibility, and reached out to touch his cheek gently. He wouldn't remember. The next day it would be nothing more than a hazy dream.

"You'll be all right, Brendan," she said softly, a concern she didn't want to feel welling up inside her, unbidden. Of course he would be. Nothing could stop Brendan Craig.

His fingers groped out from beneath the sheet and fastened onto hers. The touch of his hot, callused fingers sent a stab of exhilaration right through her, making her heart beat crazily and her lungs cry out for air. "Cassie?" he murmured, his voice still fuzzy and incredulous.

"Hmm?" Tomorrow she would regret this, but tonight...tonight...

His fingers tightened. "Cassie." A satisfied smile fleetingly lit his face, and his eyes fluttered closed again. "It's about time," he mumbled hazily. Then, still smiling, he drifted into sleep.

About time? About time for what? Even when he was drugged senseless he could still discomfit her, Cassie thought irritably as she drove home through the dawn-lit streets, slick with unseasonable rain. Damn. And damn him for recognizing her! It was her hair, of course. The kinder people remarked on it for its startling gold halo effect; the discreet ones—the majority—said nothing, just stared. Only Brendan had called her "Ol' Marigold" until she thought she would lose her mind.

The trouble, she remembered, was that there was nothing about Brendan that she could use to retaliate with. If he'd had zits or big ears or been uncommonly clumsy, she would have given as good as she got. But what could she say about a rugged boy with hair like a raven's wing, eyes like blue lagoons and a body that put the models in her father's anatomy books to shame.

And now, she thought with no satisfaction at all, he looked even better. Was there no justice?

She turned into the driveway of her low-slung, Spanish-style house, remembering with disgusting clarity how cute he had been even when he was five years old. It was probably his devilish grin that had first attracted her to him—that and his offer to let her hold his pet tarantula. She wrinkled her nose, remembering Horace. Letting her hold Horace was the last nice thing he had done for her, and even then he seemed shocked that she hadn't taken one look at the spider, shrieked and run away. *I probably should have,* she thought wryly. *Then maybe he wouldn't have spent the next thirteen years trying to shock me.* Fat chance, she thought as she got out of the car and locked the door, not really seeing the flagstone walk or the thick bougainvillea that climbed the trellis by the front door. Instead, her mind was filled with visions of gap-toothed grins and sparkling mischievous eyes that caused her to shiver years before she had any idea why. "He's so cute," her friend Nancy, who was light-years ahead of Cassie in the interpersonal-relationships department, had said. So who would have thought that such a cute little boy would have deliberately spilled Hawaiian punch down the front of her dress at Bobbi Boone's seventh birthday party? Well, probably Dr. Hamilton Craig might have, she admitted as she let herself in the front door. He had always been suspicious of his son's innocent grins, but the neighborhood mothers hadn't been so wise.

"Brendan Craig? A delightful boy!" She could remember her own mother uttering that very absurdity the day after Cassie had fallen out of the eucalyptus tree while trying to get her bike down. Three guesses who had hung it there. Of course, his stock had taken a decided drop with the local mothers once he had got old enough to date their daughters. Then he was wilder than wild. But Mrs. Farrell hadn't had to worry about Cassie. Cassie Farrell was definitely not Brendan Craig's sort of girl.

"All brain, no bust," he had described her to their assembled journalism class in high school, causing Cassie's face to go a fiery red that did not at all enhance her unusual hair. She had wanted to say what she thought all of him was, but she valued her citizenship grade far too much. It seemed to her that Brendan valued nothing at all.

Except maybe busts. He seemed to have a thing for them, she remembered as she kicked off her Topsiders in the entry hall and padded down the thickly carpeted hallway past the boys' room and her mother's to her own. Every girl he went for in those days had been well endowed. Bobbi Boone, for example. Brendan, grinning like a fool, had called her Bobbi Boobs, but it didn't stop him from dating her. Cassie wondered if he was still looking for big-chested women. Or had he found one?

She flicked on the lamp beside her wide bed and began tugging off her bright blue French-cut T-shirt, frowning at her still-underendowed bosom. It wasn't much even now, but Michael hadn't minded. But then Michael had generally been preoccupied with other things. Highly skilled, dedicated cardiologists like Mike were above that. He was gifted, driven almost, and if he hadn't had much time to be a husband and lover, neither had Cassie had much time to be a wife. They had had two sons, two thriving practices and virtually no time for each other. In fact, in retrospect, she wondered if their marriage would have lasted if Michael hadn't died two years before in a plane crash.

Was Brendan married, she wondered. There hadn't been any sign of a wife at the hospital. No relatives at all. No friends. Hadn't he had anyone to call? That didn't sound like Brendan. A loner he was not. She eased out of the jeans she had slipped into when they first called her from the emergency room hours before and pulled a sheer nightgown over her head. What had caused his accident, anyway? He hadn't been drinking; that was clear. Good, she thought wryly. Maybe there was hope for him yet. Accustomed to always thinking the worst where Brendan was concerned, she was relieved not to have to think that alcohol was one of his problems. She sighed and slid between the sheets, reaching over to turn the bedside lamp off. *Stop thinking about him at all,* she advised herself. There were enough other things to think about—the fact that she was going to have to get up again in scarcely more than an hour for one thing, that she had a full schedule of office patients and two surgeries the next day for another, and, oh, yes, Keith's baseball game. She had missed the last one due to an emergency, and he had been very understanding. She didn't want it to happen again. Keith was very dedicated to baseball.

Just wait, she thought with a wry grimace, until he heard that his mother went to school with Lefty Craig! *Stop thinking about him!* This time it was an order. She rolled onto her side, punching her pillow into submission. In fifty-nine minutes the alarm would go off, and life would start up again. Another day just like the last one. Too much work, too many demands, too little time. She closed her eyes and saw again the faint scars, the navy-blue eyes, the thick mustache, silky and soft.

No, it would not be a day just like the last one. They never were when they had to do with Brendan Craig.

Chapter Two

Raw... Stiff... Aching... Brendan tried to turn his head, to move his shoulder, to blink his eyes. Anything. Nothing. There was nothing about him that didn't hurt. *Hurt?* Hell, that didn't even begin to cover it. He felt as if he had been beaten and left for dead. Death, he thought, once he had marshaled enough words for a coherent thought, would probably be preferable to this.

The night before, he had been dead. He was sure of it because he had seen Cassie. How else would he have come to see her again after all these years? Cassie Farrell had haunted him for years—her gamine grin, intense eyes and blazing tangled curls mocking him at the damndest times. Trust her to haunt him even after death! God, and she had been so real. She had even touched him. Her fingers had been cool against his cheek, and there had been the faint smell of spring flowers as she had bent over him, telling him softly that he would be all right.

All right? He pried open one eyelid and gazed about a strange, impersonal, institutional yellow room. A hospital room. What had happened? He grimaced, trying to force his muzzy, reluctant brain to figure it out. Dog. He could remember a dog. Barking. Running crazily into the street. Rain. Slick pavement. And, oh, God, yes, the motorcycle. It all came back then—the terrier racing into the street, chasing him as he rode past, veering in front of him. Then he remembered swerving on the wet street, losing traction in the damp gravel of the shoulder, the sense of losing control, of helpless flying, smashing, scraping.

His eyes focused on the thick white plaster covering his arm. *His pitching arm.* Bile rose in his throat, and he swallowed hard, trying desperately not to be sick.

Why wasn't he dead, he wondered achingly. Then at least he would have had Cassie.

"Ah, you're awake, Mr. Craig," a voice interrupted, and a white-garbed behemoth loomed into view. "What a lucky man you are," the nurse went on as she laid out a tray of suspiciously nasty-looking equipment and popped a thermometer into his mouth. She bobbed around his bed, fussing at him like a giant broody hen, until Brendan thought he would get ill just watching her, so he shut his eyes. "Don't go to sleep on me now," she admonished. "We need to get you all cleaned up for the doctor."

Brendan tried to remember the doctor. It hadn't been Gene Phillips; he knew that. He had wanted Phillips, had demanded him and had got some smart-mouthed hag instead. "A specialist. Dr. Phillips's partner," a nurse had reassured him. All the same, he hoped she wasn't the doctor this biddy with the voice like a bassoon had in mind. She whisked the thermometer out of his mouth, clucking over his temperature, and he prayed that she wouldn't try whisking him around the way she did the thermometer. He could guarantee her the howl of a lifetime if she did.

Thankfully, she was more gentle when it came to moving him. She oohed and aahed over his scraped-up body, making him feel as though she, at least, appreciated the scope of his pain as she eased him over enough to strap a blood-pressure cuff on his arm.

"Whi-which is my doctor?" he managed. God, even his vocal cords hurt! "Phillips?" He nodded hopefully.

"No. He's still out of town. You have Dr. Hart."

Heart, huh? Her name was probably the only one she had. "The one who set my arm?" he pressed.

"Yes. She'll be along any time."

"Swell." Now he would have to ask her all the questions he had been saving for Phillips. Gene, being team physician, would have been able to answer him easily. He imagined the hag, even if she knew the answers, would enjoy making him pry them out of her. Well, at least she must be a good doctor, he told himself grudgingly; otherwise, a man with a reputation like Gene Phillips would never work with her. He just hoped she knew something about how to treat a pitcher. He needed to know how long he would be there, how long he would have to remain in a cast, when he could begin therapy and start throwing again. It was his future, for God's sake! The nurse lifted off one of the dressings on his hip, and he winced.

"Jeez, be careful, lady," he snapped, jerking away from her touch.

She scowled at him, then looked up over his shoulder and smiled. "Ah, doctor, come in. We're just now ready for you," Brendan heard her say, and he twisted his torso as best he could to look over his shoulder to glare at the hag. The night before he hadn't been able to hold his own at all. He had so much pain and so much medication he was all but incoherent. But if she thought she could intimidate him that day... Well, that was another story.

But his intentions collapsed, and his mind somersaulted at the sight of the slender woman in the tailored, pale blue linen suit and white silk blouse who was checking over a chart as she came through the door.

"Ca-Cassie?"

Dr. Heart? The hag? It couldn't be. But if not, this woman was Cassie Farrell's twin—a regal-looking, poised twin, with her marigold curls disciplined into a tight French twist and her freckles masked with whatever women used to camouflage such human flaws. She was jotting something down on the chart as she approached; she hadn't looked up yet. When she did, if her eyes were pools of intense jade, then—*then* he would know.

She did. They were. He caught his breath.

Cassie smiled, a cool, professional smile, not at all the sort he had dreamed about—or had thought he had dreamed. Had it been real?

"Yes, it's me, Brendan," she said matter-of-factly, her voice calm and steady, betraying none of the turmoil he himself felt. She set the chart on the bedside table and reached for his free wrist, taking his pulse with total concentration. Then she lifted her eyes briefly. "How do you feel?"

Stunned. Wiped out. "Okay," he croaked, managing a shaky grin, though he still reeled under the impact of seeing her in the flesh and not just in his imagination. He wondered what kind of reading she had got from his pulse. His heart was racing like a bolting horse! "I can't believe it's you."

"Dr. Cassie the Bandage Lassie?" she said with a smile of wry self-mockery that succinctly reminded him of all his youthful taunts. His ears burned. "None other," she said easily, dropping his arm back onto the sheet. Then, with utmost care, she lifted his plastered arm from the pillow pile. He couldn't stop the groan that escaped his lips as his whole body tensed.

Cassie's expression softened. "You're still having a lot of pain," she acknowledged, her gentle fingers touching his swollen, throbbing ones. "Can you make a fist?"

He tried; his fingers barely moved. Encased in plaster only as far as his first knuckle, they felt painfully immobilized clear to the tips. "I can't," he muttered, tasting defeat. How could he ever hope to pitch?

"You're not doing too badly," she approved, running her fingers over the tips of his. "Can you feel that?" He nodded, fingers tingling, whether from Cassie or from his sense of touch, he wasn't sure.

"Watch him for more swelling," Cassie said to the nurse. "You can have them split his cast if you need to.

Now—" she turned back to Brendan and took a deep breath "—let's have a look at the rest of you." She lifted the sheet covering him so that the cool air hit his raw, exposed hip. He watched her closely, her professional concentration unnerving him. He'd always known that she had intended to follow in her father's footsteps and become a doctor; her single-minded dedication had been one of the most irritating things about her. But she had also been incredibly shy and naive, a perfect object for a boy who liked to tease. But he couldn't see any signs of the shy, naive Cassie Farrell now. What had happened to the girl who had practically blushed at the sight of him without a shirt and the one who had handed her father the sutures to sew up his rear end with her eyes averted all the while?

His mouth curved into a remembering grin as he watched her now. Her slim hands betrayed only the slightest tremor as she examined him. It might be coffee jitters or even lack of sleep, but he chose not to consider that. He preferred to think that he was affecting her, after all.

Her soft fingers slid down his thigh, turning him to get a better look at one of the abrasions. Gentle, cool hands on hair-roughened skin. He bit his lip as a current of desire surged through him. God, did she have any idea what she was doing to him? He shot her a quick glance.

No, none. She was studying him with about as much interest as she had the slides of dead cell tissue in their shared biology class. He, on the other hand, had never felt less like dead cell tissue in his life! And Cassie had only to roll him back over onto his side and she would have a very good view of why not.

She did, a dark red flush staining her cheeks. Pulling the sheet over him hastily, Cassie groped for his chart. "Not too bad, considering," she said in clipped tones.

Brendan smiled. The girl who could blush was still there. "Considering what?" he asked, a suggestive grin lurking at the corners of his mouth.

"Considering the way you looked just a few hours ago," Cassie snapped. Then, as if the memory of his accident rose in her mind, the flush vanished abruptly, leaving her pale and with intense eyes that were now the wide green pools of compassion about which he had dreamed. "You could have been killed," she said in the barest whisper of a voice. Then, just as quickly, she blinked and seemed to recollect herself. "But then you always did have more lives than the proverbial cat."

Brendan's grin, which had faded at the sight of her distress, appeared again. "Fate," he told her blithely. "I had to survive so I could meet you again."

"Garbage," Cassie replied, ducking her head to avoid his gaze, just the way she had done a thousand times in the past.

"You knew Dr. Hart?" the behemoth asked, staring at him with amazement wreathing her leathery face.

"Intimately." Brendan winked at her. Cassie's teeth snapped shut with a decided click. Just like old times. He smirked at her, satisfied that in essence she hadn't changed.

"Mr. Craig is on heavy pain medication," Cassie told the nurse sharply. "His mind wanders. You can't account for anything he says. We knew each other briefly as children."

"Ah." The nurse nodded, unconvinced, her gaze moving speculatively from Cassie to Brendan.

"I wonder if you would check down in Mr. Baylor's room for my otoscope," Cassie said sharply, moving the nurse toward the door like a cowboy with a reluctant steer. "Or if it's not there, check with my other patients. Thank you very much."

The nurse, though a good four inches taller and fifty pounds heavier than the doctor, lost no time in vanishing. Brendan grinned wryly. Cassie's authority certainly hadn't diminished any over the years. It was one of the attributes he'd had no use for when they were young. Cassie Farrell, who had always known exactly what she wanted and where she was going in life and had no doubt about how to achieve it, had intrigued him. She had also scared him to death.

Only in retrospect did he wonder if he had missed out. As college and the baseball circuit brought him a never-ending supply of pliable, dim-witted, sexual wonders, he suspected that he might have. Once they were out of sight, he could never remember their names. But he had always remembered the sharp wit, intense drive and marigold curls of Cassie Farrell.

It was probably an aberration, he told himself. An obvious example of the grass-is-greener syndrome. But now that they had met again, he wanted to find out. Starting with why she was now Cassie Hart. That meant, he thought with uncharacteristic annoyance, that there was a husband around to complicate things. He wondered who would have had the guts to marry her in the first place. He was probably a colossal achiever like herself.

"So who's Mr. Hart?" he asked as Cassie turned back to face him, the flush still high in her cheeks.

Trust Brendan to jump in with both feet, Cassie thought grimly, her back to the wall. "*Dr.* Hart," she corrected firmly. "Dr. Michael Hart, a cardiologist." There was no need to tell him that Michael was dead. She could see in his eyes that if he thought she was available, he would make it a point to tease her about it just as he had when they were teenagers. Brendan's eyes narrowed, and he scowled at her. She smiled.

"It hurts," he muttered. She wondered if he meant his arm, his rear end or the knowledge she had just given him.

"Have a pain pill," she said.

Brendan's eyebrows arched. "I'd rather have some sympathy from an old friend," he answered.

Cassie tried to ignore the plaintive tone, the obvious lines of pain in his face. With one hand she hugged the chart against her chest. "No. I'm your doctor now."

"Lose your compassion in med school, did you?" he asked, the blue eyes probing hers relentlessly.

"I didn't lose anything," Cassie retorted, wondering how on earth he could make her feel inadequate in ten words or less. "I just think it would be best to keep our relationship on a purely professional basis. I don't want you bringing up our past with the staff."

"Our past?"

Damn him and his teasing, insinuating inflections! "You know what I mean." She wished she had never brought it up. She should have left the room herself instead of getting rid of the nurse and trying to tell off Brendan. Something else that hadn't changed—it was impossible to tell off Brendan Craig!

"Okay," he agreed, placing a hand over his heart. "I solemnly swear not to tell the staff any details of our lurid past."

"Thank you," she said tightly.

"So where did you meet Michael Hart, cardiologist?" he asked in the next breath.

"Stanford. Tell me about your accident." She changed the subject abruptly.

"I swerved to miss a dog."

Cassie stared. "That's all?"

"Why?" Brendan said sharply. "Did you think I was chasing a Playboy bunny and lost control?"

Cassie had the grace to blush. "Something like that," she allowed, wishing for a moment that he had. It would be far easier to despise him then.

"I don't have to chase women," he told her.

Probably not, Cassie thought. Girls used to fall at his feet like bowling pins when he walked by. She wondered again if he had married one of them. He wasn't wearing a ring, and there was no next of kin on the hospital record, so short of asking him—heaven forbid!—or checking the office record, she had no way of knowing. She hoped he was. If he were, she would feel safer—though whether she meant safe from him or from herself she didn't want to think about.

"Lucky you," she said acidly. "I suppose now that you're a famous baseball player you even have groupies." As soon as it was out of her mouth, she knew she shouldn't have said it. One just didn't give Brendan Craig openings like that.

"Jealous?" The very expressive eyebrows arched, and the mustache lifted at one corner, making him look even more roguish than usual.

"Of course not!"

He smiled.

"You can have a thousand groupies for all I care!" she snapped.

"Oh, surely not," a feminine voice interrupted from the doorway. "I don't think even Brendan can handle more than ten at a time!"

Cassie spun around to stare at the husky-voiced Joan Collins look-alike who glided into the room and, with an amused glance at her, made directly for Brendan and gave him a kiss.

"Definitely not," Brendan agreed, lifting her long dark hair from in front of his face to give Cassie an infuriating grin. "Besides, it's not the quantity that counts, Cass. It's the quality."

"I doubt you'd know much about that," Cassie retorted sharply, still rooted to the spot.

Brendan's grin turned to a frown. "You'd be surprised," he said.

Cassie, feeling as if she were the one who was being censured, scowled back at him, then turned to leave. Obviously, this was either his wife or his girl friend. Be glad, she told herself, annoyed that instead she felt a surge of dislike. "I'll check on you this evening," she said, trying to get back on a professional footing, dismayed that she had strayed so badly in the first place.

"Wait!" Brendan was struggling to lift himself up, straining past the woman who was still clucking over him and stroking his plastered arm. "Cassie!"

Cassie turned back reluctantly. What was he trying to pull now?

"This is Susan Rivers," he told her. "She writes a sports column for the *Press Dispatch.*"

And my Aunt Harriet is a midwife for giraffes, Cassie thought. Anyone who looked less likely to know a bat from a ball would be hard to find. And she didn't look like a Susan, either. Where was truth in labeling now? This woman should have been a Suzette or Chantal at least. "How nice," she said, disbelieving.

"She is," Brendan insisted. "Show her your press card, Sue," he commanded. "This is Dr. Hart. Cassie Hart."

Susan looked at Brendan as though he had lost his mind, then shrugged and pulled her wallet out of an overstuffed carryall. "*You're* his doctor?" she asked with an equal amount of skepticism as she proffered her ID.

Cassie barely glanced at it. "Yes."

Susan was studying her with undisguised curiosity. "Do you have a badge to prove it, too?" she asked, grinning. Cassie knew she was being offered an olive branch, but somehow she couldn't smile back. Women like Susan always made her feel as if she'd stood behind the door when sex appeal was passed out. Ordinarily, it never bothered her. She was, after all, an intelligent woman. Emphasis on "intelligent," she knew Brendan would say. "I'm afraid not, Ms. Rivers," she said stiffly.

Undaunted, Susan whipped out a pen and notebook. "What's his prognosis?" she asked. "I'll need all the particulars."

"I haven't even discussed them with Mr. Craig yet," Cassie said crisply. "When I have, you may speak with him. I'm sure he'll tell you whatever he wants you to know." She nodded politely to them both.

"Don't I even get an ounce of sympathy, Cass?" Brendan called after her.

"I'm sure," Cassie said tightly, "that Ms. Rivers will give you pounds."

Pounds and pounds, Cassie thought as she walked

down the hallway. If Susan Rivers was any indication, Brendan's taste hadn't changed a bit. Susan was just another Bobbi Boobs, grown up. Snorting, Cassie hurried down the stairs to the parking lot. *Stop thinking about him,* she advised herself for the hundredth time. *What difference does it make what his taste is? He's your patient, not your problem. You've got problems enough without Brendan Craig.*

She did have, too. A steady stream of patients and two emergencies kept her busy every minute until well into the supper hour. Keith's ball game came and went, scratched because of someone else's game that resulted in a broken leg. Damn, Cassie thought as she finished setting it and hurried to find a phone to call and let her mother know that it would be at least another hour before she got home. Unless one of the boys broke a bone, she might never see them. They would be grown up and wonder who the skinny carrot-haired lady was who had rushed in and out of their lives. Thank God, she thought, dialing, that they had her mother around to depend on. Elsa Farrell was everything her daughter was not—a doting feminine charmer who thought one's life only complete with the addition of a man. Cassie begged to differ. And though it was a topic they never wholly resolved, they rubbed along together in the same house much better than they had separately when Elsa was a lonely widow and Cassie was trying to be a doctor and raise the boys alone. That was why her mother's news came as such a bombshell.

"You remember Raymond, dear?" Elsa blurted, practically breaking into Cassie's excuses and apologies for missing the game with urgent news of her own. "Raymond from the bank?"

Cassie remembered. He was the widower her mother had met when she was rolling over her last CD. If he had been thirty years younger, Elsa had said with her most flirtatious smile, she would have brought him home for Cassie.

"Well, he's invited me to go to Hawaii with him for the summer!"

Cassie was glad she was sitting down; otherwise, she'd have been flat out on the hospital's highly polished floor. "Hawaii?" she echoed dumbly. "The summer?" *Mother?*

"His son lives there," Elsa went on, her enthusiasm bubbling over Cassie's hollow mumbles. "They have a little cottage on their property that we can stay in!"

"You and Raymond?" Cassie asked, wanting to get it straight. She felt as though she were in a time loop—her morals suddenly far more Victorian than her mother's!

"Who else?" Elsa wanted to know. "Pity it's me rather than you, though," she went on. "You're the one who needs a man."

Here we go again, Cassie thought, rolling her eyes to the ceiling. "Not a man, Mother. I don't have room in my life for one; you know that. But I am going to need a grandmother replacement for you. The boys will be off school in three weeks. What'll I do with them?"

"We'll advertise for a mother's helper," Elsa told her blithely. "No problem at all. Besides, how many young boys can a grandma cope with when they're not in school all day?"

Cassie laughed. "All right. But I hope you know what you're doing, eloping with Raymond," she teased.

"Oh, we're not eloping, dear," Elsa explained. "Shacking up, I think you'd say."

"Mother!" Cassie burst out laughing.

"Well, one of us has to take a few chances in life," Elsa countered briskly.

"I'll be taking a chance, too," Cassie reminded her. "Where will I ever get a mother's helper as wonderful as you?"

"Don't worry, love. We'll find someone. Everything will work out fine. You simply have to trust in fate.

We'll see you when you've finished your rounds,'' Elsa said, and rang off.

Trust fate? Not likely, Cassie thought as she slowly hung up the phone. Just that morning fate had brought her Brendan Craig.

Chapter Three

"Why didn't you tell me you were a widow?"

All the way through her evening rounds Cassie had steeled herself, preparing to be brisk, matter-of-fact and thoroughly professional when she encountered Brendan again. She had studied his X rays carefully and had spent time in the hospital library with three journals containing articles on arm injuries and sports rehabilitation. She was prepared to answer any or all of his questions. Except that.

Stupid, she chided herself, and tried looking away from the man in the hospital bed who was leaning up on his one good elbow, his deep blue eyes capturing and holding her as easily as if he were gripping her arm. She should have known that a good professional offense wasn't enough of a defense against him; and she should have known that hospital gossip would catch up with her. "It never occurred to me," she lied.

"That your husband died in a plane crash coming back from a meeting at Mayo two years ago," Brendan went on, as if she didn't know. But his voice was soft, not accusing, and she saw his mustache curve downward in a sympathetic frown. He sighed. "I'm sorry, Cass."

There was no doubt that he meant it, and a sincere Brendan was even more of a worry than a teasing one. "Yes," she said briskly. "Michael was a fine surgeon. He's been sorely missed." She averted her gaze finally, picking up his plastered arm carefully and studying the color of his fingertips. They were dark and swollen.

"Was he a fine husband?" Brendan asked. She didn't have to look up to feel his eyes probing her.

"Of course he was. Your fingers are swelling. I'll ask them to split open your cast tonight. We really can't have you under that much pressure." She was talking too much and too quickly, and she knew it, but she needed to change the subject. She could not talk about Michael to Brendan.

"You've got two boys, the nurse said."

"My, you have had an earful." Cassie had trouble keeping the irritation out of her voice as she took a pen out of her pocket and made a note on his chart. "You ought to have been sleeping."

"Talking about you was far more interesting." Brendan gave her a sleepy smile that made her heart thud against her ribs. She stepped back, wondering if he could hear it, too.

"You shouldn't gossip about your doctor," she informed him severely, "and neither should the nurse. I'll have to speak to her."

"Don't." Brendan's right hand shot out and caught her by the arm before she could put some distance between them. "She only told me because I asked. Besides, Cass, you're not just my doctor. You're part of my life."

God, I hope not, Cassie thought. "Not anymore, Brendan," she said firmly. "I'm only passing through." *And so are you,* she added silently, crossing her fingers.

"We'll see." His expression was enigmatic, and he lay back, regarding her thoughtfully. "What do you think about my arm?"

That was the question she had been waiting for. Briefly, and without pulling any punches, she told him what he could expect. She saw his jaw tighten, determination setting in as she outlined the six- to seven-week period in the cast, followed by a lengthy personal exercise program to facilitate rehabilitation.

"But do you think I can pitch again?" he demanded when she finished.

"I *think* so. I cannot make any guarantees. You did a nasty piece of work on that arm."

Brendan swallowed, nodding slowly, apparently digesting the game plan for his summer. Cassie watched the play of emotions across his face, wishing she could give him better news but pleasantly surprised when she didn't see any depression in his features. "All right." His voice was resolute. "If that's what it takes, I'll do it." Then, almost as if, committed to it, he dismissed the worry from his mind, he grinned at her, saying, "Obviously you thought of me today."

Constantly, Cassie thought with irritation. "Only professionally," she assured him. "I'm a busy woman. And speaking of busy, so's my office staff, and your boss is calling every five minutes."

"Ballard?" A look of resignation settled on Brendan's face. "The owner?"

"That's a truism if I ever heard one," Cassie agreed with distaste. She had experienced Ballard's possessiveness before, whenever she had treated one of his players, but she'd never grown used to it. She bristled at the thought of him. "He acts like you're his new toy and you've just got broken," she told Brendan. "He had my receptionist in fits. The nurses here tell me he's been hounding them, too."

"Amen." Brendan's head sank back wearily against the pillows, and Cassie saw clearly how fatigued he really was. "He showed up here first thing in the morning, right on your heels. He's been back about five times since." He shrugged awkwardly, then winced with the pain of it. "I suppose he's checking me for signs of improvement," he went on wryly. "I'm a pretty expensive toy. He probably wants to see if I'm still worth it. He'll want to ask you before he throws me out."

Cassie scowled, then shook her head. "I'm not giving him that kind of information. My relationship is with you and with Gene as the team physician, not with him, no matter how rich he is. You can tell that to Ballast, or whatever his name is, the next time you see him!"

Heavy footsteps approached the door behind her, and Brendan let out an audible groan. "Save me the trouble," he said. "Here he comes. Tell him yourself."

Cassie turned to see the only man she had ever met who could make Brendan Craig wilt. Ballard glided into the room trailing expensive cigar smoke and wearing a silver silk suit that made him resemble a tailor-made locomotive for a high-speed train. He zeroed in on Brendan at once. "What's the news?"

Brendan looked at Cassie for deliverance. "Lem, you know Dr. Hart," he said. "She set my arm."

Cassie had been scrutinized fairly often in the course of her medical career, but never with such offensive thoroughness as Lemuel Ballard managed every time she met him. She'd had physicals that were less complete, she thought with annoyance, and hoped that her own disdainful perusal of Lemuel Ballard caused him just half the discomfiture that his was causing her. "How do you do, Mr. Ballard," she said icily, hoping she betrayed none of the agitation she felt.

Apparently she didn't, for Ballard drew deeply on his cigar before asking her flatly, "Should I trade him?"

Cassie felt Brendan's grip tighten alarmingly around her wrist and saw a tense whiteness joining the pain lines around his mouth. "Whatever for?" she asked, suddenly wanting to defend him from this silver barracuda.

Ballard's eyes narrowed. "Are you telling me, Miss Hart, that Craig isn't even worth a trade?" His tone was ominous. Brendan was cutting off the circulation to her hand.

"*Dr.* Hart," Cassie corrected. "And I am telling you that your comments are precipitous and presumptuous. Mr. Craig's accident occurred less than twenty-four hours ago. His prognosis is far from decided and far from hopeless. When Dr. Phillips returns, I will be discussing it with him. Between him and Mr. Craig, they can give you all the information they wish."

Ballard looked at her as if she had lost her mind. "I *own* him," he informed her.

Cassie drew herself up to her full, most righteous five feet seven inches. "Slavery, Mr. Ballard, went out of vogue a hundred and twenty years ago." Gently prying Brendan's fingers loose from her wrist and laying his hand back on the bed, she began to advance slowly across the room toward his "owner." "Please leave now," she said. "Mr. Craig is my patient, and he is in no shape to have any more visitors today."

Ballard looked hard at her, then turned to stare at Brendan, his scowl deepening. "I need a pitcher," he said flatly. "Come September—*if* we're still in the pennant race in September," he added with a sarcasm that even Cassie could identify as implying that it would be Brendan's fault if they weren't, "I'll need you. Will you be there?"

Cassie saw Brendan's whole body stiffen. "I intend to be." He met Ballard's stare head on. Only Cassie knew how much it was costing him.

"Good evening, sir," she said firmly, moving as inexorably as an avalanche to bear him out the door with her. "I'm sure you want him to heal as quickly as he can, so you'd better leave now. He can talk with you another day, when he's feeling better." About three months from now, she added silently.

Ballard's thick gray brows drew together. "You'll be hearing from me soon, and I'll expect a full report from Phillips," he told her with a backward glance at Brendan. "As soon as he gets back," he added, then turned abruptly and stalked off down the corridor.

"No doubt you do," Cassie muttered, stuffing her fists in the pockets of her lab coat and going back into Brendan's room feeling as if she had just chased the town bully away. Brendan seemed to feel the same way. He grinned at her weakly from his bed.

"If I had two hands, I'd clap," he told her. "You still wield a sharper tongue than any woman I know. And dare to use it, too."

Cassie sagged against the door and gave him a faint smile. "If that's a compliment, I think you can keep it." She shoved a hand through her hair, which had long ago abandoned the discipline of the French twist and now sprang in a riot of curls all over her head. The variety of emotions Brendan sparked in her was a complete puzzlement. Even now she didn't know how she felt. Irritation warred with attraction; the need to keep him at a distance was challenged by the desire to comfort and protect him that she had just experienced. She shook her head, hoping time would help her sort her feelings out. It was easier to see how Brendan felt. The fatigue and pain from his accident were fast catching up with him, and as she straightened up and moved away from the door, coming toward him, he sank back into the pillows and shut his eyes.

"No compliments, then," he mumbled. "How about just 'thanks.' I didn't need another onslaught today."

"The penalty of being famous?" she asked, trying to make her voice light and teasing, though the closer she got, the more she was overcome with that entirely unprofessional desire to stroke his brow and ease his pain. She clenched her fists at her sides.

"Oh, yeah." His voice was derisive. "Like vultures around a corpse. Half a dozen sportswriters, the general manager, some of the team. A whole bloody zoo!" he added, his voice rough with exhaustion.

Her fingers unclenched, and she laid her hand on his bare shoulder, squeezing it gently in compassion. "I'll take care of it, Brendan," she promised.

The blue eyes opened to regard her hazily; then a faint, almost-trusting smile lifted the corner of his mustache. Cassie's heartbeat quickened. The skin on his shoulder was smooth and taut, warm under her fingers, and she wanted to leave them there or let them roam southward toward the medal nestled in the curling black hair on his chest. Realizing the direction of her thoughts, she yanked her hand back as though she had been burned.

"I'll tell the nurses no visitors," she said. "You need to rest. We can't let all those people in here. You'll never recover if we do, will you?"

The smile deepened; his eyes warmed, then almost closed as he shook his head slowly. "Th'only person I want is you, Cass," he mumbled. "Only you."

Cassie swallowed hard. "Nonsense," she managed around the golf-ball-sized knot in her throat. But Brendan was already asleep. She doubted he even heard what she said.

She, however, couldn't forget his words. *The only person I want is you.* How odd. She wasn't at all Brendan's type, not if past history and Susan Rivers were anything to go by. But then maybe he was just teasing. That would be typical. Except the circumstances and the tone indicated that his intent was not jocular at all. It was better, she decided, to take his words as a warning. He just might mean them, and being the object of prey where Brendan Craig was concerned did not appeal to her in the least.

He would have been easier to resist, she thought the next morning after she had seen him on her rounds, if he were not so vulnerable. When she had arrived to see him, she found that the second-day stiffness had set in and he was barely able to open his eyes. When she touched him, he grimaced; if she moved him, he groaned in pain. She wanted to be brisk and efficient, but the sight of him simply wouldn't let her. It was fortunate, she decided when she made her escape at last, that he hadn't been in any shape to pursue things, because seeing him that way, she doubted she'd have had the good sense to fend him off.

"He's just another patient," she reminded herself in the fashion of a litany every time she caught herself thinking about him that day. "Aren't you a professional?" she asked herself in the mirror when she went to bed that night. And, of course, she was. But where Brendan Craig was concerned, she began to realize that first and foremost she was a woman. A very susceptible one.

In that sense, things hadn't changed much, either. She remembered as though it were yesterday the last time she had felt so susceptible to a man. It had been the same man, as a matter of fact, though he had been scarcely more than a boy then. And then, as now, her attraction hadn't made much sense. No one, of course, knew about it. That an intellectual giant and social midget like Cassie Farrell would even entertain fantasies about a stud like Brendan Craig would have been laughable in the extreme. Sometimes she even wanted to laugh about her feelings herself. But it hadn't stopped her thinking about him, even when his irreverent teasing brought her to the brink of fury time and time again.

The peak, of course, had been the day Ernestine bit him. Cassie had been lying on her beach towel, minding her own business and reading a chemistry textbook, with Ernestine slumbering peacefully beside her for the better part of the afternoon. Only occasionally had she even lifted her head to look over her shoulder at the line of surfers just beyond the waves, and if she noticed that Brendan was among them, she certainly didn't dwell on it. Or not much, anyway. She had imagined a brief scenario in which he saw her on her towel and wandered up the beach accidentally on purpose to sit down and talk, not tease, for a change. But it hadn't happened yet, and she wasn't going to hold her breath, so she closed the book and put her head down on the towel, closing her eyes instead. When she felt the first drops of icy water on her back, she jumped, leaping to her knees before she remembered that she had untied the knot at the neck of her bikini top. Brendan, never one to waste an opportunity, yanked on the other one, which crossed her shoulder blades. That was all it took.

"Brendan!" she shrieked. "Bring that back! Damn! Ernestine, get him!"

And Ernestine had. Neither Cassie nor Brendan had expected that. Ernestine, annoyed either by having her sleep disturbed or by the flagrant attack on her mistress, lunged across the sand after Brendan, leaping and flattening him into the sand at the same moment that her teeth caught the seat of his red cotton trunks and a significant portion of his behind.

So much for fantasies. Instead of conversing with him in a civilized, adult fashion, Cassie had found herself knotting a towel around his hips and leading him up the steps and along the road to her parents' house where, fortunately, her father was home. While Brendan leaned over the desk, Dr. Farrell had cleaned the bite and sewed him up, all the while giving Cassie a straight-faced medical lecture, though there was a discernible twinkle in his eye. After that there was a noticeable change in their relationship.

Cassie never said a word about the dog bite, even when rumors were rife about why Brendan stood all through his classes for a week. She thought the incident might bring them closer together. They did, after all, have something in common now. But it didn't. In fact, his teasing even stopped. He was polite, he said hello if they met, but more often than not his eyes slid away before she could reply. And six weeks later, when he graduated, he disappeared from her life altogether.

And the same thing will happen again, if you let it, Cassie told herself firmly on the third day of her reacquaintance with Brendan Craig. *Already he has started the teasing. He's just as vulnerable now—if not more so—than when the dog took a chunk out of him, and as soon as he's over it, he'll be gone. So don't get involved,* she repeated over and over. *You have absolutely nothing to gain.*

HE OUGHT TO BE THINKING about his arm, his career, his future—and he knew it. But the only thing Brendan wanted to think about was Cassie Farrell Hart. His mind was full of her—the feel of her fingers silken soft against his skin, the scent of her perfume lingering in his room long after she'd gone, her marigold hair that he itched to tangle his fingers in, her sharp remarks that were designed to put him in his place but that invariably made him laugh. But mostly he thought about her eyes, her compassionate, beautiful eyes. They never lied to him, though her mouth told him daily that he meant nothing more to her than the broken arm in room 274E.

"I dream about you every night," he told her that morning when she bustled into his room in her most preoccupied professional manner, scarcely looking at him as she scribbled furiously on someone's chart. "I bet you dream about me, too."

She looked up then, clearly annoyed. "Of course I do," she said, "only they're called nightmares." She jerked the dressing off his hip with unnecessary vigor, and he yelped through his laughter.

"I told you I wanted you, Cass," he reminded her, enjoying the blush that she couldn't prevent staining her cheeks. "Day and night," he added huskily. The more he had seen of her, the more he thought he was right. She was worth the battle it took to get under her skin. She made him feel alive.

"Put this under your tongue and be quiet." She whipped out a thermometer and stuck it in his mouth, then concentrated all her attention on his abrasion.

"You're the only doctor I know who uses a thermometer as a defense mechanism," he teased, shoving it to one side of his mouth.

Her eyes shot emerald fire at him. "If you're not going to close your mouth, I can find another place to put that thermometer," she told him sweetly, her hand moving purposefully over his exposed buttock.

Brendan grinned but shut his mouth. It was enough that she was touching him, that he could watch her as she moved about, every movement economical and efficient, no wasted effort. He wondered what she would be like in bed, loving him. He couldn't imagine her lying passive, letting things happen. Cassie had always been a mover, a shaker, a participant. He felt his loins tighten and the heat of desire begin to consume him. He licked his mustache.

Cassie scowled at him. "I thought I told you to close your mouth." She removed the thermometer, read it, shook it down and replaced it in the drawer of the bedside table. "Not too bad," she told him. "In another few days you can go home."

Home? He hadn't given it a thought since he'd found out who his doctor, the hag, was. After Cassie had reappeared in his life, he hadn't wanted to be anywhere else. There was no way he was going back to his apartment, which was nothing more than a stop-off point, anyway, and let her disappear from his life. Not until he'd discovered more about the real Cassie Hart beneath the starchy exterior, anyway. "I can't," he protested, contriving to look ill. "I hurt too much. I'll die."

Cassie rolled her eyes. "You're healing fast. And your arm will do just as well at home now that your abrasions are healing. You will need to have someone around, though, just to give you a hand," she added. "Do you, uh, live with anyone?" She looked as if she would rather not have asked that last question, and Brendan shook his head, grinning.

"You mean Susan or one of my 'groupies'?" he teased. "No, I'm all alone."

He thought he saw a flicker of relief in her eyes, but he wasn't sure. She simply shrugged and said, "Well, you'll have to get someone to come and help out for a while. Your parents, perhaps?"

"My mother died six years ago. And I can't see my dad doing it, can you? He disapproves of me enough as is. Can you imagine what he'd say about me being laid up after a motorcycle accident?" He lay back against the pillows and shook his head.

"For a minister your father never seemed quite Christian," Cassie said.

Brendan snorted. "He's not a minister; he's a theologian. It's the practical application that makes all the difference." He sighed as he always did when he thought about his relationship with his father. Hamilton Craig was a firm believer in St. Paul's edict that children when they grew up should put away their childish games. Baseball and motorcycles were, of course, among them. Brendan was not his favorite son.

"Never mind. We'll find someone," Cassie told him. "My friend Lainie Thomas is the hospital social worker. She knows people who can come in and help out temporarily. I'll have her drop by and talk to you." She gave him what he supposed was meant to be a reassuring smile, patted his arm and left. As if she couldn't wait to escape. Damn.

He shifted on the sheet, trying to straighten a wrinkle out beneath him so that he could lie in relative comfort and pass the rest of the morning daydreaming about Cassie. He tried to imagine where she was going next, how she would spend the afternoon, counting the minutes until she would appear again. He remembered all the times when they were growing up that he had baited her, teased her, tormented her, just to get a rise out of her, because she was so dedicated, so purposeful, so at odds with his devil-may-care approach to life. Well, he'd learned something about perseverance in the intervening years, too. And now he was going to make up for all the opportunities he had missed. *If* he could ever get near her.

SHE MUSTN'T let him near her, she thought as she drove home that night. During the three days he had been a part of her life again, she had found herself mooning like a love-sick adolescent one minute and sniping at him like the Wicked Witch of the West the next. It was not a proper sort of behavior at all. Damn him. He had been able to get a rise out of her since he was three and a half feet tall; and apparently he hadn't lost the knack.

The difference was that in the past, even at her most socially inept, she had been able to handle it. Then his attacks had been primarily aimed at her seriousness, her intensity, her no-nonsense approach to life. Now they were blatantly sexual, and that—competent doctor and skillful surgeon that she might be—she could not deal with. She didn't have the experience, for one thing. No one had ever come on to her the way Brendan was coming on to her now. Even Michael—*especially Michael*, she amended as she stopped at a red light—had been tactful and discreet in his pursuit, treating her as a lady and not an object of prey. She revved her engine in annoyance. The carload of college men that had pulled up alongside her honked and hooted.

"Wanna drag, lady?" one of them yelled. Another said something far more graphic, his thoughts running along the same lines as Brendan's.

Cassie grimaced. More specimens of the adult male! Did men *ever* grow up? Somehow she doubted it. The only one who had ever impressed her as being as serious and dedicated as herself had been Michael, and sometimes she doubted that he had ever actually been a child. The light turned green, and she eased away from the intersection purposefully and sedately. *The way I ought to run my life,* she thought, *not letting it get cluttered up with the likes of Brendan Craig.*

Brendan receded into the back corners of her mind the moment she got home. There other problems awaited her—her mother's imminent departure for Hawaii first among them. No amount of talking was going to convince Elsa that a summer spent caring for her grandsons was worth more than one in Oahu with Raymond, and Cassie didn't have the heart to try. For all her mother's flightiness, she had a heart of gold, and she deserved something good in her life, even if, in Cassie's mind, "shacking up" with Raymond didn't exactly fit into the category. The problem wasn't her mother; it was finding someone to fill Elsa's shoes in the child-care department.

"We'll have to advertise," Cassie told her sons that night, trying to forget all the previous advertisements before her mother had come that had ended in disaster for all concerned. "What shall I say?" She knew she wouldn't get what she wanted, which was a drill sergeant with a smile, but if the boys were satisfied, maybe they wouldn't make the helper's life so difficult that she would be looking for another in three weeks and feeling guilty because she was failing as a mother all the while.

"Not some dumb girl," Steven said emphatically, bouncing his soccer ball off the dining-room wall to pound home his point.

"Absolutely not some girl," Keith seconded with ten-year-old stubbornness. "How about Jerry Fisk's older brother?"

Cassie shook her head. As Jerry Fisk's older brother had just been arrested for possession of an illegal substance, she ruled him out. What she needed was someone the boys could look up to, not someone she would have to go down to the jail and bail out. "No," she said.

"Not a grandma, either," Steve went on as he dribbled the ball around the table. He grinned at his own grandmother, who was putting together a jigsaw puzzle on a card table in the living room, silent but close enough to keep an ear on the proceedings. "We already got one of those, and I don't want to make her jealous."

"Get a grandpa," Elsa suggested suddenly, swooping down on a piece of the puzzle and fitting it in, smiling smugly as she did so.

"A grandpa?" Cassie echoed, finding the idea intriguing. The boys, after all, could use a male influence.

Her mother shrugged her birdlike shoulders. "Why not? You know how the boys like going to ball games with Raymond."

"How about Raymond?" Cassie teased, leaning

back against the crushed velvet of the recliner and kicking her shoes off.

"Not on your life. Raymond's mine. I saw him first. Still—" Elsa paused and scratched her salt-and-pepper curls thoughtfully "—there must be some nice grandfatherly types around. And you know how much the boys need a father."

"I'm not marrying this man, Mom, just hiring him," Cassie said, almost groaning at the all-too-familiar refrain. Once Elsa had decided that Cassie should marry again, she had been relentless. When Cassie hadn't agreed, protesting that she had absolutely no time for another man, her mother hadn't stopped. She had simply changed her tactics. Now husbands weren't mentioned, but every chance she got, she pointed out how desperately the boys needed a father. Apparently even "grandfatherly" ones, Cassie thought with a smile.

"A very old, grandfatherly man," she acquiesced. "Or maybe we could find a male college student, someone who could keep up with these two." She reached out and ruffled Steve's auburn hair, refusing to think about the students in the car she had seen earlier that day. Surely there had to be some responsible ones around. "How does that sound?" she asked the boys.

"Great," Keith said. "Hey, is it true you got Lefty Craig for a patient?"

Cassie winced. Every time she thought she had banished him, he came back into her life. "Yes. So what?" she said, a trifle more belligerently than she intended. After all, it wasn't Keith's fault his mother was acting like a schoolgirl.

Keith's eyes widened. "Can you get me his autograph?" he wanted to know.

"I guess," she said reluctantly, already imagining the smirk on his face that would appear when she asked. But maybe if she gave in on this point, that would be the last of it. She would have to ask her mother not to mention that she had once been rather well acquainted with Lefty Craig.

"WHY," CASSIE DEMANDED two days later when she was grabbing a midmorning snack in the hospital cafeteria with Lainie Thomas, "does everyone think that the sun rises and sets on Brendan Craig?"

"Well, he is gorgeous," Lainie pointed out, cutting off a piece of apricot Danish, popping it into her mouth and chewing in a manner that reminded Cassie of Albert Finney in *Tom Jones* savoring a leg of chicken. Somehow she knew it wasn't the Danish Lainie was tasting.

"Stop that!" she commanded, clenching her coffee cup like an anchor in a stormy sea. "So he's attractive. So what? It doesn't make him better than anyone else!"

Lainie smiled her wise old owl smile. "You want his body, too, don't you?"

Cassie's cheeks flared red. "I do not!"

"Nonsense," Lainie countered, wagging her dark, shoulder-length hair. "I've never seen you so flustered by a man in your life. He's just what you need."

"Huh!" Cassie thumped her cup on the table, spilling the coffee. "There's a laugh! What I need is another me—someone who can be home to watch the baseball games and bake brownies for the cub scouts while this me is making rounds and doing surgery. I definitely do not need a man like Brendan Craig complicating my life!"

"He fancies you, I hear," Lainie went on as though Cassie hadn't said a word. "I hear there are bets going that—"

"I don't want to hear it!" Cassie cut in. She had heard the same thing—that one of the emergency medical technicians had a pool going about when Brendan would score with her. "I just want him out, Lainie. And that's where you come in. Find him a nursemaid or someone to stay with him, someone who will help him cope while he's in the cast and who can do his therapy with him after he's out. Not," she underlined, "one of his groupies."

"Jealous?" Lainie teased.

"Garbage!"

Lainie shook her head at Cassie in mock dismay. "I swear, there's no hope for you. You're going to grow up into a workaholic old crone."

"Thanks very much," Cassie replied with false sweetness. She loved Lainie dearly; they had been friends for three years, but they would never agree about what made the world go round. Lainie thought it was love. Cassie knew better.

"Well," Lainie said, getting up and dropping her crumpled napkin on her plate. "I'll just go see your gorgeous gent right now and try to work something out." She winked. "Never a problem too big or too small, I always say!"

Cassie smiled, relieved that Lainie had agreed to do something. "Thanks."

"You're welcome. But I still think you could use a man."

"A grandfather," Cassie agreed, following Lainie out of the cafeteria and turning toward the parking lot. "Some nice old man who whittles and tells stories and can take care of my boys."

"What happened to your mother?"

"Mother has a man of her own. She's going to Hawaii with Raymond from the bank," Cassie admitted, embarrassed but honest.

"Terrific! She's got more sense than you!"

"To each her own opinion," Cassie said stiffly. "Think whatever you like. You will, anyway. Just get Brendan Craig out of here."

"There's a man for you," Lainie said, grinning. "Take him home."

"God forbid." Cassie shuddered. "See you tomorrow. I'm already late for my appointments. I have a job to do."

She was certain that the job would get easier when Gene Phillips got back. When she handed Brendan over to him, the source of her confusion and of the upheaval in her life would be, if not eliminated, at least minimized. Unfortunately, Gene had other ideas.

"What do you mean, you want me to stay on as his primary physician?" Cassie demanded when she confronted Gene for the first time outside the operating room the following afternoon. She had been singing her way through rounds, delighted that the day had arrived when her partner was back and she could get Brendan off her hands, and when she had emerged from assisting Gene in surgery, he had sprung the news on her. She ripped off her surgical mask and glared at him.

Gene shrugged, his loose, lanky frame contrasting completely with her tight, strung-up posture. "You're the expert," he told her. "Wrists are not my area. It only makes sense. Besides," he added with a distinct gleam in his eye, "Brendan seems to want you."

"Well, I don't want him!" Cassie almost wailed, ignoring the curious looks she was getting from a group of passing nurses who had certainly never seen Dr. Hart lose her cool before.

"We're not talking about Brendan Craig the patient, then, are we?" Gene asked perceptively, raking a hand through his thinning brown hair.

Cassie sighed and shook her head, waiting until there was no one nearby. "No," she admitted, because she and Gene had always leveled with each other. "No, we're not."

Gene looked interested. "First time I've known you to take a 'more than professional' interest in a patient, Cass." He considered her carefully as they walked down the corridor together.

Cassie knew he was seeing her confusion, her desire, her soul. "I'm not!" she protested. "Or at least I'm trying not to," she amended a trifle more honestly. "For heaven's sake, Gene, I've done all I can for him. Why won't you take him back?"

Gene stopped in midcorridor and looked at her squarely, putting his hands on her shoulders. "Because I talked to him this morning at length. This is a career-threatening injury he has, and you know it. He knows it. And I want him to have every possible chance of pulling through it all right, of pitching again. And frankly, Cass, I think he'll try harder for you."

"For me?" Her heart tightened. This was not exactly Brendan Craig the patient Gene was talking about, either. "Why?"

Gene smiled gently, squeezing her arm reassuringly. "Come on, Cass. I don't really have to tell you that."

That, Cassie decided, was the last straw. First Brendan, then Lainie, now Gene. She had never felt so manipulated in her life! Well, she might be stuck with him as a patient, but she wouldn't let it drop there. She would be only too pleased to give Brendan Craig a piece of her mind.

After ripping off her surgical gown, she stomped up the stairs to his room. Still seething, she jerked open the door. "Why did you tell Gene you wanted me?" she demanded, surprising him with a forkful of spaghetti halfway to his mouth. It fell on the bed sheet, and the fork followed it.

Brendan grinned, and she immediately regretted her choice of words.

"Because I do, Cass," he said, his eyes burning into her. "I've been lying here thinking you're my ideal woman. I want to find out if it's true."

Well, she could say this for Brendan Craig: at least he was honest. There was no beating around the bush with him. He told her; he told Gene; he told the whole world. But she wasn't sure she liked his wanting her to be part of his ongoing recovery and therapy, and she told him so.

"Gene thinks you'll work harder for me, though," she admitted gruffly, wanting to get things straight at the outset.

"I will." The glint in his eyes said a great deal more.

"Well, don't think you're getting my body as a reward." She scowled at him, and Brendan laughed, obviously delighted. Cassie went crimson.

"How about a kiss, Cass?" He winked at her.

"Stuff it, Brendan," she said sweetly, and left.

BUT IF BRENDAN'S PRESENCE was still going to play havoc with her professional life, at least her home life was smoothing out. The ad she wrote netted her four candidates for a mother's helper, and the boys sounded reasonably pleased with all of them. Surely one would work out, she thought as she moved briskly down the hospital corridor toward Lainie's office. And of the other three she might even find one suitable to be a helper for Brendan. So far Lainie hadn't had much luck finding one. There seemed to have been a surfeit of awestruck groupies and little old ladies but no one able to simply drop in on a one-armed baseball player once or twice a day to tie his shoes and make him a hot meal.

"Any luck?" she asked, poking her head into Lainie's office. She didn't need to spell it out; Lainie was quite well aware of whom she was referring to.

"Ballard's promised to help out," Lainie told her.

"You're kidding!"

Lainie tipped back in her chair and laughed. "Not helping actually. But he said he'd provide someone. 'To keep an eye on him,' he said."

"Oh?" Cassie wasn't sure what Ballard meant by that. He hadn't been hounding her much that week, but she knew he wasn't neglecting his investment. The Mustang trainer had conferred with her twice, and she knew Ballard had been in touch with Gene.

Lainie shrugged. "Well, it solves your problem, doesn't it? Unless you'd rather take him home with you?"

"No, thanks!" She gave Lainie a grin, the thought of being able to walk through the hospital without the sniggers and giggles accompanying her suddenly almost a reality. She felt enormously relieved, like an ox who has slipped the yoke at last. She fairly danced out of Lainie's office and went down to the nurses' station to fill out his discharge papers. Then, still elated, she decided to stop by his room and bid her nemesis good-bye. She could afford to be magnanimous now that he was getting out of her life. A man she saw twice a month only to check his progress and to supervise his therapy in conjunction with Gene and the trainer wasn't going to be nearly the threat to her emotional peace of mind as the Brendan she saw twice a day.

"Lainie tells me she's found you someone to help you out," she said, beaming at him as she entered the room.

Brendan was leaning back against the pillows, his bed tilted so that he was sitting up. The nurse had talked him into wearing a pajama shirt, but he still refused to button it, and Cassie's breath caught as she stared at the muscled expanse of his chest. Thank God he was leaving, she thought. "Oh?" He hadn't seemed to have heard anything about it.

"Aren't you glad?"

"To be leaving you?" He looked at her as if she'd lost her mind.

Cassie scowled. "Let's have a look at you, then," she said, resorting to a starchy professionalism, the only defense she had against him when he looked at her like that.

Brendan grinned ruefully. "You only think of me as a bunch of scabs and a broken arm," he grumbled. "Don't doctors ever succumb to sex appeal?"

If you only knew, Cassie thought, a tremor shooting through her as Brendan obediently rolled onto his right side and let her lift the sheet and ease down the pajama bottoms he was wearing. She swallowed hard the moment her fingers touched his smooth hip, his hair-roughened thigh. What would it be like to make love with him? To be permitted the liberty of exploring his body with loving care instead of professional obligation? She saw his thigh muscles tense as her palm skimmed over him, and she knew she was playing with fire. He had already said he wanted her. But she knew she couldn't have him—whether she "wanted" him or not—not if she wanted to keep any semblance of normalcy in her life at all. She had to back off. *Now.*

"Very good. You're coming along fine." Her mouth was dry, tasting of cotton. "I'll see you once more in the morning before you leave." She tugged the pajamas back up and flung the sheet over him, wishing he would stop lying there devouring her with his eyes. Her fingers trembled as she reached for his broken arm, and he saw them but only lifted his eyebrows without comment. Then he bent his fingers for her to show her how much they had improved.

"Good," she croaked again, wondering why she thought that knowing he was going to leave would grant her instant immunity to his attraction. She stepped back away from him as quickly as she could.

At once, Brendan's good arm went around her, holding her fast. "It *would* be good, Cass," he whispered, drawing her against him, sitting up so that one leg hung over the side of the bed. "It would be very good."

Cassie felt surrounded, his maleness overpowering her as his dark head bent closer and the warmth of his breath touched her cheek, then her lips. No, she thought, but before she could shove him away, his lips touched hers. Gently, with light, teasing strokes he cajoled, persuaded. And that was her undoing. If he had forced her, pressured her, she could have fought him. But he didn't; he simply gave her pleasure, the warmth of his lips and the blunt hairs of his thick mustache touching and teasing until her resistance melted away.

Gradually, his arm tightened, bringing her hard against the wall of his chest. Then his lips met hers with more persuasion, deeper desire. Cassie felt her knees give way, and she clutched at him, her fingers gripping the pale blue cotton of his pajama shirt. Her lips parted, giving his tongue the freedom to explore her mouth, to slide over the straight line of her teeth and tease the sensitive nerve endings behind them. Her fingers loosed their hold on his shirt and crept up to bury themselves in the silky thickness of his hair. It was so soft, its glossy blackness spilling over his forehead, brushing her face and filling her nostrils with the scent of hospital-issue shampoo and a male muskiness that could only be Brendan himself. Cassie made a mewling, primitive sound far back in her throat as his kiss deepened further. The taste of him, the smell of him—all of it overwhelmed her. His kiss was everything she had fantasized, and feared, that it would be. And still she couldn't stop herself. The tiniest bit of her mind that was still rational justified the foolishness. He'll be gone tomorrow, she thought. Where's the harm in a kiss? But my God, what a kiss! When—and where—she wondered, would it stop?

There was a discreet cough behind her. Brendan groaned, his breathing coming in ragged gasps. "Stop!" Cassie hissed at him, trying to stand on legs that had melted several minutes before. She turned, trying to reestablish her dignity, expecting to see one of the floor nurses standing there.

She saw a man instead. He was tall and broad shouldered, with thick, straight wheat-colored hair and sable eyes. A gorgeous dimple grooved his left cheek. "If that's how they kiss and make it better, Brendan," he said in amusement, "I think I've been going to the wrong doctor for years!"

Cassie gulped down her embarrassment, but the man just grinned. Brendan took a deep, shuddering breath and scowled, though his voice held a trace of a laugh. "You owe me one, Tucker. By God, you do!"

The man called Tucker came in and held out his hand to Cassie. "How's the old beast treating you? Besides what I just saw, I mean."

"M-Mr. Craig is a bit of challenge," Cassie stammered, looking up into laughing eyes, thinking that the warm brown color looked familiar to her.

Brendan started to laugh. "Don't you know who this is?" he demanded, looking from one to the other of them. Cassie and Tucker stared at each other, then at Brendan, mystified. "Griffin Tucker, meet Dr. Cassandra Farrell Hart!" he introduced, and settled back to watch them, grinning.

"Griffin?" Cassie stared. This was the tall, silent boy who had helped Brendan tree her bike, who had got expelled from school for refusing to back down when the principal demanded that he not print a controversial story in the literary magazine?

"Cassie?" Griffin did a double take. "Of course. Our Miss Marigold!" He ruffled her curls, then tossed a wicked glance at Brendan. Brendan, obviously less than pleased to have his past taunts brought up at that moment, scowled fiercely.

"Dr. Hart to you," he said to Griffin, and arranged his broken arm on top of the sheet so that he looked wounded and imperious at the same time.

Cassie laughed, then turned to Griffin, who was leaning against the bedside table with an amused tilt to his mouth. The dimple was lovely, and she thought how nicely he had turned out. "What are you doing now?" she asked.

"Keeping him honest." Griffin jerked his head at Brendan.

"He's a man in blue," Brendan stuck in, his distaste visible.

"A policeman?" Cassie was intrigued.

Griff shook his head. "No. An umpire."

"And you're probably not supposed to be here right now either," Brendan said roughly. "They'll hang your hide for consorting with a player or some damn thing."

"Let me worry about that," Griff said. He studied Brendan's arm sympathetically. "You don't look like you'll be doing much playing for a while. I hear you've had it rough."

"The worst is over," Brendan replied, his hand snaking out and grasping Cassie's wrist. "Besides, I've had marvelous help healing." He winked at her.

"Anyway, tomorrow he's going home," Cassie put in, trying to pull away from him. She hoped Griffin would ignore the innuendo in Brendan's voice, but after that kiss, she didn't suppose there was much hope.

"Came just in time, then, didn't I?" Griff mocked, and Brendan looked annoyed.

"I'll just be on my way now," Cassie said, prying Brendan's fingers off her arm. "You two enjoy your visit. Hope to see you again, Griff."

"Oh, you will," he assured her, his eyes twinkling as he saw her rub her wrist and as Brendan's fingers clenched on the sheet beside him. "What are you doing tomorrow night?"

"Don't ask," Brendan snapped, his eyes icy and narrow.

"Like that, is it?" Griff grinned and shrugged. "See you then, Cass."

"Cassie!" Brendan's voice was sharp, causing her to pause in the doorway and turn to see what he wanted. "Remember what he interrupted."

Cassie glared at him.

"Keep it in mind. I'll get you yet."

BUT HE WOULDN'T HAVE TIME to get her, Cassie thought smugly the next morning as she approached his room with none of her usual trepidation. In fact, she entered the room with a sunny smile on her face. Brendan didn't return it. His expression was surly, his whole body tense. She didn't need a blood-pressure cuff or a thermometer to tell her that something was wrong.

"I thought you'd be champing at the bit," she said lightly, masking the niggling concern she felt when he didn't speak but just looked at her glumly while she fitted the cuff onto his arm. "Not ready to go home, huh?"

For a moment Brendan didn't answer. For a man as innately loquacious as he was, that was worrisome. Cassie squeezed the pressure pump quickly, her eyes darting from Brendan to the gauge, assessing. "Ballard was here this morning," he said finally, his voice tight.

"Ballard? Already?" It was only just past seven. "Why?"

"Making plans for my life." Brendan's voice was bitter. His blood pressure, while not alarming, wasn't what it should have been, either.

"What plans are these?" Cassie unwound the cuff and motioned him to lie back so she could listen to his chest.

"He's got some damned marine—some physical-fitness freak—who's going to take over my life!"

Cassie frowned. "Oh? Why?"

"To help me stay in shape, he says. To protect his damned million-dollar investment!" Brendan slammed his good hand down on the bed. "Does he think I'm an idiot? My future depends on being able to pitch, damn it! I don't need some drill sergeant dogging me every step!"

"Of course not," Cassie said. "A drill sergeant is exactly what you don't need." He was strung up enough without that. Mental attitude would play a big part in Brendan's recovery, in his self-confidence. Gene had known that when he'd asked her to keep Brendan as her patient, she thought, smiling wryly. Apparently, though, Ballard had other ideas.

"Tell him so," Brendan urged.

"I doubt it would help." Ballard's faith in Cassie was grudging at best. Even the fact that his top right-handed reliever, Dave Dawson, owed his continuing career to Cassie's competence as a surgeon didn't seem to have softened Ballard's initial skepticism. Her word didn't go far. Besides, who else could she recommend? Actions spoke louder than words with Ballard, and short of taking Brendan home with her, she couldn't see anything else to do.

Take Brendan home with her? Oh, no. Forget it. How could she think such a stupid thing? How?

"You could take me home with you," Brendan said.

"No!"

A corner of his mouth twitched, and Cassie wished

she had been a little less hysterical in her response. "That's what I like about you, Cass. Always so calm and reasonable."

"Brendan!"

He gave his plaintive, one-armed shrug, designed to make her feel sorry for him. "Well, why not? I mean, seriously, look at the advantages."

Advantages? Cassie thought she might die laughing if she weren't so busy trying to construct a mental defense against his proposed invasion of her home. "What advantages?" she croaked.

Brendan frowned, obviously trying to think what might be considered advantages from her angle. She was glad he didn't know she was looking for a mother's helper. Undoubtedly he would try to pass himself off as God's gift to the working mother if he only knew. He probably would be, too, she thought glumly. Certainly Keith and Steve would be enthralled with the prospect of having Brendan Craig around all day. She had interviewed four men and had almost settled on a very satisfactory retired oil geologist. Keith and Steven liked him a lot. But not nearly as much as they would like having Brendan around the house. *Don't even think it,* she told herself.

"I'd always be there when you wanted me," he told her, grinning. He was baiting her. She bit.

"I don't want you!"

A dark brow lifted skeptically. "No?"

"No!"

"Then it wouldn't matter to you if I was there or not?"

"Of course not!"

"Well, then... Why not let me?"

Hooked. Cassie stared at him, her mouth opening and shutting like a fish.

Brendan lifted himself up on his right elbow, leaning forward in entreaty, the teasing light in his eyes absent. "Look, Cass, I mean it. I cannot stand life with a drill sergeant. I know Ballard means well, and in his own misguided way he thinks he's doing what's best for me. But it isn't. And no amount of protesting from me is going to mean a damned thing," he went on, his fingers clenching the sheet. "There's some clause in my contract about him having the last word on medical matters that would affect my pitching."

"So what good would my saying anything do?" Cassie argued.

"You're my doctor!"

"He could fire me."

"Not without firing Gene or creating a rift and causing one hell of a stir!"

Not any worse than the stir you'd cause in my house if I let you in it, Cassie thought. "It doesn't make sense, Bren," she told him, but some of the vehemence had gone out of her voice. She was, damn it, beginning to feel calm and rational again, in control—as if she could manage him, as if under the circumstances it might be making sense.

"Yes, it does, Cass. Think about it." He was looking squarely at her, his quicksilver eyes earnest, pleading, almost. Convincing, almost.

She sighed.

"What would it hurt?" he went on, his fingers reaching out and wrapping around her wrist, but with none of the subtle stroking that would have betrayed a sexual interest in her.

What would it hurt? *My equilibrium,* she thought. *My peace of mind.* She stopped short of thinking, *My heart.* Her heart wasn't involved with Brendan Craig. This wasn't love; it was hormones. And surely Cassie Hart, doctor of orthopedic surgery, woman of the eighties, ought to be able to control *them.* Mind over matter and all that.

"Well?" Brendan prodded.

"I'm considering." She shouldn't be. She should be signing him out right now, bequeathing him to whatever martinet Ballard had in mind. Serve him right. But would it, her other half argued. Whether it was her professional half or her crazed, emotional half, she didn't know. She only knew that it was telling her that given a live-in dictator of physical fitness, someone who would be pushing him at every moment, Brendan would balk. He might not intend to; he certainly wouldn't *want* to. But he would. His arm's recovery was an iffy proposition at best. He needed to put stress on hold for the time being; he needed to give himself time to heal, not be continually monitoring his improvement. That was the quickest way to depression she could think of. No, Brendan needed to have his mind on other things for the time being.

Like you? she chided herself scornfully. But medically speaking, of course, it wasn't a bad idea. It was a terrible idea, she countered immediately. He would drive her crazy at home. But would he? Especially if she was never there—and God knew how seldom she was. A slight smile curved her mouth as she considered it. She might actually see less of him there than she saw of him now. Well, perhaps that was an exaggeration, but still it might have its advantages, even if they weren't the advantages Brendan had in mind.

For one thing, medically she could keep an eye on him, and that would make both Brendan and Ballard happy. It would also let Gene know she was taking his request seriously. And—she was warming to the idea now—it would give her a "mother's helper" to end all mother's helpers! The boys would be ecstatic. They would probably also behave. They could run and fetch for him, tie his shoelaces and scrub his back—all things he couldn't do for himself until he got in a short cast. And as for his "advantage"—her smile widened—she could prove how controlled she was. She could let him live in her house and prove she didn't want him at all. It would be good for her, in fact. An exercise in willpower. Lent for her hormones.

Brendan wasn't saying a word. He was watching her intently, and she wondered if he could actually see the struggle going on within her from the expressions on her face. Well, if so, he didn't seem to know the outcome.

Cassie took a deep breath and sent a prayer winging to heaven before she lowered her eyes to meet those of her own personal demon. "All right, Brendan. You can come home with me."

Chapter Four

After she had committed herself, Cassie had second thoughts. And third, fourth, fifth and sixth thoughts. And every one of them told her that she was out of her mind to consider letting Brendan into her house. Unfortunately, since she had also bumbled into telling him that as long as he was coming, he could be her new mother's helper, she had inadvertently given him a whole stockpile of ammunition. And since Griffin had come to give him a ride to her house in midafternoon, he also had plenty of time to gain three allies before she got home. But she was stuck, well and truly, and the most galling thing was that everyone—absolutely everyone—thought it was a terrific idea.

"True devotion to duty," Gene teased her when he stuck his head in her office door that afternoon.

"He just didn't want the marine," Cassie said defensively. "And I don't think it would be good for him, either, and—"

"Nor do I," Gene agreed. "But I'm glad you thought of it." He grinned. "It would've been more than my life was worth, suggesting it to you."

"Too true," Cassie acknowledged. "But it's purely business."

"Of course it is," Gene agreed, and if his eyes told her he thought differently, she didn't want to know.

Gene was good practice, though, for confronting Ballard on the phone later that afternoon. He called and demanded to know what she had done with his pitcher, and it took every ounce of professional stalwartness that she possessed to bull her way through that conversation. Whether Ballard was actually mollified or not, Cassie wasn't sure. He said, "I'll be keeping close tabs on this," with rather more the inflection of a puritanical minister than a baseball magnate.

"Do that," she said, and hung up. She still didn't feel comfortable with the idea of letting Brendan come home with her, but Ballard went a long way toward assuaging her feelings. At least until she opened her front door that evening and found Brendan Craig, in person, sitting in her living room. Then reality began to set in, and she wondered again just what she had done.

"Wow, Mom, he's super!" Steven threw himself on her almost before she had time to shut the door.

"Thanks, Mom!" Keith said, eyes shining like a child's at Christmas.

Cassie managed a wan smile and wondered fleetingly if Brendan's arrival might not be a bit like bringing home one of Steven Spielberg's gremlins. She shot him a worried glance, but he gave her only a benign, tolerant smile, and she thought that if she didn't know better, she'd think she had imagined their kiss. "You're welcome," she said, returning Steve's hug and then disentangling herself, noticing as she did so that Brendan's suitcase was still in the living room. He'd apparently only just made it through the door before the welcoming hordes descended on him. She should have known.

"Brendan and I have been catching up on old friends," Elsa told her daughter, beaming at Brendan. Obviously, she had been won over, too. "I'm just delighted that he's come to stay. He's just what you need, Cassie," she said.

"A mother's helper, you mean," Cassie replied, knowing that it wasn't what her mother meant at all. "Yes, you're right. I see they haven't let you get settled in yet," she said to Brendan, cutting off any possible expansion that Elsa might have thought necessary to add to her remarks. "Come on. I'll show you where your room is."

Brendan nodded politely and picked up his suitcase to follow her.

Cassie led him down the hallway to the bedroom directly across from her own, wishing as she did so that the spare room was at the other end of the house. "This one," she said, opening the door. The room had barely been occupied since they moved in five years before. Michael had used it for a study on the brief occasions when he was home long enough to work there, and their occasional guests had slept in it. But it had no past, no steady inhabitant that Cassie could think of when she spoke of it, and it immediately assumed the identity of "Brendan's room" in her mind. She wished it hadn't.

Brendan seemed pleased as he tossed his suitcase on the wheat-colored, woven Irish bedspread and stood back to take in the heavy Spanish-style furniture and the medical texts lining the bookshelves. "Thanks, Cass," he said. His face lit with the soft, sensual smile that was designed for—and succeeding in—making her melt on the carpet, and she wondered where the polite, nodding, houseguest-cum-mother's helper was now. This was the Brendan who could devastate her. She closed her eyes and prayed for immunity.

"Did you talk to Ballard?" he asked as he opened his suitcase.

"Yes."

"And?"

"And he's going to be watching us closely," she snapped. "I think he's worried about your virtue or something!"

Brendan grinned. "Don't I wish!"

"I don't," Cassie said flatly. "And you won't, either, if you know what's good for you. This is recuperation, nothing more. And don't you forget it."

"Yes, ma'am," Brendan dropped his eyes, but the grin still lurked at the corner of his mouth.

And please, God, I won't forget it, either, Cassie thought, backing toward the door.

Brendan looked up from his suitcase, his quicksilver eyes arresting her in flight. "You won't regret letting me stay," he promised.

Cassie gave him a weary, almost-defeated smile. "That's what you think," she muttered more to herself than him, and she left the room. "I already do," she mumbled. Regret was only a part of what she felt. A soft-spoken, gentle Brendan like the one she had just encountered was harder to deal with than a brazen, overconfident one. The latter was bad enough, but with him she could at least bluster back. This one had her completely stumped. She was every bit as scared of him as he had accused her of being. He was a danger to her way of life. The best thing to do would be what she had decided at first—she would simply have to avoid him.

He couldn't work his magic on her if she wasn't there. And even when she was, he would probably be busy with the boys. At least she could contrive not to be alone with him. The boys would take care of that. They seemed pleased, at least. If that day was anything to go by, Brendan would be the greatest mother's helper in the world. Good. He could deal with them, and she could get on with being a conscientious doctor. And never the twain would meet.

"You can do anything you put your mind to," her father had always told her. And so far she had always proved him correct, often over formidable odds. Well, tomorrow she would set her mind to coping with and resisting Brendan Craig. She wondered if she had ever encountered such formidable odds.

THE SUNNY MORNING was in direct counterpoint to Cassie's mood. She ran her stocking, burned the toast and nearly dropped her beeper in the coffee. Her mother, full of morning sunshine, good cheer and "I told you so's" left her gnashing her teeth, and the boys' obvious jubilation that Brendan would be there when they got home from school soured what little optimism she could muster. Of Brendan, thank God, she saw nothing. But that didn't really matter, for she had dreamed of him all night. She had had a rotten night's sleep—full of dreams about prickling mustache kisses that invaded her mind the way an injured left-handed pitcher was invading her life. If the rest of the nights were going to be like that one, she thought she might rent a room at the Y.

She ran a stoplight, got a ticket, left her beeper on the kitchen table and only discovered she had when she got to the hospital. Gene groused for twenty minutes about having to set some wrist bones that morning because no one could get ahold of her. Guess why, she thought wearily, and sank down onto one of the sofas in the doctors' lounge and contemplated sneaking forty winks.

"I hear you're living in sin!" Lainie poked her head in the door and grinned, then retracted it when Cassie tossed an empty paper cup at her. Then, with exaggerated caution she edged into the room and plopped into the nearest chair. "Did you really do it?" she demanded, then turned red. "Take him home with you, I mean?"

"Yes." That was all she was saying. If word got around that she was lamenting and regretting it, she would look like even a bigger fool than she must look already.

Lainie grinned, triumphant. "See! I told you he was gorgeous."

"That is *not* why I took him home."

"Well, it wasn't for 'medical purposes,'" Lainie said knowingly.

"Says who?" Cassie gave her a hard stare. "Anyway, stop worrying about my life for a change. Tell me about yours."

Lainie smiled an enigmatic smile.

Cassie grinned. "A new man?" Lainie went through men like Cassie went through splints. She was friends with them all, serious about none, and Cassie had never seen her smile in quite that way before.

"A new man," Lainie agreed happily.

"Who?"

"That scrumptious friend of Brendan's. The blonde."

Cassie's eyes widened. "Griffin?" Surely not.

Lainie made her "I could devour that man alive" face. "The very one."

"But Griff is so—so—" She wanted to say, so much of a loner, so unlikely to respond. But what did she know about anybody else's aberrations? It was perverse enough that Brendan Craig should happen to be hers.

"I think he might be it, Cass," Lainie confided conspiratorially.

"Have you even gone out with him?" Cassie asked, still trying to put her bouncy, devil-may-care friend together with serious, dogmatic Griffin Tucker. For her money, Lainie would have made more sense with someone like Brendan.

But she didn't like the feeling that thought gave her, so she was glad when Lainie replied, "Just had coffee with him once. I came in to see Brendan, and *pow*, there he was! I forgot what I was there for. Know what I mean?"

Up until Brendan had walked back into her life, Cassie would have said no. Now she thought she had a very good idea. "And that's the extent of it?" she asked skeptically.

"No. We're going out tonight after the game. Then he goes out of town again." Lainie actually drooped at the thought. "Maybe you and Brendan and Griff and I could—"

"No." Cassie was emphatic. "No more 'Brendan and I.' You and Griff, fine. Brendan and I, never!" She got to her feet and smoothed down her yellow cotton skirt. "I've spent as much time loafing as I dare. There must be office appointments stacked up clear to the ceiling."

"You work too hard," Lainie said. "You and the kids

and Brendan ought..." Her voice trailed off at Cassie's hostile glare. Then, shrugging, she smiled brightly. "See you tomorrow, then."

"Not if I see you first," Cassie warned, but Lainie only laughed.

It was past ten o'clock before she dragged up the front walk that evening. Initially, she had wanted to avoid Brendan by working overlong hours, but even she hadn't intended such a day. The appointments had, indeed, been stacked to the ceiling. Then Gene had dropped into her office to talk about the prognosis of the wrist he had done. Their conversation had gone on so long that they simply picked up hamburgers at a fast-food restaurant on the way to the hospital and ate them in the parking lot before going up to do evening rounds. They were about to leave when the first emergency call came through. By rights it should have been Gene who stayed; Cassie had been on call the night before. But his older daughter was in a ballet program, and he'd promised to go. Remembering the look on Keith's face when she missed game after game of his, she told Gene to go on while she stayed and set three broken bones, two easy and quick and the third requiring an open reduction that left her exhausted and thinking longingly of her home and bed much before she actually made her way there. Even the knowledge that Brendan was waiting at the other end didn't faze her now.

She was glad, though, that he was nowhere around when she finally opened the door and crept in. Someone had left a light on in the kitchen, but otherwise the house looked asleep for the night. Cassie kicked off her shoes and padded through the kitchen, enjoying the feel of the cool tile on her cramped feet as she poured herself a glass of iced tea and sat down at the table to leaf through the day's mail. She was grateful for the silence. It was the first time all day she had heard nothing more demanding than the dripping of the faucet and the ticking of the clock. Finishing her tea, she tiptoed down the hall past her own room to peek in at the boys. Keith was lying on his back in his customary sprawl, a slight smile curving his mouth and a Brendan Craig baseball card clutched in his fist. Refusing to remove it, Cassie turned and went into her younger son's room. Steve was huddled, hugging his pillow in football-tackle style, the sheet nearly pulled over his head. Had they had a good day, she wondered as she ruffled his auburn hair. Probably. She sighed with a mixture of guilt and envy. Usually when she couldn't make it home before they went to bed, she did manage to call them. That night she hadn't, even when she'd had the chance. Brendan might have answered the phone. "Sorry, guys," she mumbled, ashamed of herself as she kissed Steve lightly and went back to do the same to his brother. "Your ma is pretty dumb sometimes." It wouldn't happen again, she vowed. There was no way she would let Brendan come between her and her sons. She had a difficult enough time being a part of their lives as it was. Brendan didn't know how lucky he was, she thought briefly, to get to see them all day.

She wanted to sleep, but her mind was too busy, her body too taut. Her thoughts spun with worries about her sons, her job, the man behind the door across the hall. Even the knowledge that it was safely shut didn't give her the peace of mind to just crawl into bed exhausted. She stripped off her blouse and skirt, hanging them up, wondering momentarily if, when they needed it, Brendan would be the one to take them to the dry cleaners. Then she contemplated the pink nightgown on the hook. Shaking her head, she rejected it in favor of a flaming red-orange bikini. She had been mentally and emotionally exerting all day. Physical exertion was what she needed now.

She crept stealthily down the hallway, warily glancing back at Brendan's door, almost expecting it to spring open at any moment. Blessedly, it did not. The door to the patio was still unlocked, and she slid it back silently, then followed the path through the moonlit garden down to the pool. She hovered for a moment, toes curling around the edge of the tile, drawing in the mingling scents of chlorine and night-blooming jasmine. Then, bending her head and raising her arms, she sprang forward in a clean dive.

The water was like heaven, cool and soothing, quenching the burning in her body that she had felt for—for how long? Days, it seemed. Ever since Brendan had come back into her life. She plowed through the water, back and forth, lap after lap, the rhythmic movements of her body soothing and easing away the tensions of the day. At last, satisfied and exhausted, she surfaced in the deep end, resting one arm on the side of the pool as she shook the water out of her eyes. Turning her head, she watched the play of the moonlight on the expanding ripples.

"If I didn't know better, I'd think you were avoiding me." Brendan's voice filled the silent air.

Cassie jerked around. He was sitting in a deck chair, a dark shape silhouetted against the moonlit night. "How long have you been there?"

"Since the boys went to sleep. You walked right past me."

"Why didn't you say something?" she demanded, tempted to turn away and swim to the other end of the pool. But it would be in vain. Brendan would still be between her and the house, and she had no doubt that if he wanted, he could wait longer than she could.

"You didn't look like you wanted conversation." His answer was easy, soothing even. And Cassie, prepared to snap at him, paused abruptly when she realized that he was right.

"I didn't," she admitted.

He braced his one good arm on the side of the chair and shoved himself to his feet, crossing the tiles to where she had tossed her towel; picking it up, he moved lithely to the edge of the pool. Reaching down, he offered her a hand up. For a moment Cassie stared at it outstretched in the moonlight. It was a capable hand, strong and masculine, with long, callused fingers and a roughened palm; so different from Michael's hands. Cassie sighed. So different from Michael.

She put her hand in his, feeling the warm, rough skin close around hers as he lifted her easily to the side of the pool where she stood shivering in the moonlight.

"Thanks." She continued to tremble, though it had nothing to do with the cold, only with Brendan. He slipped the towel awkwardly around her shoulders with his right hand, draping it across her breasts. Then his fingers tightened at her nape, tugging slightly on her curls so that she tipped her head back and looked up at him. The harsh lines of his face were softened in the moonlight, his mustache shadowing his mouth so she couldn't tell his expression. Cassie sucked in her breath, remembering the feel of that mustache against her lips, wanting to feel it again.

"Cass," he murmured, and the mustache twitched slightly. "Oh, Cass, what are you doing to me?" It was almost a groan. His hand skated across her shoulder, then followed the towel down her arm, slipping beneath to touch her bare midriff. The callused fingers branded her like an electric current, spreading a warmth instantly throughout her body. Instinctively, she moved against his tantalizing hand, wanting it to continue its exploration.

"Brendan." Her voice shook. She knew she should tell him to stop; she knew she should move away; she knew she should be doing anything but standing there letting him have his way with her. *Have his way with her!* She almost laughed at her Victorian terminology. Not even her mother talked that way. Mother, she knew, would be cheering Brendan on right now. His fingers kept up their delicious stroking, moving up to the bottom edge of her skimpy bra, then slowly and teasingly down to the line of cloth below her navel. The warmth was growing within her, the tension building until, almost inexorably, Cassie's hands lifted and brushed down across the springy hair that curled on Brendan's chest. Then they raised again to stroke his cheek, brush across his mustache and tangle in his hair. It was insanity—all the while she was doing it, she knew that. It was everything she had been trying to avoid since he had plunged back into her life. But it felt so good, so right. And soon she would stop.

She felt a tremor shake him, and his hand, which had been lightly teasing her stomach and making delicious forays beneath her bra, now wrapped around her, drawing her firmly against him. Her damp trembling legs collided with strong thighs clad loosely in navy sweat pants and nothing else. Strong evidence of his desire pressed into her, making her ache to feel him even closer. He murmured her name again and again while she slid her arms around him, across the smooth, tense muscles of his back, and buried her face against his shoulder, reveling in the singularly Brendan mixture of male perspiration, after-shave and lemon-scented shampoo. His hard plaster cast was crushed between them, and Cassie moved back to give him room.

"No," Brendan muttered. "Don't go. Stay, Cassie. Want me." He groaned, burying his face in her hair, his lips moving against her ear. "Want me the way I want you."

She did want him; there was no conceivable way he could believe she did not. But she couldn't have him. Not now. Not this way. They were too different, too much at odds. She might not have done well at marriage, but that didn't mean she wanted an affair. And nothing she knew about Brendan proved that he wanted anything more. Consciously slackening her fingers, loosing their grip on his hair, she dropped her hands reluctantly to her sides. Her heart heaved in her chest as she shook her head and stepped back. Brendan touched her chin, tipping it up once more so he could look into her eyes.

"Cassie?" His voice was ragged and uncertain, stumbling over rapid breathing that made her feel guilty for having let him go on so long. She had never been a tease. She didn't want to start now.

"I can't, Brendan." She dropped her eyes, refusing to meet the glazed passion in his. But at eye level was his mustache, and that didn't make her resolve any firmer, so she resolutely stared out over his shoulder into the moonlit night at the house silhouetted behind him. In it were her sons, her mother, a whole way of life that her profession had brought her. She had no intention of abandoning it for a few moments of stolen physical pleasure. "I won't," she added more firmly, taking a deep breath. "I don't want it."

"Don't want it?" he echoed dumbfounded. "That's idiocy, Cass! How can you say that? You *do* want it. My God, that wasn't one-sided what just happened between us."

She hugged the towel more tightly, shivering in earnest now. The caressing breeze had suddenly turned into a cold wind. "I know that," she said stubbornly. "You're a very attractive man, but—"

Brendan snorted in disgust. "But you don't want me," he finished sarcastically.

"Not so. I do want you," Cassie admitted, trembling to her toes. "Or part of me does. The physical part."

Brendan's eyes glittered angrily. "Thank you very much. And you think Ballard is only interested in my body!"

"That's not the same thing at all. What I meant is, *I* don't want any complications in my life!"

"Complications?" Brendan's voice dripped scorn. He hitched his sweat pants up more securely and glowered at her.

Cassie tore her eyes away from his hand, which was struggling with the drawstring of his pants. "Definite complications." She gulped.

"I don't think so, Cass." His tone became persuasive rather than angry. "I don't want to complicate your life. I want to make it better." He paused, letting the words sink in. "I could, you know."

"No." She didn't believe him for a minute. Brendan promised danger, excitement, quick satisfaction. And whatever Cassie might be missing in her life, she didn't mind forever missing that.

"I can," he insisted. "Your mother thinks so. The boys do. Lainie does."

"There's nothing wrong with my life the way it is." She met his eyes defiantly.

Brendan's mouth curved into a gentle smile beneath the mustache, its expression so sweet that she blinked. "Isn't there, Cass?" he asked softly. Then, before she could even imagine how to respond to that, he slipped his right arm around her shoulders and led her up the silvery path toward the house. "Come on. You'll catch a chill out here. You need something to warm you up."

But Brendan's arm alone was warming her despite her wish that it would not. Stiffly, reluctantly, she walked beside him, refusing to give in to the desires of her body. But she waited for him while he locked the patio door, not going on ahead as she knew she ought. And when Brendan's hand settled once more against the cool skin of her back, she couldn't deny how right it felt. She only knew she mustn't give in.

He stopped in the hallway between their bedroom doors, turning her to face him. His athlete's body emanated both power and masculine desire held tightly in check. "Think about what you have, Cassie," he said evenly. "Two fine boys, a thriving practice, a lovely mother, a beautiful home. It's a lot, granted. But is it *all* you want, Cass? Is it really enough?"

He bent his head, and his lips brushed hers with the lightness of a butterfly's wing. Then he turned and went into his own room, shutting the door behind him with a soft click. Cassie stood alone in the hallway, the memory of Brendan touching her lips and her heart.

Chapter Five

More than once during the next ten days Brendan wondered where he'd got the nerve to even suggest that Cassie might have time in her life for more than she was already dealing with. My God, he'd never seen a woman go through life at the pace she did! She was up by six every morning, if not before, zipping through a quick breakfast designed more to sustain a bird than a human being before she crept in to kiss the boys goodbye and vanished to the hospital. From there, judging from the few times he had tried to get ahold of her, she went flat out all day, usually managing to call the boys sometime after they got home from school, often on the run from one appointment to another and frequently with the news that she had an emergency or a surgery that would require her to be home even later than usual. While Brendan had had dinner on the table by six every evening, so far Cassie had got home in time to eat it only twice. The rest of the days he had left it warming in the oven and then had stood over her when she got in, making sure she ate it.

He knew she resented his watching her. She scowled at him while he stood there, suggesting that he go watch television or play catch with the boys, but he steadfastly shook his head. "If I don't watch you, you'll throw it down the garbage disposal," he told her.

Cassie looked offended. "Would I do that?"

"You've *done* that," he reminded her.

"Only when I was in a hurry to get to Keith's ball game."

That was true, but Brendan didn't think that even Keith's game ought to come before her eating. Cassie disagreed. "I've missed dozens of them, it seems," she told him on the way to the ball park. "Lots of parents get there for every one."

"You're too busy," Brendan had argued even as he admired her obstinacy.

Cassie shrugged. "But I'm not tonight, so I should go. Shut up and drive. I don't even know how to get there."

Her life was so hectic that if he hadn't known better from personal experience, he would have thought she'd be raising maladjusted children. She certainly didn't have a quantity of time for them. But when the chips were down, she came through. She shuffled her schedule and arrived only ten minutes late for Keith and Steven's end-of-the-school-year awards assembly, slipping into a chair at the back and clapping enthusiastically when Steve's class won the award for first place in the dodge-ball tournament and beaming when Keith played trumpet in the absolutely dreadful beginning band. And afterward she took them out for hamburgers and ice cream. If she seemed reluctant to make Brendan a part of that celebration, he was sure he was the only one to notice it. Her reserved attitude was lost on the boys. He wished it were lost on him—or that he had a thicker skin. For the longer he lived with her—in the most remote sense of the word—the more he thought about her and the deeper he fell in love.

He was positive she would fall over laughing if he admitted it. Cassie clearly didn't think he was at all acquainted with the finer emotions in life. And, he had to admit a bit ruefully, for the most part she would have been right. But that was before she had come back into his life and he had become smitten. Smitten? He'd been knocked right off his feet!

Just how far gone he was came home to him vividly and forcefully on his birthday. During one afternoon by the pool the first week he had been there, when he and the boys were sharing hopes, dreams, fears and significant moments, he had told them when his birthday was. After that, he hadn't given it a thought. Birthdays, since his mother had died, had largely gone unnoticed in his life. His father was never one to make an event out of such a profane occasion, and while his brother, Duncan, and his wife usually remembered to send a card and Griff occasionally did the same, there was never anyone else in his life long enough to go to the trouble of helping him celebrate. He didn't expect anything any different this year.

In fact, his birthday landed on a Thursday, which had been designated by Cassie as his "day off" because it was also hers. In her words, she could "deal with the boys then," which meant he was supposed to disappear for the day, because she didn't want to "deal with" him. Usually, though, he hung around the house, anyway, because he had nothing better to do and he kept hoping that she might forget her defenses long enough to at least smile at him.

Idiot, he told himself impatiently as he hung about in the doorway to the patio that afternoon, watching her as she sat by the pool playing Scrabble with Keith while Steven dived about porpoiselike a few feet away. But acknowledging his idiocy didn't make it any easier to turn his back and walk away. She obviously thought he'd gone off somewhere long before, if she ever even thought about him at all. She was sitting at the poolside table, hunched over the Scrabble game with the concentration of a surgeon about to perform a life-or-death operation. He sighed and shook his head. Her intensity positively amazed him.

Just then Keith must have got a particularly good word, because he grinned at her triumphantly, then jumped up and did a mock bow. As Brendan watched, Cassie hopped to her feet and rounded the table, laughing as she grabbed her son around the waist and tossed him into the pool. Then she dived in after him. Brendan's gut ached with wanting her. He chewed on his lip, watching them roughhouse in the water, the desire to join them gnawing at his innards.

The phone rang. Tearing his gaze away from the pool, he went to answer it, almost annoyed when he heard Susan's breezy voice on the other end.

"Hi, sweetheart," she said the moment she heard him answer. "How're you doing?"

"Fine," he lied blithely, stretching the phone cord taut so he could stand by the patio door and watch Cassie.

"You don't sound fine," she informed him. "I know just the thing to cheer you up. I'm doing a story on the intercollegiate diving trials today. Want to come along?"

He should, Brendan thought. Staying around the house mooning over Cassie, who either didn't know he was alive or pretended not to, wasn't doing a thing for his ego. Except destroying it, maybe. If he went with Susan, he would have a day out with a woman who, if she didn't exactly drool over his body, at least acknowledged that he had one. Ever since Cassie had admitted to wanting his and he had told her she was just like Ballard, she had been looking at him as if he had the biceps of a paper doll. Besides, nobody should have to stay home and feel depressed on his birthday.

"All right," he agreed with as much enthusiasm as he could muster.

"Terrif'," Susan enthused. "Pick you up in an hour."

If he had spent a more miserable birthday, Brendan couldn't remember it. Even his ninth, when his father had sent the party guests home early because Brendan had spray painted the cat with his model-airplane paint, didn't hold a candle to this one. Then only his bottom had hurt from his father's well-placed smacks. Now his mind did, and his emotions, and, not least, his loins. Briefly, he wondered if he ought to ask Susan to forgo the diving and spend part of the day in bed with him. At least it would take care of one of his aches. But he knew immediately that it would be no solution. He would be seeing Cassie's face no matter whose body was in the bed. And if it wasn't Cassie's, he had more than a little doubt that he could actually become aroused at all.

Susan, fortunately, seemed oblivious to his distress. He supposed in part it was because she had a story to write about the outcome of the trials, but it also meant that she really wasn't interested in him, either. So he sat alongside her for the rest of the afternoon and the early part of the evening, acutely aware of his own misery and wishing that he were back at Cassie's where, even when she ignored him, he could at least feast his eyes on her.

Susan offered him supper out, but he declined. "I should be getting back," he told her, though there was no earthly reason why he should, except to torture himself further with visions of Cassie.

Susan looked at him oddly. "Are you getting sick?" She searched his face over the gearshift of her Triumph sports car, studying him carefully, he supposed, for spots or rashes or something.

"Not really," he said uncomfortably. "I'd just like to get back."

"Becoming a regular homebody, that's what you are," Susan chided him with a grin. "She must be some lady." She quirked her eyebrows at him, expecting confirmation. He'd always given it to her before. Now he looked at her blankly.

Susan shrugged. "Okay, don't tell me." She studied him a moment longer. Brendan felt like a specimen beneath a microscope. "You like it there, don't you, Lefty?"

He didn't even answer that for a moment, weighing in his mind what she would do with it if he did. But her blue eyes were guileless, and they had been friends for a long time. "Yeah," he mumbled. "I do."

"Good," she said easily, darting the tiny car out of the parking lot and weaving it through traffic with such abandon that Brendan felt they'd left his stomach behind. "You deserve something good, Lefty," she went on, "what with your arm and all." Her voice hung expectantly as if waiting for him to pick up the conversation.

He couldn't. Or wouldn't. There was nothing but worry where his arm was concerned, and nothing he could do about it, either. If it recovered, he would know in a couple of months. If it didn't, he would know that, too. And if it wasn't going to, he didn't want to think about it now. Thinking about Cassie was misery enough. "Tell me," he asked, changing the subject, "have you got your lead for this story yet?"

Susan shot him a look that said he wasn't fooling her a bit, but she gave in, telling him her ideas. Then he chipped in some, and fortunately the discussion lasted until she pulled up in front of Cassie's house and Brendan eased himself out of the close confines of the car.

"Thanks a lot," he told her. "I enjoyed it."

Susan laughed. "Sure you did," she said, as unconvinced as she was unoffended. "Take it easy, buddy." And whipping back out of the driveway, she squealed the tires and roared away.

Brendan stood staring after her in the waning sunlight, feeling the warm June breeze on his face and the aching deep within, and wished he had fallen in love with someone as uncomplicated as Susan. What business did he have with a high-powered woman like Cassie, anyway? Hunching his shoulders, he turned and ambled slowly up the drive to the house. Had she even missed him?

He had barely opened the front door when he heard a suppressed giggle and a loud "Shh!" Mystified, he crossed the darkened living room to the fully lit den. His eyes widened. There were balloons and streamers everywhere. Hundreds of them, quite literally, hung from the ceiling, the light fixtures, the fan, the drapery rods, bobbing about in the breeze from the patio doors.

Suddenly, through the doors, Keith and Steven burst in, whooping and grinning.

"Happy birthday!"

Brendan grabbed for the back of the nearest chair, steadying himself as much from astonishment as from their onslaught. The weight of both of them hit him at once, warm, strong arms hugging him so that all he could manage was "Wha—" His eyes sought Cassie, blinking wildly as they scanned the room, feeling a kind of giddy relief when they finally lit on her just as she stepped into the room from the patio. There was a small, almost-embarrassed smile on her face.

She shrugged, her embarrassment obviously increasing by the minute. "They said it was your birthday," she told him awkwardly. "I'd forgotten the date myself," she added, "but we, um, er, baked a cake and—" She waved her hand at the rainbow explosion of balloons and streamers as if she had no adequate words to explain it.

It was the quick ascent from misery to ecstasy that was making his eyes water, Brendan decided. He blinked furiously, wrinkling his nose. A grin cracked his face. "It's all for me?"

Cassie looked as if she might vanish from sheer embarrassment at any second, so he rushed on, not wanting to discomfit her further. "It's great. Hey, you guys." He turned to Steve and Keith, who were bouncing around the room just like the balloons. "Did you really blow up all these?"

"Yeah. An' we decorated your cake, too. See?" Steve grabbed his hand and dragged him over to the bar between the kitchen and the den where a tall two-layer cake with a veritable mountain of chocolate frosting presided on a crystal pedestal cake plate. In blue squiggly letters someone had written Happy Birthday Brendan, the last letter disappearing over the side. There was a forest of candles stuck into the frosting, and his lifted eyebrow when he saw them all brought a hurried, flustered explanation from Cassie.

"They are great sticklers for accuracy," she told him, the color high in her cheeks. "I couldn't convince them that three and three could symbolize thirty-three. Sorry."

Brendan grinned, and Cassie averted her gaze.

"Want me to light 'em?" Keith asked, beginning before he got an answer. It took nearly five minutes before he had the blaze roaring, and while wax dripped onto the frosting, they all sang happy birthday to Brendan.

Brendan swallowed hard, his eyes seeking Cassie's, wanting to tell her that even though he realized her participation was grudging, he was still grateful. But Cassie wouldn't look at him. Her eyes were fixed determinedly on the conflagration before her. Brendan's lips twisted. God, she was such a puzzle! On the one hand, she was the most capable, energetic, frighteningly competent woman he had ever met; on the other, she seemed at times totally vulnerable and unsure of herself. *Especially,* he thought, *around me.*

"Cut the cake, Bren," Steve urged, thrusting a knife at him so that he jumped back to prevent being run through with it.

Cassie drew a sharp breath and exclaimed, "Steven, for heaven's sake, be careful!"

Obediently, Brendan cut large slices of cake over which Keith heaped vanilla ice cream. Then, at Brendan's suggestion, the boys took theirs out on the patio to eat. For a moment Cassie looked as though she would follow them, but when he nodded to the sofa, she acquiesced, sitting in the far corner of it, keeping her eyes on her plate.

"It's very good," Brendan told her after he crossed the room and settled into the leather armchair farthest from her. It wasn't his first choice, but he didn't want to unnerve her, and he could savor a full view of her from there in any case.

"It's just a mix," she mumbled, not looking at him.

Brendan shrugged. He kept his hands busy cutting

off bits of cake. He would have liked to have set it down and gone across to her, sitting beside her and running his hands over her, easing the tension in her shoulders and making her come alive in his arms. Dream on, fella, he thought. "Isn't everything a mix these days?" he asked lightly. "It's still great."

"My mother would have made it from scratch," Cassie said obstinately.

"You're not your mother," he countered.

Cassie looked up then, meeting his eyes with an unfathomable expression. All he could see was a conflict that he didn't understand. "Ain't it the truth?" she agreed in a tone just as light as his, but the shoulders stiffened even more. Then she unfolded herself deliberately and rose from the sofa, patting her stomach. "I'm stuffed," she announced, and carried her plate to the sink, rinsing it and setting it on the sideboard. "Happy birthday, Brendan." She gave him a fleeting smile and stuck her head out the patio door. "Time for baths, fellas. School tomorrow. Last day!" Then, without looking at him again, she left the room.

"Cass?" He half rose from his chair to go after her. But she turned at the sound of his voice, and he sank back down at the sight of the wary expression on her face.

"What?"

He pressed his lips together. There was a lot he wanted to say. Then he smiled. "Thanks."

Cassie blinked. Then, with a slowness born of caution, she returned his smile with a perfectly beautiful one of her own. Brendan sucked in his breath. "You're welcome," she replied quietly. Then she was gone.

Brendan closed his eyes, expelling the breath slowly, reluctant to let go of the image of her smile. He felt again the familiar tightening in his loins, the quickening in his heart that accompanied all his thoughts of her. Damn, what she could do to him! He shook his head in a sort of rueful dismay. Maybe it hadn't been so smart, after all, getting himself this chance to come and live with her. Not if he wasn't ever going to be able to touch her! It must be punishment, he decided, for a lifetime of sins. His father would undoubtedly be pleased.

CASSIE THOUGHT that if nothing else, the ten days she had spent with Brendan under her roof had taught her the true meaning of "approach-avoidance conflict." The longer he was there, the less she could justify running scared; after all, he didn't seem to be chasing her! But then, the longer he was there, the more frighteningly susceptible she felt to his boyish, intriguing charm. Like tonight. It had probably been a mistake, she thought as she bolted herself inside her bathroom and began running the water for a bath, to give in to the boys when they clamored to make him a cake. But she didn't want to seem unfeeling and uncaring to them, even though, she thought grimly while she stripped off her jeans and wide-striped red-and-white boat-necked top, the problem was actually that she felt and cared far too much! In fact, she didn't know how many more exchanges like the one she had just had with Brendan Craig she could take. He was far easier to resist when he was coming on strong or teasing her into a fury. But when he looked vulnerable and touched, as he had that night and the night she rescued him from that barracuda Ballard, she felt herself growing far too fond of him.

She stepped into the warm water, then deliberately turned on the cold, trying to put a little perspective in her life. What she had told him that night by the pool was true: she did have enough in her life. She barely had a free minute between her work and her children. She didn't need the complications that a man like Brendan would involve.

And what would it involve, that irritating little voice that seemed always to be sticking up for Brendan demanded of her.

It would involve cutting down on other things, she

replied as she scrubbed herself vigorously with a thick lavender washcloth. Important things! And it would mean letting him matter *more* than they did.

And you're too busy, the voice demanded with rightful skepticism.

The washcloth paused halfway down her sleek calf. No, she admitted with more honesty than she would have preferred. It was only partly that she was too busy. Mostly, she was scared.

Ah, the voice said.

Cassie scowled. No more questions? No more soul-searching or probing? No more demands to force her to look deeply within herself. Was the voice stopping there? Just *ah*? She slapped the washcloth against the side of the tub, splattering herself in the face with icy water. Then, shivering, she bent forward and ducked her head under the faucet. What was that song? Something about washing that man right out of her hair? She smiled. It wasn't a bad idea. But somehow she didn't think that Brendan would be so easily removed. He was insidiously everywhere, rather like a bad case of lice.

She never had a clearer example of it than the next afternoon when she rushed home from the office to bake pistachio dreams to take to the end-of-the-year potluck at the boys' school. She was late, as usual. A broken hand shortly after noon had set all her appointments back forty-five minutes, and any other day she would have called home and offered excuses and said, "Let's just forget the whole thing." But there was no way she was going to miss this event with the boys. They would be crushed, for one thing; and she had to admit that she would be upset, too. Just how much had come home to her the day before while she helped them bake the cake for Brendan.

She had thought that when he left for the day that would be the end of him. In fact, it was simply an excuse for the boys to tell her all the neat things they had done with Brendan since he had arrived. It was "Brendan this" and "Brendan that" and "Brendan says you shouldn't swim right after eating" and "Brendan is gonna teach me to pitch sidearm," until she thought she would scream. If she had counted on a nice day of just mother and sons, she was heartily disappointed. And not a little bit jealous.

It didn't take long to figure out that Brendan was a far more significant person in their lives at the moment than she was. That had never happened before. Mike had taken care of them, but he hadn't had any more time than she had. And their grandmother was, of course, a favorite, but grandmas didn't teach you to pitch sidearm. So Cassie listened to their enthusiasm and saw the glow in their eyes and felt shivers of jealousy that made her resent Brendan and feel anger at herself. She needed to be a part of their lives! So today, barring disasters of the first magnitude, she was going to make those pistachio things that Elda in the office had given her the recipe for and spend a nice fun evening with her sons. That it would take place without Brendan went unsaid.

"You're late!" Steve accused when she dashed into the living room, flinging her bag into the corner of the sofa and kicking off her shoes.

"Tell me about it," Cassie said. "No fear. I'll just get changed and then fix Elda's pistachio goodies and we can—"

"Brendan already made brownies, Ma." Keith ambled out of the kitchen holding up a thick one, half-consumed. "We can take them."

Cassie halted midway down the hall in the process of peeling off the jacket to her suit. Brendan? Her stomach did a somersault. "He what?"

"Made brownies," Steve repeated, because Keith's mouth was full. "When you didn't come home like you said you would, he didn't think you'd have time and—"

"I thought Brendan wasn't coming." She could barely get the words out.

"I'm not."

She whirled at the sound of his voice behind her. He came out of his bedroom, buttoning up a dress shirt one-handed. "I'm going to a sportswriters' banquet. A retirement dinner." He made a face that said he'd rather not, but Cassie thought that he was probably going with Susan, and she couldn't dredge up much sympathy.

"Umm, yes," she mumbled awkwardly. "Well, thank you for making the brownies." She knew she still sounded put out, but she couldn't help it. She wasn't an actress, after all.

"No problem," Brendan assured her, blessedly overlooking her impolite behavior. He grinned at her sons. "I had plenty of help. They stirred." He flopped his plastered arm a bit to demonstrate his helplessness, and Cassie felt an even bigger heel.

She avoided his eyes. "Thank you," she repeated. She wanted to move past him down the hall to her room, but he wasn't moving. To get by, she would have to brush by him, touch his arm, breathe in his after-shave. She backed against the wall, edging toward him while he regarded her with obvious amusement. Why couldn't he just move? "Excuse me," she said irritably to the shoulder in front of her nose.

Brendan did a double take, as if he hadn't been totally aware that she was trying to pass by. "Oh, sure." He stepped back then, but not much, and she still brushed against his arm as she darted by.

Her heart thudding, she hung her suit in the closet and changed into a pair of faded jeans and a canary-yellow cotton pullover sweater. She had to get a grip on herself. He was the baby-sitter, for God's sake! She ran the brush through her curls, leaving them loose. It made her look more motherly, she thought. Less like a chairman of the board.

"You look about twelve years old," Brendan said, pushing open the door to her room.

"Don't you ever knock?" Cassie glared at him in the mirror.

"I did." He was crossing the room toward her, a tie in his hand. For a second she had the skittish feeling that he was about to lasso her with it. "You must have been day-dreaming," he teased. The gentle smile that she hated because it melted her defenses lit his features. He held out his tie to her. "Can you knot this for me?"

Oh, Lord. Her fingers clenched around the handle of the brush. She drew a deep but, she hoped, indiscernible breath. She had knotted Michael's ties lots of times. *Lots of times.* One tie was just like another. One man was just like another. Right?

Wrong.

She took the tie from him, the smooth silk cool against her palm. Brendan stood obediently in front of her while she threaded it through the button-down collar of his pale blue shirt. Her fingers touched the dark hair that just lapped his collar in the back, and she sucked in her breath. Another mistake. Deep breaths drew in powerful scents of something undeniably Brendan. She expelled her breath quickly and concentrated on breathing shallowly. Then she realized that she was panting. Idiot, she thought, and jerked the tie.

"Hey!" Brendan's voice was mildly reproving.

Cassie felt her face burn. "Sorry," she mumbled. "I'm out of practice." Now her fingers were right under his chin, her knuckles brushing against newly shaved skin. Torture. Did he *know* what he was doing to her? She lifted her lashes momentarily, trying to catch a glimpse of his expression without giving away her own. His jaw was taut, his features composed. Her eyes dropped to his chest. He, too, was barely breathing. Oh, yes, he knew. And the feeling was apparently mutual. Knowing that didn't make her feel any better. She slid her fingers up the length of the tie, knotting it firmly. Then her hands dropped to her sides, and she bowed her head, steadying her rampant emotions.

The highly polished loafers didn't move away. The regimental striped tie moved closer, and she felt something—his lips?—brush her forehead.

"Thanks, Cass." He sounded as winded as she felt.

Cassie reached blindly for the hairbrush again, then quickly stepped away from him. "Don't mention it," she said, hoping she sounded more breezy than breathless. "Have a good time tonight." She put the thought that he would probably be with Susan again out of her mind. What difference did it make, anyway, she reminded herself. You're not interested in him. Much.

Brendan smiled. "You, too," he said.

She did have a good time. She and Keith won the three-legged race, Steve got a shirtful of egg yolk in the egg toss, nobody asked her to diagnose any illnesses, and everyone complimented her brownies.

"You'll have to give me the recipe," one harried mother told her. "I'm Nathan's mother. I do deviled eggs." She winked. "They're easy."

Cassie didn't dare say she didn't even do brownies. Especially not after she heard Steve telling a friend, "We brought brownies. Ma was gonna make some pistachio junk. Nobody *ever* eats that!" So she smiled and told Nathan's mother, "I'll have Steve bring you a copy." Brendan the chef could dictate it to him!

Damn Brendan! She supposed she ought to feel indebted to him. He was, after all, making her seem a far more competent mother than she actually was. If he hadn't baked the brownies, they'd have been late, and they'd also undoubtedly have had to carry home a plateful of pistachio junk that no one would eat. Still, it didn't stop the feelings of resentment and inadequacy she felt growing inside her. Did other mothers know that pistachio was out, she wondered. How did Brendan know? Was she really losing touch with her sons?

"It was a super party," Steven told her sleepily as she bundled him into bed that night. "Didn't you think so?" he asked, regarding her with a green stare that was almost a mirror of her own.

Cassie blinked. "Yes, yes, I did." She bent over and ruffled his hair, remembering all the times she had come in and kissed him good-night after he was already asleep, whole weeks when, it seemed, she had scarcely seen him at all. He was almost nine years old. In nine more, he would be off to college. Where had so much time gone? And what did she have to show for it?

"Can we do it again?" Steve asked, shoving himself up off his pillow as she turned to leave the room.

"Sure," she promised. "Sure we can." But she wondered, with more than a bit of wistfulness, if it was a promise that she could keep.

She was sitting in the den still wondering when the clock struck eleven and she heard the front door open quietly and Brendan came in. She sat up with a start, wondering if she ought to make a run for her bedroom before he came into the den. But she knew he would hear her scurrying like a rat in flight, and anyway, she didn't have the energy for it. She felt hollow, depressed somewhat, more aware than usual of what she was missing. So she sagged back against the soft leather sofa and took another sip of her rapidly cooling cup of tea.

Brendan's eyebrows lifted when he saw her sitting in the dimly lit room. "Did I miss curfew, then?"

Cassie shook her head, a slight smile touching her lips. She felt a pull like the tide emanating from him so strongly that she almost got up off the sofa and crossed the room to put her arms around him. *It's late and you're tired,* she told herself. But he looked warm and inviting, his sport coat slung over his shoulder, the tie she had so carefully knotted now loosened and the top buttons of his shirt undone.

"Something wrong?" Brendan asked.

Cassie sighed. "Just thinking."

He crossed the room and sank down onto the couch barely a foot away from her. Any other time she would have drawn herself more tightly into a ball. But now, in her wistful, almost-bemused state of mind, his presence warmed her. His movements were slow and easy, calming, not threatening. He fiddled with his tie, loosening it completely and then stripping it off. Then he dropped it on the coffee table and stretched out his legs in front of him so that her eyes followed the length of navy-blue material as it shaped his thighs.

"Everyone loved your brownies," she told him, trying to keep the slight hurt she had felt out of her voice. She must not have been entirely successful, however, for Brendan shrugged and said, "I didn't mean to usurp your rights."

"No. No, it's fine," she assured him, laughing a little shakily. "I found out that pistachio isn't big among the elementary-school set. You saved my reputation!"

Brendan's mustache lifted in a grin. "That's a first."

Cassie returned the smile. "I'll bet." Saving reputations had never been a part of Brendan's repertoire. She remembered him at Keith's age when he and Griff had been playing ball at the park and had hit a high hard one through Mrs. Cameron's dining-room window. No one knew who had done it, but Brendan looked as innocent as Griffin did stoical. There was no question about which one of them took the blame. She looked at Brendan now in the dim light and thought how short a time ago that seemed.

"We're getting old, Bren," she said, laying her head against her arm as it rested against the back of the sofa.

Brendan's jaw tightened, and he clenched the fingers of his broken arm. Cassie felt a guilty stab as she realized that he had problems with time, too.

"I mean, I was looking at the boys tonight. They're growing up while I'm at work. I'm not sure I know them anymore." Or myself, either, she added silently. Needs and wants she had never recognized before were suddenly assuming a huge significance in her life. "Is it enough?" she remembered the echo of Brendan's question.

"I know what you mean," he said slowly, lacing his fingers through his hair. "In another ten years they'll be gone."

Cassie was silent. Then she slowly unfolded herself

and rose to her feet. "Exactly." She carried the stone-cold cup of tea to the sink and dumped it. "And in another ten years, where will I be?" The question swam in her head as she turned to go down the hallway. Is it enough? Where will I be? And how did Brendan fit in her life? Or did he? "Good night," she called over her shoulder. She needed to do some thinking—without any help from the man she left slumped on the couch.

BRENDAN FELT as if the tie on the table were still choking his neck. He stared at it, then at the back of the woman who was disappearing down the hall. And what about me, he wondered as his eyes went from her down to his white plastered arm and back again. What in the hell about me?

THAT NIGHT Cassie had nightmares. She was a barren, lonely old woman in a sterile room. Everything was antiseptic and stainless steel. The boys were grown and gone, and there was no Brendan anywhere. Everywhere she looked in the dream he was beyond reach. She could catch the elusive scent of his shaving lotion, hear the rough amusement of his laugh, but Brendan himself wasn't there. She awoke at dawn tired and strangely bereft.

In fact, the very opposite was true. Everywhere she looked there was Brendan. He was in the den, on the patio, in the kitchen. He was whistling in the shower or singing off-key while he clipped the grass and Keith pushed the mower up and down the lawn. His wristbands were in the junk drawer of the dining-room buffet; his insurance card was among the unpaid bills; his baseball cap was on the back seat of her car. She couldn't have escaped him even if she had tried. And she had to stop trying, she decided, if she wanted to keep up a good relationship with her sons. They were where Brendan was; and if she wanted them, she would have to learn to keep her emotions under control where he was concerned.

It would be nice, she thought, if she could turn him into a friend. But looking at him that morning as she sat at the breakfast bar sipping orange juice and eating toast while he made himself some dreadfully healthy concoction in the blender, she knew it wouldn't be easy. She tried to dredge up the momentary ease she had felt in his presence the night before. But it wouldn't come. Instead, she was all too conscious of his lithe, tanned body. And why shouldn't she be, she wondered wryly, when he was hardly wearing any clothes? All that covered the essential parts of him was a pair of royal-blue jogging shorts that now, as he leaned across the counter to plug in the blender, rode high enough up his thigh to bare the new pink skin where his abrasions had finally healed.

You've seen it all before, Cassie reminded herself firmly. But Brendan had particularly tantalizing buttocks, and she felt a heat course through her body that owed nothing to the warm June morning.

"How can you drink that stuff?" she asked him irritably when he turned, giving her a full view of his chest with its whorls of dark hair as he tipped the container to his lips and drained the entire ghastly mess.

Brendan grinned, froth dotting his mustache. "Good for you," he said, winking at her. "Try it. It puts hair on your chest."

Cassie rolled her eyes. "Just what I need."

"No. You don't." The light of desire kindled in his eyes. "Your chest is terrific just the way it is."

She would have liked to remind him of some of his more juvenile comments about the relative flatness of her chest, but it was a subject she didn't want to pursue. It was all too obvious where such a conversation would lead, and with Brendan she always finished second best. He had a mouth faster than his fast ball, she bet. Fortunately, she was saved by Keith handing Brendan a copy of the *Los Angeles Times*, which reviewed a movie he wanted to see.

Brendan dutifully read it and looked up. "Sounds

okay to me. If you guys want to, we can take in the matinee."

"Super!" Keith bolted for the patio to tell his brother, then stopped and turned back. "You wanta come, Mom?"

Cassie's eyes flickered from her son to Brendan. Coming meant getting to spend time with the boys, which she wanted. It also meant spending time with Brendan, which she didn't. Decisions, decisions. She met his eyes, catching the dare she read in them. "All right," she said firmly. In ten years the boys would be gone. And so, almost certainly, would Brendan. *Don't let him get to you,* she told herself. *He is a here-today, gone-tomorrow sort of guy. He is as undependable as he is attractive. And you have lots of willpower. You can cope.*

It was a great pep talk. Unfortunately, she never had to discover whether she would have coped or not. Twenty minutes before they were about to leave for the movie, the phone rang. There had been an accident on the freeway. Cassie was on call. Could she come?

"You know," Brendan told her as she stuffed her feet into her shoes and headed for the door, "you and Gene ought to think about getting another partner. You're gone more than you're home. Something's got to give."

Cassie looked at him, seeing the dare replaced by concern on his face. She shrugged, uncomfortable with his caring. "Maybe," she said, unsure. He was right about one thing, she thought as she drove to the hospital, visions of broken bones, woeful little boys and silky dark mustaches swirling in her mind. Something definitely was going to give.

She wondered if the something would be Cassandra Farrell Hart.

Chapter Six

"I can't believe you're really coming, too," Steven said to his mother as he bounced on the back seat of Brendan's BMW as Cassie backed it out of the driveway.

Cassie couldn't believe it, either. The thought of spending an entire day at Knott's Berry Farm Amusement Park in the company of Brendan Craig completely unnerved her. It wasn't what she'd had in mind at all, she thought as she shot a quick glance at the lean, powerful man sprawled in the other half of the front seat of her car. She had made a simple suggestion at dinner the night before that she take the boys to the Griffith Park Zoo on her day off the next day. But instead of it being met with cheers from her sons and a sigh of relief from Brendan, who could have had the day free, it was received with groans of dismay.

"But we were goin' to Knott's Berry Farm!" the boys had chorused. "We don't wanta go to the zoo!"

Then Steve had said, "Why don'tcha come with us?"

Brendan had looked at her over a plate of spaghetti and said, "Yes, why don't you?"

The look in his eyes positively dared her, and after her failure to go to the movie and three other places he had taken the boys to, she knew she was committed. So she had jutted out her chin and said airily, "All right, why not?"

And there she was, cruising down the San Diego Freeway, trapped by her own obstinacy into spending a day with a man she found almost impossible to resist.

"Are we there yet?" Keith asked even before they had got south of Palos Verdes.

"No," Cassie said, wishing the car had bucket seats. Brendan's thigh was just millimeters from her own. His plastered arm lay along the back of the seat, his fingers almost—but not quite—brushing her curls. She inched closer to the door.

"How much farther?" Steve asked moments later.

Cassie groaned, imagining another hour punctuated by similar questions. But Brendan turned sideways in the seat, grinning back at him. "Ages," he said cheerfully. "Hours and hours. Want to hear a story?"

"Yeah! Yeah!" came the duet from the back seat.

Cassie was intrigued in spite of herself. Brendan told stories? Well, she guessed that fit. He had always been glib. And in school he'd never told the truth if fiction sounded better. She wondered what sort of stories he told these days. Not X-rated ones, she hoped. "What about?" she asked him cautiously.

Brendan laughed, his grin telling her that he'd read her thoughts. But Keith chimed in, "Great ones, Ma! Mysteries. Brendan's got this sleuth called Fellwell and—"

"Fellwell?" Cassie shot Brendan an amused glance. "Wasn't he our rather klutzy journalism teacher? The one who poked his nose into everything?" The one who had threatened Brendan with expulsion every other week at least. And not without cause, either, as she recalled.

Brendan's grin widened. "This Fellwell is a gumshoe with a sharp mind and two left feet. Sound appropriate?"

Cassie laughed. "Very. Do go on. I'm all ears."

"Not quite." Brendan's eyes roved over her body, teasing her before he deliberately turned back to the boys and began his tale. Cassie kept her eyes on the road, but her mind was focused on the man sitting by her side.

By the time they reached Knott's Berry Farm, Cassie

had decided that he was indeed a man with a silver tongue. Glib didn't begin to cover it. "If you don't pitch again, you can always be a TV commentator," she told him unthinkingly as they walked from the car toward the amusement park.

He stopped flat. "Don't pitch again? Why not?"

Cassie turned to see a white, stricken look on his face. "I'm sorry," she said quickly. "I didn't mean that. I wasn't thinking." Damn, he looked positively grim. She hadn't realized he was so touchy about the possibility. He never mentioned his arm at all now. Or he hadn't until she'd opened her big mouth. She hoped he would just forget it, but he caught ahold of her hand, clenching her fingers so tightly that they hurt.

"You're my doctor, Cass," he said roughly. "What are you trying to say?"

She shook her head, confused as much by his nearness as by the tautness of his tone. "Nothing. I just meant that you are marvelously gifted with words. You were always a good writer. I—I remember the things you wrote for the paper and the literary magazine in high school." She was running off at the mouth, but she couldn't help it. He looked so vulnerable.

"Will I pitch, Cass?"

She faced him straight on then, turning her hand so that their fingers were linked, not crushed. "I have every reason to believe that you will," she told him honestly.

He swallowed. "From everything you've seen?" he persisted.

"From everything I've seen, you're healing up nicely."

"But you said, 'If you don't pitch...'" He was ignoring the shouts of the boys to hurry and the stares and nudges of several intrigued bystanders who seemed to recognize him as a celebrity in their midst.

"You will not be able to pitch forever, Brendan," she replied. How like him not to have even thought beyond his baseball career. "Not even Satchel Paige did that."

"But a few more years?"

He sounded like one of the Lost Boys pleading for a few more years until he had to grow up. She smiled. "God willing, yes," she said. "Now, come on. We're attracting a crowd."

Brendan still stared at her, his eyes probing as if trying to see into the depths of her heart, to read the truth written there. And for once Cassie tried to show it to him. He needed to believe in her sincerity for his own sake, even if he saw too much in her.

"All right," he said finally, apparently satisfied. He glanced around at the group of people who had gathered, and a faint grin touched his lips. "I'm sorry, Cass. It's just that I wonder sometimes. And it looks as if I'm not the only one!"

Cassie soon discovered that with Brendan, even wearing sunglasses, it was hard not to attract a crowd. He was famous, oddly enough almost beloved by an adoring public. And as the day wore on, he gained more and more of her respect, for while he never seemed to crave the adulation accorded him, he never shunned the people who stopped to wish him well, to commiserate about his accident or to ask him to pat their children on the head. He always obliged with a smile, only going so far as to say once, "I never realized that there was an advantage to breaking my arm."

"What's that?" she asked as they stood in line with the boys to ride on one of the stagecoaches.

"No one asks me to sign autographs."

Cassie laughed. "The eternal optimist," she teased.

"When life gives you lemons..." Brendan quoted, grinning as he helped her onto the front seat of the coach and scrunched against her to make room for the boys. Cassie was overwhelmed by his nearness, the feel of his denim-clad thigh pressed against her own and the warm strength of his suntanned arm as he wrapped it loosely about her shoulders.

"Life didn't give you lemons," she argued. "It gave you caviar."

"Fish eggs by any other name." He winked roguishly at her, lifting a corner of his mustache in a teasing grin. The stage lurched forward, bouncing Cassie against him, and his arm tightened. There was no arguing with him, she thought. He could talk circles around her or render her speechless with a touch. She could never win at all.

By early evening she wasn't even sure she wanted to. She couldn't ever remember being so carefree in her life. Despite her initial wariness about him and about her attraction to him, she nevertheless found that she was growing more comfortable with his lighthearted teasing, the boyish grin lurking just beneath his dark mustache and the warm, bubbly feelings he evoked in her as the day progressed. It reminded her of the feelings that teen magazines had always promised she would experience on the "ideal date." During her sporadic and spectacularly uneventful dating career, she had ended up more often annoyed than bubbly. She couldn't ever remember feeling truly comfortable with any man she had dated except possibly Michael. And their dates had consisted of studying together in the library, and the teen mags never promised anything ideal about that. But that day she seemed to have found the missing ingredient. And what was that, she asked herself wryly as she and Brendan leaned against a souvenir stand, licking ice cream cones in the late-afternoon sun while the boys clambered onto the merry-go-round. Was it her two little boys? Had she needed them to make her dating life sparkle? Or, she considered the possibility reluctantly, had she needed Brendan?

"Let's ride the merry-go-round." He broke into her reverie just in time. She was too close to probing the truth of that supposition, and she knew that any such probing had better be done alone, not in the presence of Brendan Craig.

"Merry-go-round?" She looked at him, amazed. He had boysenberry ice cream on the fringe of his mustache and the light of anticipation in his dark blue eyes.

"Even Keith thought he was too old for the merry-go-round," she protested.

Brendan winked. "Keith is too young to know what I know," he told her, tearing off two tickets and dragging her after him toward a vacant white horse. "Up you go." He tossed her the reins. And shrugging, though she wondered just exactly what she was letting herself in for now, Cassie flung herself up onto the horse. The next instant she felt Brendan settling himself on the horse with her.

"Brendan! You can't!" She quailed at the feel of his hard chest pressing against her back and his muscular thighs rubbing intimately on her own.

He grinned unrepentantly. "Of course I can!" His breath stirred the hair beside her ear, and she shivered. Brendan turned to the ticket taker, who looked as though two people on a horse was against every rule he knew. "Can't I?" Brendan asked, innocence personified. "I need her to keep my balance. Because of my arm," he added.

And while Cassie fumed and bristled at this falsehood, the boy nodded seriously and said, "Yes, sir, Mr. Craig, sir," and Cassie realized that there were perks to fame she hadn't thought of till then.

"You are an unconscionable liar," she told Brendan as the music started and the horse began to move. His right arm tightened around her just beneath the swell of her breasts, and she thought she might never breathe again.

"Glib," he corrected. "I think that's a kinder word."

"It doesn't do you justice," she snapped, her face flaming. Brendan ducked his head and laid his cheek alongside her ear, his breath stirring her curls in the same way that the warmth and nearness of his body was stirring longings buried deep inside her.

"Good idea, hmm?" he murmured.

Cassie wanted to say no, it was not a good idea at all. But the longings once stirred were warming her, melting her from within, and her resolve was going down in flames along with the rest of her. The rhythmic rise and fall of the white stallion, the lilting tune, the smell of Mexican food and Brendan's tangy after-shave all combined to defeat her. "Not bad," she whispered back, and allowed one hand to drop down to rest against the side of his denim-clad thigh. Brendan's muscles tautened, and he sucked in his breath as if he were going to say something.

For a second he didn't speak, and she wondered if her moment of daring had been a colossal mistake. But just as she was about to withdraw her hand, he covered it with his own. "Does this mean we're going to be friends?" he asked, a note of gentle amusement but no sarcasm in his voice.

Cassie fumbled in confusion, her eyes fastening on their hands. She could see the differences emphasized there. Rough, callused ballplayer's fingers alongside deft surgeon's ones. But there was something complementary about them, too, and a comfort as well as a spark whenever they touched. "Yes," she agreed softly, not daring to lift her head or turn her gaze to meet his. "Yes, I guess we are going to be friends."

"At last," she thought she heard him mumble. Then he hugged her against him with his heavy plastered arm until the music ceased and Cassie planted her feet on the ground once more.

On the way home Steve asked over and over, "Wasn't that neat? Didn't you have a great time, Mom?"

And Cassie could only agree. She was curled in the passenger seat now, letting Brendan drive. She hadn't argued when he'd lifted the keys from her fingers. She might have had her feet on the ground, but the rest of her was sky high, basking in the sunshine of his smile and wondering if Knotts put uppers in their chicken dinners or if there was another, more personal, reason she felt so euphoric.

"You're high," Brendan teased her. "You're the

only person I know who gets an upper from boysenberry ice cream."

"It wasn't the ice cream." Cassie's eyes met his again, and if she blushed under his gaze, it wasn't because she was embarrassed or incompetent for once but because she felt that everything was right and that the day had brought her a delicious anticipation of things to come.

Just how things had changed she wasn't entirely sure. Probably, she reflected as she leaned against the back of the seat and watched while Brendan deftly pulled around a Chevette, it had been coming on ever since their confrontation by the pool. Until then she hadn't really considered that she was missing anything vital from her life. It had certainly seemed full. But after that, all her running had seemed like so much time on a treadmill. There was time for work, time—albeit little—for the boys but precious little time for her. And it was daily exposure to Brendan that made her realize it. Besides being just what she ordered for the boys, she thought that he might be the right prescription for her, too. Not in any permanent sense, she hastened to add, just in case her mind decided to go in for too much fantasy. But at least to point out to her a bit of what she was missing. That day she had simply given in to what she'd discovered she wanted all along. And the feeling was delightful. The question, of course, was where did she go from here?

If she were a teenager, she could go home and read the next installment in the magazines that had first alerted her to the existence of the perfect date. But thirty-two-year-old widows, she imagined, were expected to rely on their instincts and vast experience and not expect a set of diagramed play-by-plays. It was a pity she didn't have more faith in her own instincts.

There was a full moon by the time they'd arrived home, and stars twinkled romantically behind the palm trees that lined the curve of the street. Cassie thought a

Hollywood set designer couldn't have done better until Brendan pulled the car into the driveway and she saw Susan Rivers standing on the front porch.

"What's *she* doing here?" Cassie demanded, sitting bolt upright and glaring, feelings she didn't want to put a name to flooding her entire being.

Brendan shrugged. Cassie wished she could see annoyance in his face. Earlier she had been more than understanding of all the people who had sought contact with him, but she didn't feel at all understanding now. He waved a hand at Susan and hopped out of the car, neglecting, Cassie noticed, to come around and open the door for her. Not that he had done it before, either, she acknowledged gruffly. It was just that she had been expecting it, had spent the whole ride home in some sort of fuzzy purple daydream that obviously now had no bearing on reality at all.

She got out, shutting the car door with a bang, herding the boys quickly toward the house with the instincts of a well-trained sheepdog protecting its charges from a lurking wolf.

"You remember Susan," Brendan said, turning to her as she brushed past him, nose in the air.

"How do you do, Miss Rivers." She kept right on walking, chilled to the bone, and knew that her words sounded even colder.

"Hi, Miss Rivers," Keith said enthusiastically. "You should have come along today. We had a great time. Even better than the day you came with us to the beach."

The knot in Cassie's stomach tightened further. They'd been to the beach with Susan? She steered Keith through the door by his nape. "Say good-night, boys."

"Join us for a glass of wine on the patio," Brendan called after her, and she heard a note of uncertainty in his voice.

"Thank you, but I'm tired." She had absolutely no intention of joining them. There was no way she could compete with the likes of Susan Rivers, and there was no point in even trying. As if it weren't bad enough to pit Little Orphan Annie against a Joan Collins look-alike, there was also the incredible gap in their social skills. Cassie simply didn't have any. When it came to man-woman small talk and the charming little things that developed relationships, she was a disaster. "First pajamas, then brush your teeth," she commanded the boys. That was why she and Michael were so well suited. They both went their own ways, intent on their careers, passing in the hall on the way to individual success. That they had Keith and Steven owed more to exploratory biological experiments than impassioned lovemaking. And looking at Brendan with the very lovely, seductive Susan, she couldn't imagine him understanding that. Nor could she imagine that he would really expect her to reappear and be gracious and genial to Susan. He knew she wasn't good at that sort of thing—never had been. And, she thought angrily as she chivied the boys off to bed and tossed their dirty clothes in the hamper, most likely he really wouldn't want to be bothered, either. She had no doubt that he and Susan could keep very well occupied together with no help from her at all.

She kissed the boys good-night and closed their doors, pausing in the hall and listening, feeling like a spy in her own home. She heard voices on the patio, the clink of glasses, John Williams playing Bach on the guitar. Damn, if he had had to entertain a sportswriter, why couldn't it have been a cigar-chomping, potbellied one?

She retreated to the bathroom, hoping that a long, cool soak in the tub would help her become her calm, sensible self once more. It didn't. In her mind she kept hearing Brendan's voice, droll and amusing, as he told them the Fellwell story. Then she visualized the stricken expression on his face when she made her thoughtless comment about his pitching career and the way he looked at her with desire in his eyes while she licked drips of boysenberry sherbet from her fingers. She recalled the roughness of his arm beneath her breasts on the merry-go-round, the heady scent of his after-shave, the warmth of his hand covering hers on the soft, faded jeans he wore. And then she remembered Susan.

She yanked out the plug and wrapped herself in a lavender-sprigged bath sheet, rubbing herself briskly, trying to blot out memories as much as bath water. Then, putting on a sheer green gown whose color reminded her that she ought to call the hospital and check on a patient, she padded back into the bedroom and picked up the phone.

She would have been smarter, she thought, to have gone to the hospital that day than to have let herself fall into the romantic trap of mooning over Brendan Craig. Her instinct to run had been right all along. *Dumb move, Hart,* she told herself. *There are some things you are cut out for and some you're not.* Moonlit nights and soft guitars were obviously not on her list. If she got smart, she would stick to reducing fractures and repairing nerve damage and leave the hearts and flowers to someone else.

Without warning, the door crashed open, and Brendan stood in the doorway, glaring at her. Cassie dropped the phone back onto the hook and wrapped her arms defensively across her chest. He strode in and kicked the door shut behind him.

"You haven't changed a bit," he accused, his blue eyes glinting dangerously.

Exactly what she had been thinking herself. Cassie lifted her chin coolly. "I don't remember inviting you in here, Mr. Craig." Her toes clenched on the soft pile of the carpet, but she stood her ground.

"You are just as big a damned snob as you ever were!" he went on, ignoring her comment. He ran agitated fingers through already-disheveled hair so that it stood up in spikes before flopping across his forehead.

"Snob?" Cassie didn't know whether to be outraged or laugh. "Who's a snob?" She stood up, glared, real-

ized he could see every curve and then some through the diaphanous material of her gown, and promptly wadded herself into a ball again on the bed, pulling the gown over her drawn-up knees and wrapping her arms tightly around them. It was as close as she could get to turtle posture, and it would have to do.

"You. You are a snob." He seemed to take great delight in drawing out the words, putting heavy emphasis on each and every syllable, his mouth twisting into a mocking smile. "What do you think Susan is? Dirt?"

Ask a loaded question, Cassie thought, but she had no intention of saying so. "I do not think Susan Rivers is dirt," she said succinctly, not committing herself to more until she knew where the conversation was going.

"Then where do you get off waltzing past her like some damned prima donna, like you couldn't be bothered to even say hello!"

"Prima— *Me*?" Cassie couldn't believe her ears. "Are you serious?"

"Damned right I'm serious. Just because you're some lord high doctor with all your damned degrees, does that mean you can't even be polite to us lesser mortals?"

Cassie stared, numbed. Brendan glowered, a flush emphasizing the high cheekbones and the sharp angularity of his face. "Is *that* why you think I walked past?" she asked, stunned.

"Isn't it?" He didn't look as though he had a doubt in the world.

"No."

Neither of them said any more. Eyes fenced, dueled, parried. Neither looked away. Finally, Brendan sighed and stuffed his hands into his pockets. Cassie couldn't help noticing the way they stretched the material across his thighs, emphasizing a raw masculinity that she had no way of dealing with. She sighed, too. That was precisely why she had turned the field over to Susan without so much as a fight. "Why, then?" he asked.

Cassie rocked back and forth on the bed, gathering

courage. "Exactly for the reason you said," she told him honestly. "Because I haven't changed."

Brendan opened his mouth, but she cut him off. "That doesn't mean what you think it does. It's not because I'm a snob."

"No?" He didn't look convinced. One dark eyebrow lifted in obvious skepticism. "You've had your nose in the air for years."

"I am not a snob," she repeated, knotting her fingers together, wishing she had the savoir faire to put him off but knowing that while honesty might not be the best policy, for her it was the only available option. "I just cannot compete with Susan. I never could—just like you suggested. And I still can't."

Brendan looked stupefied. "Who the hell's asking you to compete?" he demanded. His brows drew together in a frown, and he crossed the room to stand next to the bed, looming over her.

"For God's sake, sit down," Cassie said irritably. "You're intimidating enough without hovering over me like that!"

"Me?" Brendan looked incredulous. "*I* intimidate *you*?" He almost laughed. But he sat. Unfortunately, Cassie thought, on the bed. Not even a foot away. She edged back uncomfortably.

"Yes. You always have." There, she couldn't be more honest than that. She wondered what he would make of it.

He looked surprised, then amused. "Would it help if I said the feeling was mutual?"

Cassie snorted inelegantly. "Be serious." A werewolf wouldn't intimidate Brendan Craig.

He rested his elbow on his knee, then turned his head to regard her past the dull white plaster on his other arm. "I am completely serious," he said softly, and she could almost believe it, seeing the intensity of his clear blue eyes. "You terrify me. You have for years. And that crap about not being able to compete with Susan is absurd. You've got more brains in your little finger than—"

"*Brains*," Cassie snapped, "are not the issue here!"

"So what kind of competition are we talking about, then?" he asked.

Cassie rolled her eyes. And how did she answer that? A dull red flush crept up her neck. Starting near her bosom, she imagined. Brendan, who was staring in that general direction, suddenly seemed to notice, for he ran his hand uneasily beneath the collar of his polo shirt and dropped his eyes, mumbling, "Oh," like a thirteen-year-old boy who has just discovered something different about girls. Then he said gruffly, "You are out of your mind," which was just the sort of non-comment that Cassie had expected.

"You get my point." She gave him an arch look that provoked one of exasperation in return.

"You mean you're desperate to be a sex symbol?" Brendan growled, his eyes raking her hunched shoulders and defensive arms as if seeking some sort of reason why her mind had ever entertained such an aberrant thought.

"I don't know what I'm desperate for!" Cassie wished he would just leave. She needed space, time to think. What had he meant, she terrified him? Because of her brains? Probably. He certainly wouldn't be the first to turn and run. She wanted to groan at the thought.

"I know what I'm desperate for," Brendan said, and suddenly he twisted, his arm catching her off-balance and rolling her back on the bed where the next thing she felt were his lips meeting hers. Hot and persuasive, they were everything she had dreamed of, everything she remembered. And before she could say, "Susan," she was kissing him back. She could still taste a hint of boysenberry sherbet as his tongue darted past her teeth, staking a claim on her. It was no teasing kiss, no prelude to passion. It was passion itself. His hips against hers were urgent; his knee thrust between hers as he covered her body with his, his cast anchoring her so that his free hand could tangle in her marigold hair.

"Brendan?" Her voice was jerky, as though he had drawn all her breath out of her body, when at last he lifted his lips from hers. Cool night air caressed her cheek, but she only wanted to feel again the roughness of his and the velvety lips on her own.

"Do you get *my* point?" he rasped, his eyes, just inches above her own, dark with desire.

Cassie looked at him, bewildered. What point?

"You're all the sex symbol I want, lady. There's no competition between you and Susan."

He had kissed her to make a point? "Let go! Let me go, Brendan!" She tried to pull away, to sit up, but he held her fast, the heavy cast pinning her down while he caught her chin in his hand.

"Cassie." His voice was low and patient, like that of a father talking to his child. "You're a very attractive woman."

She concentrated on the moon beyond the wide louvered window and on the crickets chirping by the pool. "I am a very intelligent woman," she corrected him tonelessly.

"The hell you are! You're dumb as a crutch about this!" Brendan exploded.

Cassie's eyes jerked to look at him.

"I don't want Susan." He enunciated every word. "I never did. I do want you. Is that clear enough for you?"

"Why?"

Brendan looked as if he might tear his hair out. Or hers. "Why not? I'm a normal male with all the normal male instincts and—"

"They why don't you want Susan?" Cassie countered.

"Because I don't sleep with the press, all right?" he snapped, irritated, his weight pressing her into the bed.

"But you do with your doctor?"

He glared at her. "Maybe I won't sleep with you," he said pleasantly. "Maybe I'll just strangle you instead."

Cassie's mouth twitched into a smile at his words. She shoved against his chest with her hands, and this time he pulled back enough to let her sit up beside him. They regarded each other steadily, eyes studying, deciphering, trying to find words that neither would say. She saw passion in his eyes, the flames now banked and controlled, and she saw respect. She saw amusement and tolerance and something more. And she wanted to give something in return. For the first time in many years she thought she might have drawn a bit closer to Brendan Craig. "I didn't mean to behave like a snob, Brendan," she told him in a low, clear voice. "If I seem to, it's my own insecurities causing it, not my opinion of Susan."

A light sparked in the sea-blue depths of his eyes, and slowly he bent forward and brushed his lips tenderly across hers. Then he got to his feet and hooked his thumb in the belt loop of his jeans, looking down at her with a half smile creasing his face. "Relax, lady," he said softly. "You've got nothing to be insecure about."

Maybe not, thought Cassie hours after he had gone. But then what was it that was keeping her awake all night long?

WOMEN, Brendan decided as he idly flipped a Frisbee across the sand to Steven, were a pain in the rear. Especially one woman. She was an incredibly maddening combination of Madame Curie, Queen Victoria and Shirley Temple, with enough sex appeal thrown in to make him ache like a boy. And just when he thought he'd got her figured out, she showed him another side of herself entirely. The day before, at the amusement park, she had finally relaxed with him, sharing a sparkling wit and a cheerful nature that since she was about seven years old he'd only glimpsed from afar. She had also, and he knew this for a fact, been attracted to him—whether she wanted to be or not. And then, without warning, she had turned from a kitten to an iceberg at the sight of Susan. Could she really have been jealous? Did she really feel insecure? He didn't see how she could, being clever as well as damned attractive herself. But he couldn't imagine why she would tell him she was if she was not. He leaped to catch Steve's wild toss, his weight hitting the sand with an impact that jarred his arm and made it ache.

"Go have a swim," he called to Steve. "I need a break."

The boy obediently trotted down the beach to join his brother, who was hurling himself headlong into the waves, and Brendan sank down gratefully on his beach towel, mopping his face with his discarded T-shirt and wishing his arm didn't itch. He would have to ask Cassie if there was anything she could do about it. She would be changing the cast that day, she had told him. He lay back and closed his eyes, enjoying, despite the itching, the feel of the sun beating down on his chest. He wished its warmth were heavy like the feel of Cassie's body covering him. His hand clenched briefly in the hot sand as he spun out his fantasy, letting the previous night's bedroom scene play to its appropriate conclusion in his mind. He could picture her now in that sheer gown, which hinted at the curves and softness he knew would be underneath. He wanted to peel it over her head and lie with her naked on the bed, kissing her, touching each of her freckles with his tongue, while his hands explored her body. A thin sheen of sweat covered him, and he felt it run in rivulets down his shoulders and dampen the waistband of his swimming trunks. He squirmed on the towel as his loins tightened, and he imagined her hands running over his chest, tracing the line of his ribs before dipping lower. Her hands, deft, capable surgeon's hands, would smooth across the taut skin of his abdomen and then sweep down his thighs, and slowly, excruciatingly, work their way back up and...

He licked his salt-stiffened mustache and groaned.

A shadow fell across his body. "Where does it hurt, sonny?" an all-too-familiar feminine voice drawled, and Brendan's eyes flew open to see Susan drop her huge white wicker purse onto the sand and wink at him from beneath her equally huge floppy white hat.

"Cripes." He sat up quickly, draping his plastered arm across his lap in a futile attempt to disguise his obviously aroused condition. "Give a guy some peace, can't you?" he grumbled as she sank down on the sand beside him.

"It isn't peace you want," she told him cheerfully. "Or not that kind, anyway," she added with a broad grin, and Brendan was grateful for his sunburn. At least she wouldn't see that he was blushing.

"What do you want?" he asked irritably. He wanted to say, "Haven't you done enough damage after coming by last night?" But it wasn't Susan's fault that she looked like the answer to Everyman's prayer or that Cassie had a complex about buxom women. "You got your follow-up story on poor injured me last night," he reminded her, since she had told him that was what she had come for.

"And today I got Ballard's. I thought I'd share it with you."

Brendan scowled, getting a pain in his stomach. Ballard was an irritation at the best of times, but since Cassie had banished him from the premises, he hadn't done much more than call up and demand to know how Brendan was. Out of sight had put him out of mind as far as Brendan was concerned. Obviously he should have been paying more attention. "What'd he say?"

"He's talking trades." Susan looked at him sympathetically.

"What?" His stomach knotted. "He can't! He wouldn't!"

Susan shrugged, adjusting the brim of her hat. "He can, you know. You haven't been with them long enough to have veto rights."

"Who'd trade for me?" Brendan demanded desperately. He could just imagine finishing out the season in New York or Philly or some equally remote place at the farthest end of the earth from Cassie.

"Just about anyone if you were whole and the price was right."

"But am I whole?" Brendan asked, wondering whether he wished he was now or not.

"That's what Ballard wants to know. If you can pitch, for sure there's no doubt he'll want you in September if the Mustangs are still in the race."

Brendan remembered what Ballard had said in his hospital room. He looked at Susan suspiciously. "Did he put you up to this?"

Susan batted innocent eyes. *"Moi?"* She grinned. "Too clever by half, Lefty, old man. Yes, as a matter of fact, he did." She tapped long scarlet fingernails on his cast. "He's concerned. Everyone is. And he says he can never get past your 'dragon of a doctor.'" She laughed. "His words, not mine. Are you going to be able to pitch again?" She met his eyes levelly, not looking away.

"There's no reason why not," Brendan snapped. But his thoughts went reluctantly to Cassie's unthinking comment the day before. What if he couldn't? What then? A cold sweat chilled him even in the heat of the southern California sun.

"I hope you're right." Susan patted his leg in a comradely fashion. Then she rose to her feet, showering Brendan with sand from her wicker bag as she shook it, and said, "Well, if you don't, your new sweetie can keep you, can't she?"

Brendan's jaw clenched. "Dr. Hart, you mean?" he asked coolly, trying not to rise to the bait she dangled.

Susan smiled and ruffled his hair. "Like that, is it?"

"Like that." He wasn't saying one word about Cassie. Not because he didn't trust Susan's integrity—he knew she didn't gossip—but because, he thought wearily, there was too damned little to tell.

"I wonder," Susan said. "She looked madder than a

hornet when I called in at her office and asked where I could find you."

Brendan groaned audibly. After the previous night it didn't take much imagination to visualize Cassie's reaction to Susan's question. So much for her insecurities. The way things were going, he was going to be developing some colossal ones of his own! "Thanks a bunch," he muttered.

Susan blew him a kiss. "Any time, sweetheart. Just say the word." She started back up the beach toward the car park. "Best of luck, Lefty," she called over her shoulder. "You're going to need it."

Too right, Brendan thought, sitting cross-legged on his towel, drizzling sand through his fingers and contemplating his plastered, no longer very clean cast with distaste. Experimentally, he wriggled his fingers. They moved, albeit not with any great flexibility. If he bit on them, he could feel pressure and pain. That was hopeful, Cassie would have told him. Well, good, because he could use a bit of hope right now. For God's sake, what was he going to do if he couldn't pitch?

"Too bad you can't go swimmin' with us," Steve said, racing up and shaking water all over him like an exuberant puppy. His teeth chattered, and he looked faintly blue about the lips.

"I know," Brendan agreed. "But you're not swimming anymore just now, either. You're too cold."

"Am not!" Steve protested, clamping his teeth together and trying to stop jigging up and down.

"Uh-huh," Brendan said, unconvinced. "Sit." He glanced down the beach and waved Keith in from the water, too.

"What do you want?" the older boy demanded as he scampered over.

"Take a break." Brendan patted the towel.

"Aw." Keith made protesting noises. But when Brendan glared, he plopped down and demanded, "Then tell us a Fellwell."

"A Fellwell?" Brendan was amused, then momentarily irritated as he remembered what Cassie had said the day before after he'd finished his story. All roads led to "not pitching," it seemed. "What kind of Fellwell?" he asked, groping for a starting point.

"A baseball one," Keith said instantly. "Tell us a baseball mystery."

Brendan sighed, but then Fellwell, that mysterious bungler for whom things always seemed to come up right, caught hold of his imagination. It's wishful thinking, he told himself. But a slight smile tugged at his mouth, and he began, "Fellwell had just stumbled into his office when the phone rang. He answered it to hear the commissioner of baseball on the line. 'Have I got a case for you, Fellwell,' he said..."

And by the time Fellwell had solved it to everyone's satisfaction, there was barely time for one more quick swim before they had to head home.

"Can Fellwell solve *anything*?" Steve wanted to know, still obviously awestruck at the detective's prowess half an hour later as they were driving home.

"Anything," Brendan agreed blithely.

"Like you," Keith put in with a ten-year-old's confidence.

"Don't I wish," Brendan mumbled under his breath, and turned on the radio. He wondered what kind of ending Fellwell would manage for a broken-armed pitcher and the prickly woman he wanted desperately in his life.

Chapter Seven

Cassie walked slowly down the hall from the examining room where she had just left the girl with the smashed fingers and pulled the final chart of the day out of the rack on the wall. The afternoon had been long and beastly hot, a Santa Ana wind bringing heat off the desert, and it hadn't helped a bit that she'd spent the whole time entertaining visions of Brendan at the beach with Susan.

Maybe she shouldn't have told the woman where Brendan and the boys were going that afternoon, she thought irritably for the hundredth time. She ran her hand beneath her collar to loosen the white lab coat that stuck to her rampant curls. She could just imagine the two of them entwined on a beach towel together. On a public beach, she mocked herself, annoyed at the leaps of fancy that her imagination had been taking regularly. Not very likely. Not with two boys around. Still... She glanced down at the name on the chart as she opened the examining-room door.

"Brendan?" Her voice lifted in astonishment as she read the name and looked up to see the man himself, tanned and shirtless, sitting on the examination table, his blue-jeaned legs dangling as he cradled his bare arm against his chest. The cast had obviously just been sawed off. So much for imagination, she chastised herself.

Brendan gave her what could only be described as a hopeful look. And while she might have liked to remain detached, she was so relieved to see him in front of her instead of with Susan that she couldn't help blurting out, "What are you doing here?" though the answer was perfectly obvious. She took refuge behind the chart in her hands.

His mouth twitched into a maddening grin. "Ah, I see your insecurities are out in force."

Cassie pursed her lips, aware of the red tide of color creeping up her neck. "Forget my insecurities," she said brusquely, wishing that *she* could.

He winked. "I'd love to." His blue eyes teased her. "But actually I'm here because we have an appointment this afternoon. X rays and a new cast, the nurse said." His expression turned serious, and he nodded at the set of X rays hanging before the lighted wall panel. "What do you think?"

Cassie, still stunned by the sight of him, struggled to drag her eyes from his lean, powerful body and began to study the battery of X rays before her. "So far so good," she told him when she had regained enough equilibrium to turn and give him a professional smile. After all, that was what he was there for, not because he was in love with her, despite his kisses of the night before. "Three more weeks in a short cast and you can start getting in shape again."

Brendan made a face. "That's almost the end of July. Can't I start now?"

Cassie considered the X rays again and then the obviously well-muscled man in front of her. "You can run," she told him. "With this new cast you should even be able to swim if you want. Just blow it dry with a hair drier afterward." Think of him as just another arm, she cautioned herself as she closed the distance between them and lifted his arm gently from his lap, running her fingers over the site of the fracture, straightening the elbow slowly and turning it slightly. Brendan winced.

"Hurt?" she asked, probing near the joint.

Brendan gritted his teeth. "A little."

By the look of him, "a little" meant a great deal

more than that. Cassie frowned. She laid his arm back in his lap and went to study the X rays again, squinting at the area around his elbow.

"What is it?" Brendan demanded, an edge to his voice.

"I'm curious about this tenderness in your elbow." She studied it carefully on the X rays, wondering if there was a fracture there that hadn't been visible earlier. It wasn't anything she particularly wanted to mention. There was no need to alarm him unduly. It might just be sore and stiff.

"What about it?" He was already alarmed. He hopped off the table, flinched as his feet hit the floor, but came to stand by her and peered over her shoulder at the pictures of his arm.

"We'll just have to see how quickly it works itself out," Cassie said.

"And if it doesn't?"

She saw that he looked decidedly grim, far more so than she ever remembered him being before. She recalled his momentarily stricken look of the afternoon before when she suggested that he might not pitch again. This look was far bleaker than that one, as if he had had his worst fears confirmed.

"Where's your innate optimism?" she tried to tease, but Brendan wasn't having any.

He was straightening out his arm slowly, his teeth set. Lines of pain or tension drew his face taut. "God knows." He sighed and shut his eyes as if when he opened them, the nightmare might fade away. Unfortunately, Cassie could have told him, he was wide awake. "Hell," he muttered, running his right arm over the thinner, paler left one as if it were made of the most fragile porcelain.

Torn between a need to maintain her professional demeanor and a tremendous desire to comfort him, Cassie took his other arm and urged him back to the table. "Don't worry about it now," she counseled him kindly. "Worrying won't do any good at all."

"What will?" He sounded morose, staring off into space as though the arm she was wrapping in gauze and then molding a shorter lightweight cast around belonged to someone else entirely.

Cassie looked up, her hands still pressing and smoothing the burlaplike fabric over his arm while she studied his profile, wanting to smooth the worry she saw in the lines by his eyes, to soften with a kiss the set of his lips and to caress the clean line of his jaw. Poor Brendan; even his mustache drooped. And here she had been envisioning him spending the entire afternoon with Susan, soaking up the rays and thoroughly enjoying himself without a care in the world. Odd how much more satisfying the reality was, she thought, though she felt faintly guilty for being glad he wasn't out with a beautiful woman but instead was here, looking as if she had just handed him notice of the end of the world. "I'd say a good dinner might do you some good," she answered his question, surprising herself as much as him.

"What?" His eyes turned toward her, still and wary, though his knee was now pressed intimately against her hip, and whether she was more conscious of it or of his deep blue gaze, she didn't know.

She swallowed. "I said, would you like to join me for dinner?" It was by far the hardest thing she had ever done, like a gawky schoolgirl asking the "big man on campus" to a dance.

For a moment neither of them moved. Gene's laugh boomed down the corridor, and a sharp whiff of disinfectant and institutional soap only intensified her awareness of mellow after-shave and honest sweat that were overwhelmingly Brendan. Then, as she watched, his mouth curved into a slow smile. "I'd like that," he said.

He was loafing in the waiting room when she finished cleaning up and joined him thirty minutes later. All the time she had been brushing her hair and applying lip gloss with shaking fingers, she told herself that she was only doing it because he looked as if he needed a friend. That fallacy collapsed the second she laid eyes on him again. She couldn't prevent them from feasting on the long, denim-clad legs stretched out in front of him, the smooth fit of his maroon and gray pin-striped polo shirt, which accentuated the tanned arm, lightly sprinkled with dark hair, and the rough hardness of the cast that rested on his thigh. He got to his feet easily, the look on his face still bemused despite an underlying grimness, as he held the door open for her and followed her out. His palm rested lightly against the small of her back, and she had a hard time thinking of him as a patient.

"We'll take my car." She headed for her Mazda at the far end of the parking lot, hoping that if she drove, she would forget his nearness and her out-of-character behavior in inviting him to dinner.

"Whatever you say." Brendan's tone was equable. He held the door open for her, then went around to the passenger side and folded his lithe body compactly into the seat beside her so that his thigh was scant inches from her own. She knew then that nothing would take her mind off his nearness, especially not shifting gears in a car the size of this one!

"Anywhere in particular you'd like to go?" she asked, her mouth dry. If this was how teenaged boys felt when confronted with their first date, her feelings of empathy were reaching new heights.

Brendan shrugged. "Well, I'm not exactly dressed for anything too elaborate." His mustache lifted in a self-deprecating grin, and Cassie wished he wouldn't do that. To look devastating *and* boyish was entirely unfair of him.

She groped through her memory for someplace that wouldn't require a tie but that didn't have a jack-in-the-box out front, either. Finally, she recalled a place in Santa Monica where she had attended a luncheon meeting not many months before. It was designed primarily for tourist trade, being not far from the beach, and the vast proportion of its clientele wore loud shirts and violent red or kelly-green trousers. If anyone looked out of place there, it would be herself in her tailored, robin's-egg-blue linen suit, not the casually dressed Brendan.

"I know a place," she told him. "It's just what you need." He was looking morose again, and she thought a bit of tourist hoopla might do him good, take his mind off his arm and his future, where it no doubt was right now.

Brendan didn't reply. He was oddly silent on the entire trip, giving Cassie plenty of time to regret having rashly made the invitation in the first place. She wondered if he might have had a date with Susan and if he was only going out with her to be polite, but she didn't feel sufficiently daring to ask. The only remark she did make was to ask about the boys, and Brendan assured her that the baby-sitter was willing to stay as long as needed and that everything was fine. That said, Cassie, too, ran out of conversation. The rest of the ride was endured in gratitude for her tape deck and the sounds of early Beatles music, which effectively papered over the situation.

"This?" Brendan asked, incredulous, when she turned the car between two flaming spires into the parking lot beside a lavish, rambling building that resembled a gargantuan grass hut gone mad. *"I need this?"* He echoed his own words as she shut off the ignition and bounded out of the car, determined to cheer him up whether he wanted it or not. "I must be worse off than I thought."

She took his arm and dragged him through the front doors, feeling more desperate by the minute. For the first time in her life she was almost glad when an extremely buxom brunette, wrapped in what looked like a flowered dish towel and little else, swooped down on them and draped leis over their necks, brushing past Cassie's cheek in a hurry but planting scrumptious smacks on Brendan's.

"Welcome! Welcome!" she exclaimed, and Brendan looked at Cassie from beneath arched brows, and

Cassie shrugged helplessly. It wasn't quite what she remembered, but obviously the atmosphere was going to go a long way toward taking Brendan's mind off his problems.

The hostess led them to a secluded table, obscured from the main dining area by a veritable forest of palm fronds, and handed them menus the size of pup tents before she disappeared. Somewhere behind them a tropical rainfall began. Brendan peered at Cassie over the top of his menu, eyes shimmering with amusement. "You really know how to pick 'em," he teased, good humor returning. "Did you and Mike come here often?"

Cassie looked up, startled. "Heavens, no!" Michael wouldn't have ever come to such a place. His taste ran to dark walnut paneling and heavy damask tablecloths, and somehow Cassie suspected Brendan knew that. But she couldn't take offense, because she knew, just then, that none was intended. She was trapped in his gaze like a fish in a net, very like the one on the wall behind him, and nervously she licked her lips, asking, "What would you like to drink?"

Brendan looked away from her to study the menu. She noticed that he unbent his arm very slowly, then bent it again. Testing, she thought. He frowned. "Something long and cold," he decided. "What about you?"

Cassie decided that something nonalcoholic was a must tonight. One of them had to be in shape to drive home. She turned to order and found herself staring into the navel of the waiter, who was wearing about half as much as the buxom brunette. In the back of her mind Cassie filed away the notion that somewhere there must be a health regulation prohibiting that, but at the moment the rest of her was occupied with the simple feat of managing two or three intelligible words. She wasn't managing well. Laughing, Brendan ordered for her, requesting something else for himself.

"What did you order?" Cassie asked, worried. But Brendan waved her off.

"You'll see," he told her, and she did moments later when the half-naked waiter returned bearing a tall, frosty pineapple-colored drink for Brendan and a shallow, wide glass that looked more like an Easter bonnet than a drink, which he proceeded to set in front of her.

"Enjoy." Brendan grinned over the mountain of papayas, mangoes, kiwi fruit and strawberries that sat before her.

Nonplussed, Cassie poked at it cautiously. "Is it to drink or to wear?"

Brendan reached over and speared a strawberry with the tip of the tiny Japanese parasol that was tilting out of one side of the glass. He held it out for her, waving it in front of her lips until Cassie opened her mouth and took it from him, a shiver running down her spine at the intimacy of the act. Her teeth closed on the cold fruit, crushing it, savoring the essence of strawberry and something else undefinable and therefore, she decided, alcoholic. "Very nice," she managed, swallowing.

It was, too. It was going to take every ounce of willpower she had not to dig right into it. She offered Brendan a tentative smile, groping for precisely the right attitude. Should she project friendly disinterest, she wondered, or professional ease? Or, with her heart thundering like a runaway horse and her eyes out on stalks just ogling him as he sat across from her, did she even have a choice? Wasn't she just plain, old, besotted Cassie and nothing more? Very likely, she decided, and was relieved to see the waiter back for their order. Looking at him, even in his dish towel, was far less of a strain on her libido than Brendan Craig was fully clothed.

"Do you think it's bad, Cass?" Brendan wanted to know as he poked his swordfish steak with the tip of his fork.

She didn't have to ask what he meant. It was the reason they were there, after all, whether either of them admitted it. She sighed, prodding a piece of squid with the fork, weighing her answer before she gave it.

"I'm not hedging, Brendan," she began, "when I say that I really don't know. You'll have to start exercising to develop your range of motion."

"But you *thought* it was going to be okay." He stared at her insistently, his forearms leaning on the table, the fork held awkwardly in his right hand while the fingers of his left tightened against the cast.

"I know." She took a swallow of ice water and met his eyes again. "And it might be. Everything might work out fine. It's far too early to tell."

"Then why are you taking me out to dinner?"

The $64,000 question. She cracked an ice cube between her teeth. "Because you're worried about it," she told him finally. *And because I wanted to,* she added silently. *Because it matters to me, too.*

"Yes," he admitted, "I am." He laid down the fork and leaned back in his chair, sipping his drink slowly, cradling it against his chest and looking at her over the top of it. "I keep thinking, What am I gonna do if I can't pitch."

"And what do you answer?" she asked softly.

He shook his head; his eyes lowered, regarding the pineapple froth in his glass. "God knows." He sighed heavily and took a long swallow, draining the glass. Then he looked up at her and smiled almost wistfully. "God knows," he repeated, and Cassie looked at him horrified, afraid that he might actually cry! She had never seen him like this. Not Brendan the irrepressible!

"You'll probably win five games before the season's over," she told him quickly, needing to stave off the despair she saw in his eyes. "Really, Bren, you might!" She reached across and squeezed the fingers of his left hand, impulsively needing to give him a shot of confidence so she could find some for herself.

"Yeah? And win the Cy Young?"

Cassie didn't know what that was, but it obviously meant something pretty important, so she nodded her head, willing some confidence into him. Releasing his hand, she plucked a slice of kiwi fruit out of her glass and held it out to him. "For sustenance," she told him seriously.

He leaned forward slowly and nibbled it off her spoon. "For sustenance," he repeated, his blue eyes mesmerizing her.

She offered him a chuck of pineapple. "For courage."

He took it, the powdered sugar on it dusting his mustache. "Courage." He repeated the word, nodding his head slowly. Then, before she could dip her spoon again, he caught her fingers in his and leaned toward her to touch them with his lips, his teeth, his tongue.

"What's that for?" Cassie's voice was hollow and shaky.

"I think," Brendan told her solemnly, "that it's for love."

Afterward, Cassie thought she might have dreamed it all. The setting, with its flaming spires, blue sea glass and fish nets, might have addled her brain. The steel guitars might have bent the sound waves into words she wanted to hear. But she couldn't be sure. Brendan just sat there holding her hand in his while he smiled at her. The waiter came and went unobtrusively—later Cassie thought it was an indication of how far gone she really was that a nearly naked man seemed unobtrusive when he filled her water glass or brought Brendan another drink—the music played on, and Cassie decided that the smell of orchids, pineapple and teriyaki combined to make one of the most powerful aphrodisiacs in the world.

Brendan finished her drink after he'd finished his second; his smile broadened, and his words grew softer. There was no more talk about the bleakness of his future, just silly reminiscences of spiders and bicycles and Bobbi Boobs, and for the first time Cassie could recall those days without feeling self-conscious.

It was wonderful, she thought, what maturity, distance and a few rum-soaked strawberries could do.

"We'll have to do this again," Brendan said, looping his arm around her shoulders as they strolled out to the car, the flames from the huge torches casting everything with a warm pink glow, equaled only, Cassie thought, by the rosy state of Brendan's mind. He spun her around and waved his still-plastered arm in the air. "My arm feels lighter," he told her. "Is that a good sign?"

"Definitely." She held the door open for him this time. "Your brain is lighter, too."

"Another good sign." He laughed sleepily. Resting his cast along the back of the seat, he tangled his fingers in her hair, then played with the sensitive cord of her neck while she tried to concentrate on not running down the doorman or wrapping the car around a palm.

Once in the stream of traffic, she ventured a glance at him. He was looking at her, a warm, possessive look that set off shivers of apprehension as well as warmth all through her. Two days in a row now, she cautioned herself. Two days that have been almost entirely focused on Brendan Craig. *Watch out, Cass. This could get to be a habit.* But it was hard to believe that it might be a *bad* habit when, a few moments later, she felt the soft warmth of his hair against her shoulder and heard a mumbled "You don't mind, do you?" just before he fell asleep.

She wondered how she was going to get him into the house without alarming the baby-sitter or starting a scandalous rumor, but she needn't have worried. Brendan might be drunk, she decided, but he was so practiced at it that, generally speaking, no one would ever know. He woke easily when she shook him gently after they arrived home and navigated with competence if not dexterity through the house to his bedroom, leaving Cassie to see the baby-sitter home. As she only lived three doors down, that was no problem, and Cassie came back bemused and satisfied with the results of the evening. She checked on the boys, brushed her teeth and changed into her sheer green gown and was about to put out her light when she saw a glimmer beneath Brendan's closed door. Thinking that he had fallen asleep with the light on, she crossed the hall and opened his door. Astonished, she saw him sitting exactly where she had left him on the bed.

"What's wrong?" she asked, frozen in the doorway.

He looked up and blinked, a dazed sort of expression on his face that made her wonder if he had been asleep with his eyes open while sitting there. "Wrong?" He could scarcely get his tongue around the word. He gave her a bleary smile and flopped backward on the bed as if he had died.

Well, at least he had lasted until the baby-sitter had gone home! She crossed the room and hauled him to a sitting position. "Stay there," she commanded when he tilted, smiling, though his eyes were still shut. She stuffed a pillow behind his back to keep him upright and with practiced hands unbuttoned the top buttons of his shirt and dragged it off over his head, while cursing his nuisance of a cast. Then she remembered she ought to be grateful it wasn't his old cumbersome one. Pulling the covers down on the far side of the bed, she gave him a shove, toppling him over onto it. He made a "whomph" sound as he landed and uttered something like a laugh that implied a consciousness somewhere, however remote. He was on his stomach now, and she went around to the side of the bed and took ahold of his shoulder, prying him over onto his side.

"Come on, Brendan. Roll over!" Like calling a dog, she thought. With about as much success, she decided, remembering her Labrador, Ernestine, which had taken a bite out of Brendan's butt. Brendan grumbled something and didn't move, so she yanked on his arm till he fell over on his back, sprawling across the sheet in a way that would have been far more intimidating if

Limited Time Offer!

Make sure you get this great FREE OFFER- act today!

NO POSTAGE
NECESSARY
IF MAILED
IN THE
UNITED STATES

BUSINESS REPLY CARD

First Class Permit No. 70 Tempe, AZ

Postage will be paid by addressee

Harlequin® Reader Service
2504 W. Southern Avenue
Tempe, Arizona 85282

he weren't nine-tenths unconscious. She untied his shoes and slipped them off his feet, peeling down his socks and running her hands over the fine bones and high arches of his feet, tracing his toes till his foot twitched and he muttered, "Tickles." Then she dropped it and took a step back, wondering if she dared to go on.

She was a doctor, for heaven's sake! She had seen men naked before. She had seen Brendan naked before. But she had never undressed him before, she argued with herself. Her eyes strayed upward from his feet, traveling the length of his blue jeans, pausing at the flexed knee, the tautly muscled thigh, slipping quickly to the snap an inch or so below his navel. *He'll never know you undressed him,* she told herself. That Brendan would remember anything about the evening at all seemed highly unlikely. Probably she hadn't a thing to worry about. *You hope,* she thought as she bent down and undid the snap and slid down his zipper. She lifted her eyes to his face. It was innocent, boyish, unnervingly sweet in spite of the mustache. Deceptive, she decided. If he had looked menacing, she might have been more careful. She eased the jeans down past his hips, her eyes narrowing suspiciously when he lifted himself up just enough to allow her to slide them down. "Brendan?"

"Wha'?" He struggled to get his eyes open, the smile still on his face.

She yanked the jeans the rest of the way off, left his stark white briefs securely in place and hauled a sheet over him before she gave in to further temptation. "Nothing." Her eyes lingered on his mustache, remembering the feel of it, velvety soft or bristly against her lips and cheeks. Another temptation. She hesitated, then gave in, bending down to kiss it gently, letting her lips linger for a moment in its softness, savoring the hint of pineapple and rum she tasted there. Brendan sighed, a corner of his mouth curving upward as he tried to respond to her touch. She lifted her head.

"Sleep well," she murmured, and crossed the room to shut out the light.

"Cass?" His voice came faintly from the bed.

She turned, lingering in the doorway. "What?"

"Cass?" The voice sounded less sleepy now, more desperate, and she moved back to the bed to bend over him. He reached out and caught her hand, his fingers warm and damp on her own. "Don't go, Cass."

She sank down on the edge of the bed, her instincts and her brain at war in her body; her brain saying, *Run*, while her body edged closer to the man whose voice implored her.

"Please, Cass, stay." His voice and his touch were insistent. He drew her down to him, his arms going around her in an embrace that she gave in to, wanting it as much as he did when she heard him mumble against her ear, "Oh, God, Cass, what am I gonna do?"

DAPPLED SUNLIGHT the color of pineapples woke her. It spilled across Brendan's cheek, highlighting his morning's growth of beard and the thick dark lashes that shielded his eyes. It ought to have felt strange waking in his bed. She ought to be scrambling up, running while her virtue was still intact. But nothing in her wanted to move. She caught a quick glimpse of the clock on the bookcase: 5:45. In fifteen minutes she would have to get up, like it or not, dress, grab a quick breakfast and head for the hospital. But for now, for these few minutes, she was staying right where she was—in Brendan Craig's bed.

She almost laughed wondering what her mother would say if she knew where Cassie was at that moment. Probably she'd cheer, Cassie decided, her mother's intentions having been all too clear before she left. But for once the knowledge didn't make Cassie bristle. She moved her leg, running her toe down Brendan's thigh, past his knee, loving the feel of his warm, bare skin under her foot. He shifted, muttering and flinging his arm over her, almost braining her with his cast.

"Oaf," she whispered, turning her head so the words fluttered strands of his dark hair. She blew experimentally across his forehead; his nose twitched, and he grinned unexpectedly. His arm tightened around her, and she tensed, then willed herself to relax. It wasn't hard; it was what she wanted to do, anyway.

Am I out of my mind, she wondered. Thirty-two years of sane, sensible living going right out the window in less than a month after meeting him again. But when had waking up sane and sensible felt this good? And this, she reflected, was how she felt without even making love with him. What would it be like to love Brendan, to have him loving her? A warmth crept over her, slowly, starting deep within but surfacing so that she knew her face was burning, her toes tingling. 5:56. She lifted his arm gently, laying it between them, the roughened palm up so she could see the callused pads on his fingers and wondered what he would do if—and it was a big *if*—he never pitched again. His face was turned toward her, and she saw in it vestiges of the boy she had known. There was a tiny scar by his right ear, a souvenir of a skirmish with Griff, and another just below his hairline that she remembered seeing bandaged after a fall from his bike. She couldn't ever remember lying beside Michael and cataloging his features, but then Mike was rarely in bed any longer than she was. "Up and at 'em," was his motto, and as it was now 6:00, it had to be hers, as well. She eased herself out of the bed, trying not to disturb Brendan, feeling slightly smug and just the tiniest bit pleased that she had spent the night with him. Nothing had happened, to be sure, at least nothing physical, but deep inside Cassie felt that fundamentally she had changed.

"BRENDAN?" The voice was a whisper. "Are you awake?"

He wasn't. Not really. He was having the most marvelous dreams. Truly wonderful ones in which Cassie, long limbed and naked, wrapped her legs around his and—

"Brendan!"

A drum slammed inside his head. He opened one eye. Not easily. His eyes weren't cooperating that morning. Two hazel eyes beneath a fringe of auburn hair peered back at him. Steven? He groaned, patting the bed, groping for Steven's mother. The sheets were cool and rumpled. He shut his eye, trying to will himself back into the dream. "G'way," he mumbled.

"Brendan, your friend's here," Steven insisted. His hand jiggled Brendan's shoulder, doing obscene things to the inside of his head, and Brendan's hand shot out to grab a handful of sheet so as not to be flung to the ceiling. "What's wrong with you?" Steven demanded. "Me an' Keith have been up for *hours.*"

Brendan's mind stuck on the word "friend." What friend? Not Susan surely. Susan rarely got up before noon, and though he knew it must be late, Brendan doubted it was past that. Lem Ballard, then? He groaned again, dragging the pillow over his head.

"He says he'll wake you up if I don't," Steve warned him, tugging the pillow off Brendan's face.

"Aw right." Ballard. It had to be. What other bastard would come around just the day after he got his new cast and demand to see him. "Tell him I'll be out in a minute."

Steve turned and headed for the door, whistling. Brendan's head slammed. "Make that ten," he croaked, hauling himself to a sitting position and leaning his head against his hands. "And tell him to put on some coffee."

As soon as the room had settled its spin to a moderate degree, Brendan staggered to his feet and pulled on the jeans he found folded neatly on the chair. How had he done that—folded them and hung up his shirt and got himself to bed without remembering any of it? A flicker of a memory taunted him—a glare of overhead light, a muzzy alcoholic haze and Cassie stripping off his pants.

Cassie? He gripped the edge of the dresser, swaying as he tried to bring the tantalizing recollection into sharper focus. *Aw, you're imagining things,* he told himself, and shook his head. A bad idea, that. He waited until the room had righted itself, then tugged a clean T-shirt over his head and wove his way down the hall to the bathroom. God, he never should have drunk two of whatever they were—and finished Cassie's. He must have been insane! Gritting his teeth, he bent his head, running it underneath the faucet, shivering and cursing but emerging minutes later with a tighter grip on reality.

He toweled his hair ineffectually with his one good hand and decided that Ballard could stand seeing him unshaven. The question was, could he stand seeing Ballard? A bloodshot gaze met his in the mirror and slowly shook its head. Ah, well, maybe he wouldn't remember this tomorrow, either. He padded back down the carpeted hallway to his room, unearthed his sunglasses and propped them on his nose. Now he might have to see Ballard, but it wouldn't be as clearly, and Ballard wouldn't be able to see as much of him. He ran a comb through his hair, which still clung damply to his forehead, and studied his reflection in the mirror once more. It wasn't promising, but it was passable, and Ballard wouldn't notice if he had his eyes shut, either.

Ballard, in fact, wasn't there at all. The friend who lounged in the redwood-framed deck chair had a shock of sun-bleached wheat-colored hair and a twisted grin that meant the sunglasses hid nothing at all.

"You!" Brendan exclaimed. "What in hell are you doing here?"

Griffin Tucker toasted him with a steaming cup of coffee. "Just inquiring after your health. I stopped by your apartment when I got to town. When you weren't there, I went right to Lainie's."

Brendan arched an eyebrow, then wished he hadn't. Even that hurt. What in hell had been in those drinks last night?

"So how's life?" Griff asked amiably.

Brendan grimaced. "Who knows? I died. Yesterday, I think."

"That bad?" Griff looked doubtful. He surveyed the split-level Spanish-style stucco house with its red-tiled patio and landscaped lawn and pool. "You must've gone to heaven, then," he said. "That's a surprise."

Brendan couldn't help smiling. He poured himself a cup of coffee, drawing a deep breath of its fragrance as he lowered himself gingerly into the lounger opposite Griff. "Isn't it, though?" He blew across the top of the cup, trying to cool the scalding liquid before pouring it down his throat. "I must live right."

"How's Cassie, then?"

The question shouldn't have caught him off guard. Griff, after all, had known her for years. He had every right to ask. The trouble was, of course, that Brendan didn't know what to answer. How *was* Cassie? Warm, loving, delectable. At least in his dreams. Had she put him to bed last night? Had her silken thighs really nestled next to his? He took a gulp of coffee, burning himself clear to his toes. Coughing, he set the cup down and gasped for air, squeezing his eyes shut.

Griff watched him sympathetically, just the barest hint of an amused smile lurking around his mouth. "You always did have trouble talking about her."

Brendan glowered, grateful for the sunglasses, wishing they would disguise the tide of red he felt creeping up his neck. "She's fine," he muttered. "Who's *your* latest?" He really didn't care; he just wanted to get the subject changed quickly, but Griff stretched his long bare legs out, flexing his muscles with a satisfaction that reminded Brendan of a well-fed tiger, and smiled contentedly.

"Lainie Thomas. I'm in love with her."

Brendan's jaw dropped. "Cassie's friend?" He'd wondered about Griff's sterling devotion when he'd been in the hospital. They had been friends for years, but Griff had never bothered to nurse him through any of his other myriad injuries. Odd that he hadn't noticed his friend's lustful glances after the bouncy social worker at the time. But then, he reminded himself, he had been in pain. And if he were totally honest, more than a little smitten himself—with Dr. Cassandra Farrell Hart.

"The very one." Griff's face lit up in a way that Brendan had never seen it before. "She's glorious." He went on to give Brendan a pretty thorough, if discreet, account of all the things that made her that way.

Brendan knew he ought to feel happy for Griff. In fact, he felt annoyed as hell. How come taciturn, grim-faced Griffin Tucker could wax poetic about true love with a woman he had only met a month before while Brendan didn't know where he was with a woman he had known for twenty-eight years?

"She makes me feel alive, expansive," Griff finished, waving his empty coffee cup in the air.

"Obviously," Brendan said fractiously. "You can't seem to shut up."

But Griffin was too much in love to take offense. He just got up and poured them both refills of coffee before saying, "Lainie and I are going horseback riding on Thursday. Could you come with your arm that way? You and Cassie, I mean?"

Again, Brendan didn't know what to say. For a fleeting moment he thought a morning with Lem Ballard might have been less of a strain. "I could," he said cautiously, flexing his elbow, which moved, it seemed, a bit more easily that morning. It should be that that was hanging him up, not Cassie. Yet he knew that a wrong step with her mattered more right now than with his arm. He remembered her fingers on his in the restaurant, her hand feeding him. "For sustenance," she'd said. "For courage."

He drew a deep breath. "Yes, all right. If she's off, we'll try to come."

HE WONDERED what Cassie would say when he told her. He wrote scene after scene, anticipating it in his head. He thought about all the good reasons for going. He wanted her to have a break in her routine; he wanted to share a day outdoors with her; he wanted her to be with Griff and Lainie, who, if Griff was anything to go by, were obviously in love.

And what did Cassie want? God only knew. But he was more than a little surprised when she came home that night and he broached the subject with her.

"Go horseback riding?" She had had a long, hard day and looked it. He wanted to offer her back rubs and hours of cuddling in bed, but he just nodded mutely and set a plate of pork chops, green beans and apple sauce in front of her. She gave him a beatific smile. "I'd love to, Brendan," she said.

Chapter Eight

Cassie knew exactly what she wanted—joy, lightheartedness, relief. She had spent thirty-two years in pursuit of goals that, having been achieved, were important but not, as she had originally thought, all consuming. She loved being a doctor, and she loved her sons. But her career and her children only gave her a sense of responsibility. It was Brendan who had brought some fun into her life, some sense of joy that had been missing. He had added a new dimension. And going horseback riding with him, even in the company of Griffin and Lainie, seemed somehow exactly right.

For one thing, before Brendan's reemergence into her life, she never would have done such a thing. It would have seemed too frivolous, not to mention dangerous. She might fall off and break her *own* arm, for heaven's sake! Before Brendan, she would have spent her day off reading medical journals by the pool, swimming and playing with her sons in the yard. She would never have simply hired the girl down the street to come over for the afternoon to keep an eye on them while she hopped blithely into the car and drove off to Palos Verdes for the afternoon to "enjoy herself." It was unheard of, and even as she did it, she found herself saying to Brendan, "I have to check in at the hospital by six."

Brendan seemed to accept that. "No problem. Griff has to be at the ball park. We'll get back in plenty of time." He smiled at her as they sped down the freeway, the wind ruffling his dark hair in a way that her fingers itched to do.

God, she was getting to feel just like a teenager around him all over again! *You're a case of arrested development,* she chided herself, tugging her eyes away and forcing herself to concentrate on the boring sameness of the suburbs they passed. Even since she had agreed to come, she had found Brendan's reaction to her acceptance curious. He obviously hadn't thought she would want to. And when she agreed, he had seemed taken aback. Since then he had been studying her with a kind of wary fascination, as if she might at any second change her mind, sprout wings and fly away. Cassie could have reassured him that she was having far too much fun to fly away. She had never lived for the moment before; she found it an intoxicating, heady experience. The thought of taking off midweek, even on her day off, to do something as outlandishly out of character as going horseback riding made her laugh.

"What's funny?" Brendan looked up from Lainie's hastily drawn map and made a left turn onto a narrow lane that wound up a eucalyptus-shaded hillside with a redwood mansion on the left and a broad vista of the sparkling blue Pacific on the right.

"Me," Cassie replied. "I can't believe I'm doing this."

She thought she heard Brendan mutter, "I can't either," but when she looked over at him, he just grinned enchantingly and warmed her to her toes.

Griff and Lainie were waiting at the stables, private ones belonging to the redwood mansion, which was owned by some relatives of Griff's roommate or some other peripheral being. Cassie was too intrigued by the prospect of the outing to care.

"Glad you could come," Lainie told her as they led the horses out of the stable. "It's wonderful that you and Brendan are getting together."

Cassie lifted an eyebrow. "Are we?" She couldn't decide whether she was more annoyed or pleased at the notion. She supposed the fact that it came from Lainie should warn her. Lainie always read far more into situations than really existed.

"I'd say so." Lainie grinned, winking as she studied Brendan's lean physique in snug blue jeans and a kelly-green T-shirt that hugged his back. "Judging from the way he's been hanging around you."

Cassie wondered what "hanging around" Lainie had heard about, but then she remembered that even when he was at the hospital, he had made no secret of wanting her, going so far as to maneuver himself into staying at her house. That they were there together that day spoke for itself. Cassie knew her cheeks reddened at the thought, but Lainie apparently didn't even notice, for she went right on. "He's a great guy, Brendan. He has some great friends, too." She grinned.

One in particular, Cassie thought as she watched her friend and Griffin together. Lainie had always had an eye for the men, but Cassie had never seen her seriously interested in one until then. She had expected to get a chance to visit with her friend, but it was apparent after half an hour that it wasn't a foursome but two couples out for the day. Griff and Lainie rode on ahead, knees touching, glances kindling fire, and finally Cassie reined her plodding gray in next to Brendan's chestnut and said, "Are you sure we were invited along. We seem superfluous somehow."

Brendan rolled his eyes. "Disgusting, isn't it?" He grinned, but the look on his face said something very different, and confused, Cassie kicked her heels into the gray's flanks and loped ahead without answering. She knew he wouldn't mind some of the same between them. She didn't know what she wanted just then. She only wanted to get away. But Brendan's horse, a bit more lively than her own, broke into a canter, following her, and she glanced back at him, grinning until he shouted, "Wait!"

She saw him frantically trying to control the strong chestnut horse with his one good hand, and immediately she hauled in on the reins. Her horse quite willingly slowed down. Brendan's crashed through the underbrush next to her moments later as he tried to slow his. Sweat glistened on the chestnut's neck, glinting red in the sunlight as Cassie saw him straining under Brendan's taut control.

"Sorry," she said contritely. "Are you okay?" Her eyes went immediately to his arm.

"Terrific." His tone was ironic, and he grimaced. He was sweating, too, his hair damp and spiky across his tanned forehead, the kelly-green T-shirt darkening under his arms and across his back. He looked incredibly attractive just then, the power of the man in the saddle complemented by the strength of the horse he controlled, and Cassie, in a purely professional medical way, admired the economy of movement, the play of muscles as the horse moved and Brendan moved with it. He might not really be "terrific," but he certainly looked it.

"We'll take it slow," she said. "As your doctor, I don't want to be patching you up out here." She maneuvered her horse so that it stayed just abreast of Brendan's, letting its gentle rollicking motion lull her, content just to bask in the undemanding situation. Even if Brendan did look at her with desire in his eyes, there was no way of satisfying it out there. So she needed to make no decisions for a while yet. She could just relax and enjoy his company and the beauty of the day.

"I can't believe Griff," Brendan was saying as they watched the other couple disappear over the crest of the hill. "He's usually so serious, so intense."

"I remember," Cassie said, but all the while she thought, Griff? *Yes, sure, he's changed. But what about me?* Talk about *changed*! "Maybe he's in love," she said flippantly, wondering what Brendan would say to that, expecting him to deny it.

"That's what he says."

Cassie looked shocked. "Truly? But they don't have a thing in common!"

Brendan scowled as though he would have liked to have refuted her comment or made a countering one of his own. But eventually he just shrugged and said, "So what?" and Cassie, watching as the other couple came into view again and Griffin stole a kiss behind a fir tree, thought that maybe Brendan was right. Maybe it was enough just to be attracted to each other. She and Michael had had lots in common, but they'd never enjoyed each other much.

The thought returned again when they stopped on the top of another hill and found that Lainie and Griff had dismounted and were lolling in the shade of a broad oak tree, presumably setting out a picnic lunch but, in fact, more preoccupied with nibbling on each other.

"Ah, there you are," Lainie said gaily, far less embarrassed than Cassie was by the display of affection between her friend and Griff. "Give me a hand with the sandwiches, will you?"

Cassie did, waiting until Griff had moved a ways down the hill, talking easily with Brendan as they tethered the horses, to ask, "Are you in love with Griffin Tucker?"

"Feels that way," Lainie said cheerfully, tossing Cassie a covered bowl of olives. Cassie pried the lid off and set it in the center of the blanket next to similar bowls of carrots and pickles.

"Are you going to marry him?" Cassie knew she sounded aghast at the idea, but she couldn't help thinking that the serious Griffin Tucker she remembered, the boy who had been the perfect straight man for the irrepressible Brendan Craig, did not seem like the kind of man who would want to be straight man for his own wife. Yet Lainie was a lot like Brendan. And Lainie, Cassie knew, was strong spirited. How would she be able to blend her demanding career with Griff's career, which required that he be on the road almost six months out of every year?

"He hasn't asked," Lainie replied. "But he will, I think." She went about tucking napkins under the paper plates she had brought along with all the savoir faire of an accomplished hostess, and Cassie marveled at her unflappability. If someone had cornered her about marriage, she would be stammering and blushing, but Lainie acted as if it were the most logical thing in the world.

"As for what you're about to say next," Lainie went on, "about how unsuited we are—" she met Cassie's eyes frankly "—I suppose you're right. But they do say that opposites attract. And I'm sure everything will work out."

Privately, Cassie hoped so, but she didn't say anything, just nodded and then called Brendan and Griff to come and eat.

"Delicious," Brendan decreed. He polished off his third chicken-salad sandwich and slid around sideways on the blanket so that he lay back with his head in Cassie's lap, his long legs stretched out before him while he continued his nibbling—this time on her fingers. Cassie choked on her carrot stick as the weight of his head insinuated itself against her thighs and his warm tongue and sharp teeth played havoc with the sensitive skin of her hand.

"Brendan!" she admonished, slapping at him with her napkin, shooting self-conscious glances at Griff and Lainie, who were, fortunately, far too interested in each other to notice what Brendan was doing.

"Even more delicious," he intoned. The nibbling continued up her palm to her wrist and then to her forearm. Cassie shivered at the feel of it, the air striking cool where his mouth had been, though the sun warmed the rest of her. Reluctantly but inexorably, her hand came down to tangle in the dark hair on his head, teasing his scalp so that Brendan stopped his nibbling momentarily and smiled up at her. Cassie smiled back, suspended in a web of feelings that had been growing around her, wrapping her tightly, like a fly caught and held, frightened and yet dazzled by the beauty of it all. She told herself that it was folly to feel this way, that a thirty-two-year-old orthopedic surgeon who was the parent of two children should be businesslike and purposeful, not acting like a besotted adolescent just because a gorgeous man kissed her fingers and smiled. But her brain wasn't working, and her heart was—overtime. Brendan caught her head with his hand and pulled it down as he lifted his own. Cassie's lips parted over his, and her eyes closed as they melted together, adrift on sensations of warmth, the scent of clover and green olives mixing with masculine sweat.

"I'm glad you came," Brendan whispered, loosing her only fractionally.

Cassie traced his lips with the tip of her tongue, heedless of the horses, the droning of bees and the muffled sounds of Griff and Lainie similarly occupied not far away. "Me, too," she murmured. "Me, too."

In fact, from then on she felt as if someone were blowing up a bubble of happiness deep inside her. Day by day it grew until she almost feared it would burst. "You're infatuated," she told herself daily, but she couldn't bring herself to say it in derogatory tones. She *was* infatuated; she could even admit it and enjoy it. Why not, she thought as she went about her rounds or drove home after a long, hard day. What was wrong with that?

Nothing, she decided, except that she didn't know how she was going to make time in her life for everything—her job, her sons, Brendan. The day with Griff and Lainie, far from being a single isolated experience that she could take out and fondle like a seashell brought back from a rare trip to the shore, became the catalyst for a change in her life.

She had tasted joy and wanted more. The trouble came with fitting it in. There were no fewer patients, no fewer surgeries, no fewer demands from the boys. But now, along with them all, there was an overpowering need to be with Brendan. Where it was all leading she didn't know and didn't care. For once in her life she didn't want to think beyond the next day or two.

Brendan, thank God, was accommodating. He was waiting when she got home late and now swam with her in the evenings, laughing and joking, kissing and touching her, watching her with a kind of hunger that she was growing increasingly to understand—and share. She held the hair drier and dried his cast every night, watching with concern but no comments as he gingerly straightened his arm. He caught her watching and scowled but didn't say anything, either, until a week after the horseback-riding afternoon when he showed up at her office without an appointment and, by charming Elda, her receptionist—no difficult task, Cassie acknowledged irritably—got himself let in.

"I thought we were going out later," she said, taking off her lab coat and dropping exhausted into the leather desk chair, kicking off her shoes and looking over at him.

"We can." He seemed distracted, rubbing his right hand through his hair in his characteristically disturbing way. "Cass, could you take another X ray?" He paced across her small office and turned, leaning back against the closed door with a look of entreaty on his face.

Cassie looked up sharply, concerned. "If you want." She tried to keep her voice even. Had Ballard been pestering him again? She hauled herself out of the chair and padded across the chocolate-colored carpet and reached for the doorknob. Brendan moved out of the way, but not so far that she couldn't actually feel the tension emanating from him. Turning, she put a hand on his arm. "What's wrong?"

He shrugged, scuffing his toe on the carpet. "I was talking to Dave Vincent this afternoon." Dave was another of the Mustang pitchers. He had dropped by once or twice to offer comfort and encouragement after Brendan's accident.

"Oh?" Obviously no comfort or encouragement was forthcoming that day.

"He broke his arm four years ago. He never had this trouble with his elbow. With stiffness."

"He probably didn't break his like you did." Cassie would have been willing to bet on it. Most likely he'd only had a simple fracture that just took time to mend.

Brendan shrugged. "I don't know. But he could bend his elbow. It wasn't like mine." He grimaced as he demonstrated the same stiffness she had observed daily for a week.

"Come on, then," she said, her hand still on his arm. "We'll take another look."

This look, however, was just as inconclusive as the earlier ones. "It's possible that you fractured the radial head. That's not easy to see in an X ray," Cassie told him when they had the films spread out before them.

"What's that mean?" He was glowering at the pictures as if daring them to reveal anything he didn't want to deal with. He had taken his shirt off for the X rays, and Cassie was more than aware of his bare chest just inches away, though she kept her eyes glued on the X rays.

It means you may never pitch again, she thought, but didn't say so. There was equally the chance that he might. She took a deep breath. "That you may have some trouble with extending and turning your arm," she told him.

"Snapping off a pitch, you mean?"

She nodded reluctantly. "You may not get your full range of motion back."

Brendan's good fist clenched. The expression on his face, for a moment sheer desolation, gradually shuttered as though he were willfully removing himself from the room, from her presence. Cassie put her hand on his bare arm, but he didn't even seem to notice. A muscle in his jaw jerked; then he blinked rapidly.

"I'm not through, Cass," he said, more to himself, though, than to her. It sounded like a vow, a promise. Cassie hoped desperately it was one he could keep.

If he couldn't, Brendan thought as he jogged resolutely down the wide stretch of sandy beach the following afternoon, it wouldn't be from lack of trying. The stiff breeze off the ocean cooled his overheated body, drying the rivulets of sweat that coursed down his chest and back and dripped into his eyes, stinging them as he squinted into the glare. He could just make out Keith and Steven leaping in and out of the surf far down the beach and was glad he had turned to run back. The measured thud of his feet hitting the hard-packed sand made his arm ache, but he ignored it and ran on. In another week, Cassie promised, the cast would be off. Then he would worry about the aches and pains there. Now he was concentrating on keeping the rest of his body in tiptop shape. It had been a cinch at eighteen, easy enough at twenty-eight, but at thirty-three he had to work, and he knew it. He remembered Cassie asking, "You have to quit sometime, don't you? What then?" But he shoved it aside, not wanting to think about it. His arm would come around. He would *make* it come around. All it took was conditioning. Any fool knew that.

Keith and Steven waved at him, laughing and beckoning as he approached. Brendan slowed his pace, not even breathing hard, and watched them with a fatherly sort of pride that had crept up on him insidiously. He couldn't imagine a life now of which they weren't a part. He looked forward to their conversations, the confidences and their antics. He liked playing catch with them, eating hamburgers with them, going to the beach with them. And—he slowed to a walk, his eyes dropping to watch the deliberate movements of his feet across the sand—he liked their mother.

More than liked her. And he was beginning to think that Cassie liked him, too. She had, he decided, actually spent the night with him. He couldn't really remember it all—thanks to the fish-house punch and Cassie's long, cool destroyer of reason—and he certainly didn't *ask* her if she had, but there had been a new presence about her after that night, a sort of unspoken intimacy that was too new and too precious to be questioned. And the day they had gone horseback riding, she had responded to him the same way he had responded to her. Memories of her softness, her honeyed lips, both sustained and tormented him throughout the ensuing days. He didn't see how he could stand being with her and not having her, and yet, from day to day, he managed. He managed, he knew, only because he was holding out, waiting for the right moment when he could ask for something better. He hoped.

He sighed and stopped walking, staring out to sea, remembering the times when he was a child that he had wanted to know what was out there, just beyond the horizon. He felt like that now. A desperate need to see beyond, to know the future, assailed him, making him ache everywhere his arm didn't. For Brendan, who had always lived for the moment, the tug to know the future had been momentary, easily dismissed until now. But now there was Cassie. And what, if any future, did he have with her?

He couldn't ask her to marry him. Not with his future uncertain. If he hadn't had the damned accident, he would have been a sure thing—as successful and busy as she was. But now? Now all he could do was gnash his teeth, bide his time and run like mad. And next week he could begin to get in shape for real. God willing, his arm would snap back. Then he would have something to offer.

"Time to go?" Keith asked him as he turned and waved them over.

Brendan glanced at his watch. "Yeah. If we hurry, we can pick up your mom at the hospital."

Steve stopped flinging seaweed at his brother long enough to consider the idea. "Great! Then what'll we do?"

"I don't know yet," Brendan said, tossing him a towel. "But I'm sure we'll think of something."

It had become a challenge—one that he loved. Cassie

was so delighted, so easily pleased, with crazy little things that most women would have disdained. Her enjoyment of the trip to Knott's Berry Farm had planted the idea in his head, and the horseback riding confirmed it. So now he made it a point frequently to pick her up after she finished at the hospital, sometimes with the boys, sometimes without, and to find things to do. Once they drove to Playa del Rey and parked in the dunes just east of the beach and watched as the huge jets from LAX took off almost directly overhead. Cassie had watched, astonished, as they went over, her hands covering her ears while the boys cheered as each gleaming silver monster struggled airborne.

"Is that all there is to it?" she had asked, a teasing light in her eye that reminded him that he had promised her a "hot date" when he had phoned to tell her they would pick her up. Brendan mumbled, "Simple people, simple pleasures," and dipped his head swiftly to touch his lips to hers.

Another time they had bought pizza in a fast-food place, eating it in the car—to the detriment of Cassie's seat covers—and had driven to the harbor in Redondo where they walked on the pier holding hands and pretending that the two young boys whistling and catcalling about their entwined hands and starry eyes were no relation to them.

"Tonight," Brendan told the boys after they had changed clothes and were on their way to pick up Cassie, "we are going Mexican."

"Huh?" They both looked puzzled, bouncing on the back seat and demanding to know what he had in mind.

"Wait and see," he told them. But the minute he saw Cassie, he wished he hadn't promised a thing. She looked like nothing so much as a woman who needed to go straight home and go to bed. She drooped when she came out of the hospital door. Then, seeing him playing Frisbee with the boys on the lawn, she straightened up and came toward them, a genuine smile on her face.

"Hi." Brendan flipped the Frisbee to Steve and went to meet her, wanting to fold her into his arms but reining himself in, instead hoping that she could read the expression in his eyes that told her things he didn't dare.

"Hi, yourself." She opened the car door and tossed her bag inside, then leaned against the fender, watching as the boys played, a tired smile lighting her face. "Did you have a good day?"

"Not bad. We went to the beach. I ran; they played. I wished you were there. How about you?"

She looked drained, as though she had been through a wringer. But she just shook her head, loosening her curls from the pins that held them against her head. "Just routine."

Brendan wanted to say, "If that's routine, change it." But he didn't, only nodded and pulled her over in front of him so that she leaned back against him. Her buttocks curved against his thighs, and his arms went around her, cradling her lightly. He nestled his chin against her ear, breathing in the faint scent of cologne she had dashed on many hours before and that now mingled with smells of hospital soap and disinfectant along with an indefinable essence that had always and forever brought Cassie to mind.

"Want to go home now?" he asked, all too ready to make up an excuse and tell the boys they would "go Mexican" another night.

Cassie shook her head. "No. I'm all right." She tossed her head back to look up at him, her cheek just a fraction of an inch from his own. "What's on the agenda?"

Bed, Brendan wanted to say. Loving. All night long.

They went to Olvera Street instead. Meandering down the cobblestone street of the oldest part of Los Angeles where vendors sold Mexican and Mexican-American arts and crafts, they listened to mariachi music as they moved from shop to shop. Armed with three dollars apiece and the admonition to meet back at the fountain at nine o'clock, Keith and Steven darted off to explore on their own, leaving Cassie and Brendan smiling into each other's eyes. Brendan was relieved to see that she was looking brighter by the minute. Maybe a change of pace was all she needed. She worked too hard, too long. She needed caring for, loving. The thought made his stomach ache and his throat tighten, and he thrust his fist into the pocket of his jeans and clenched the other around the hard wrapping of his cast till it bit into his palm.

"Come on," he said brusquely. "Let's go get something to eat."

An open-air restaurant yielded tasty, spicy, hot taquitos, which they ate as they walked, licking the pungent sauce from their fingers and the waxed paper wrapping.

"Is waxed paper biodegradable?" Brendan asked, fanning his mouth and taking a long draft of Coke.

"I hope so." Cassie laughed, her eyes sparkling. "I think I've eaten most of mine. These are great, Bren. You do have good ideas!"

Daringly, he bent over and whispered another one in her ear, laughing when she blushed.

"Behave yourself," she admonished him, but she quite willingly slipped her fingers through his, leaning against his arm as they threaded their way through the throngs of people milling about, eating, looking into the shops or just visiting with friends. They stopped and watched while several small children tried out their packets of jumping beans, laughing as one leaped right off the counter. Then they moved on to watch a glass blower at work, admiring the delicate strands of glass that he blew and twisted into intricate, lacy shapes.

"Aren't they lovely?" Cassie asked him. And they were—like a sea of glittering diamonds reflecting the rainbow in a thousand directions. One small piece caught his eye, and without thinking, he stepped up and purchased it from the woman who was making the sales.

Cassie, who had been absorbed in watching the man blow glass, scarcely missed him and looked up in surprise when he pressed a tissue-wrapped package into her hands. "What's this?"

"Open it and see." He felt oddly tongue-tied, like a boy bringing his prom date a corsage and wondering if he had chosen right, if it would go with what she wore.

Cassie's fingers fumbled with the paper, loosening the tape. Was it his imagination, or did her fingers tremble the slightest bit? He steered her to a nearby bench, and she sat down, still focusing on the paper that was wrapped around and around the small object. At last she uncovered it to find in her upturned palm a perfectly blown hot-air balloon, straining at its ropes, fragile and delicate as it tried to break free, catching the neon lights and candles from the restaurant and turning them into a brilliant winking display.

For years, Brendan thought, she didn't say a word. Then her eyes lifted and met his, wide and wondering.

"It's for you," he said awkwardly, then wanted to kick himself because that much must be obvious. He gave her a faint grin.

Her smile was tremulous. Were those tears, for God's sake? "Thank you," she said in scarcely more than a whisper. Then she leaned across the balloon in her lap to kiss him lightly but lingeringly on the lips. "Thank you, Brendan. It's perfect."

It was so perfect, Cassie decided, it simply couldn't last. Like the balloon she set on her dresser and looked at longingly every night, she was buffeted by winds that confused her as much as they freed her. And the longer she tried to fly free while keeping her feet firmly on the ground, the more worn out she got. The night they went to Olvera Street, she was barely able to drag herself out of the hospital she was so exhausted. It was only Brendan's solicitous care and, later, his infectious enthusiasm that had brought her around. She wanted to be with him, but she also had a job to do and sons to care for. She needed sleep more and was getting it less. She didn't know what to do.

You used to manage just fine, she reminded herself as she dressed for work a week later and wondered why everything she did seemed as if it were in slow motion these days. Yes, she agreed with herself as she hastily buttered her toast and poured a cup of instant coffee before she left for the hospital, but that was before Brendan. *So give him up,* she continued her monologue as she pulled out of the driveway with a regretful look behind her at the house where he and the boys still slept. No way, she thought as she eased her car onto the freeway. No way at all.

But something, it became increasingly clearer, had to give. She felt muddled and fuzzy minded just trying to think about it. She had had a headache for the past several days, and that was from worrying, too, no doubt. She wished her mother were home so she could ask her, or Lainie. But her mother was too far away, and Lainie was a lost cause. Lainie had only one subject of conversation lately. Three guesses what it was, Cassie thought wryly. Or *who* it was. Any day now she expected the announcement that Lainie was going to marry Griff. And, of course, it would "work out." Things for Lainie always did. It must be nice, Cassie thought with more than a little self-pity, which she immediately shook herself out of. Anyway, she was glad it was Gene doing the surgery that morning and that she was only assisting.

"Are you all right?" Gene asked her when they came out of surgery, his thin face reflecting the concern in his voice.

"Fine." She squared her shoulders and walked as briskly as she could back to the lounge, hoping that he didn't start harping at her again. After Mike had died, Gene thought it was his duty to get her to take some time off and sort things out. He didn't realize she needed to work then. She hoped he wouldn't start in again now.

Gene looked as if he doubted she was really fine but tactfully changed the subject. "When does Brendan's cast come off?"

"Tomorrow." He certainly hadn't picked an easier topic. It was a sore point between her and Brendan, he pushing, she holding back. But the moment of truth had finally arrived, and she knew he would be denied no longer. Selfishly, she had wanted him to wait—she liked things as they were. But that couldn't last forever, and for better or worse, the cast was coming off in the morning.

"How's it look?" Gene asked. He pulled off his surgical cap and raked fingers through his sparse hair.

"Not too great," Cassie admitted, though she had never said as much to Brendan. "I'd like you to take a look at it and at his X rays when we take the cast off. Will you?"

"Sure."

She gave him a wan smile. "Thanks." She didn't know why, but she suspected she was going to need all the moral support she could get.

It turned out she was right. Brendan appeared at the office almost before she did. She was jotting down notes on one of her hospital patient's records when Elda, her receptionist, informed her that he was waiting. She felt her stomach knot and wished she wasn't his doctor or that she didn't care about him personally or about his future. Damn. She closed her eyes, praying for a bit of strength, wishing, too, that her faint nausea and blasted headache would subside and that she would feel a bit more energetic. If Brendan's arm wasn't any better than she thought it might be, she knew she was going to need some. Soon.

"I'll be with him in a minute," she told Elda. "As soon as Dr. Phillips arrives."

Unfortunately, Dr. Phillips arrived almost at once. He took one look at Cassie, who was leaning against one of the examining tables, and said, "Who's the patient here, anyway?"

Cassie smiled faintly.

Gene peered into her eyes. "Are you all right?" He put a palm against her forehead, which she shook off.

"I'm fine. Just tired. Brendan's in the next room," she added, almost as an afterthought.

Gene nodded, then said with more than a trace of guilt, "I suppose I should have taken his case back from you, Cass, since we're talking elbows now."

"Too late now," Cassie said heavily, shoving herself away from the table. Much too late. She looked down at her hands with an almost-detached curiosity, wondering why they were trembling.

Gene obviously wondered, too. "I'll cut his cast off," he told her, patting her arm solicitously. "Why don't you just go lie down?"

Lie down? He hadn't even suggested that she lie down after Michael had died! Not that she would have. But now, oddly enough, she was tempted. She felt light-headed and decidedly edgy. All because of Brendan? She shoved a hand through her hair, messing it even more than it already was but not particularly caring. "No. No, that's all right." She tried a smile, not very successfully. What on earth was wrong with her?

She was still wondering as she followed Gene into the next examining room and saw Brendan sitting on the table. He looked as worried and preoccupied as she felt. With more reason, she thought. He, after all, had his arm to worry about. What was *her* problem? She let Gene remove the cast, her own trembling hands stuffed into the pockets of her lab coat as she watched, certain that she was betraying all her anxiety on her face. It was fortunate that Brendan was watching Gene, too, and not her.

"Go get it X-rayed now," Gene told him when he lifted the cast off. "Then we'll talk." He waited until Brendan had followed the nurse down the hall to the X-ray machine and then turned to Cassie. "It doesn't look bad."

"Have him move it."

"I will." He tipped back on the stool where he sat and studied her, his brown eyes warm and sympathetic.

"You're working too hard," he said conversationally, "and enjoying it less."

Cassie shrugged. "Perhaps." Another time she would have denied it. That morning she wasn't up to arguing about anything. She hadn't got the energy for it.

"I've never seen you like this before."

Nor have I, Cassie wanted to say. She'd never *been* like this before. "I'm just a bit tired," she offered, not knowing what else to say. "And I suppose I'm concerned about Brendan's arm."

"Yes." Gene tapped his fingers on the countertop, his expression thoughtful. The nurse brought in the X rays, and he spread them out against the viewer, studying them carefully. Cassie left her post by the counter and joined him. "Nothing obvious," Gene said finally, nodding his head.

"No." There was an unspoken "but" that they both knew followed even though she didn't open her mouth.

Gene shrugged. "He might be fine."

Brendan came back into the room then, his arm cradled gingerly against his chest, his eyes wary. "Well?"

Gene smiled. "Now you get to work."

Hope lit Brendan's features. "You mean it?"

Gene raised a cautionary hand. "Hard work, chum. And I can't promise what the outcome will be." He took Brendan's hand and drew it out from his body, supporting it with one hand as he straightened it with the other. He held it palm down, then slowly rotated it in an attempt to bring the palm up. He couldn't. Cassie bit her lip. Brendan frowned.

"Why can't I turn it?"

"Maybe it's just stiffness that will work out," Gene said. "Or you may have some permanent damage. Time will tell."

Brendan looked at him for a long minute. Then his eyes sought Cassie's, looking, she knew, for a more positive opinion. Her head pounded. She swallowed the lump in her throat and forced herself to nod, not wanting to, wanting only to assure him that he would be fine, wanting to promise him miracles. She also wanted, she realized with dismay, to fling herself into his arms and cry her eyes out. She blinked rapidly, fighting down the impulse. She mustn't. Oh, God, she mustn't! Doctors didn't cry, for heaven's sake! Certainly not over broken arms!

Brendan nodded his head slowly, expelling a deep breath, as if coming to terms with what Gene said. "I will work," he promised grimly. "I will." He looked at his arm, still lying in Gene's outstretched hand, ran his own fingers along the forearm, then tapped them against the back of his hand speculatively. Lifting his eyes, he met Cassie's frightened gaze with an unfathomable one of his own. Then he turned on his heel and left the room.

Gene squeezed her shoulders. "Now I know why I gave him to you, Cass," he said softly. "He's going to need all the help he can get."

Thank God he didn't look back as he followed Brendan out of the room, because he hadn't shut the door before the tears started to fall. Her head throbbed, and her eyes stung. Cassie clung to the back of the chair where she had been standing, gulping down great wrenching sobs, and wondered if perhaps she was losing her mind. Nobody cried over a broken arm! But deep down she knew it wasn't an arm she was crying about but a future.

Chapter Nine

"Exhaustion," Gene diagnosed for Brendan's benefit. He was moving purposefully around Cassie's bedroom, closing the drapes, which left them standing in the shadows, regarding Cassie's inert form lying in the middle of her bed. "Maybe a dash of flu, too. She looks half dead."

And feels it, too, Cassie thought miserably, too far gone to be offended by the accuracy of Gene's statement. She wished they would both go away. But it was her turn to do something for Brendan now—Gene had said so only a couple of hours before—and she felt too worn out to move.

"What should I do?" Brendan sounded dismayed, at a loss for once. Cassie would have liked to have seen his face, but she couldn't. He was standing behind her, out of her field of vision, and her mind felt a million miles away, so totally unconnected to the rest of her body that she couldn't even command her muscles to turn her head. All her reactions were involuntary. The only things she seemed able to do at all were to cry and to throw up, neither of which had much to recommend it.

"I'd get her out of here for a while. She needs a break. She's been burning the candle at both ends lately," Gene advised. "And you could do with some space, too, right now. Get away from Ballard and let that arm come back at its own pace."

"Good idea," Brendan said.

Cassie agreed even though she didn't say so. She closed her eyes and let him take over. For once she didn't care that her life was out of her control. She trusted Brendan. He would know what to do.

THE INTERMITTENT RUSHING and crashing sounds were as unfamiliar as they were continuous. It took Cassie a few moments to place them. Waves—pounding and relentless—and, closer, the caw of wheeling sea gulls. She frowned, opening her eyes to the dull golden glow of sunlight on pine-paneled walls. Blinking and stretching, she felt for the first time in recent history remotely human. Also confused. Her foot touched something hard, and she rolled over to see Brendan sitting on the edge of her bed, smiling down at her, his bare back glinting almost copper in the late-morning sun.

She opened her mouth, but her words came out cracked and raspy. "Where did you say we were?" She thought she remembered, but now she couldn't quite believe it.

"Oregon."

She was right. God in heaven, she didn't even *know* anyone in Oregon! "The boys?" she croaked, struggling to sit up against the old-fashioned iron bedstead.

Brendan moved quickly to her aid, saying, "Here, let me help you." He tenderly arranged three pillows behind her, then smoothed the tangle of hair off her face with his rough, callused hand. "The boys are with your mother. Remember?"

She did now that he mentioned it. Gene had brought her home from work exhausted and had told Brendan that she needed a break. Always a man of action, Brendan hadn't wasted any time. He had called Elsa and Raymond, arranged for the boys to fly over to Hawaii and at the same time had arranged for the two of them to fly to Oregon where they could, in his words, "sleep and surf." He might have been doing the latter, but Cassie, as far as she could recall, had done almost nothing but the former since they had arrived. But Gene must have been right, for after two days of almost round-the-clock slumber, she felt weak but definitely on the mend. Brendan had taken better care of her during the past two days than she had ever taken care of him.

He stood up now, stuffing his fists into the pockets of his jeans, which were the only thing he wore. Her eyes noted the pale thinness of his left arm, and she recalled with a start that he was supposed to be *her* patient and not vice versa. "Your arm," she said. 'How does it feel?"

Brendan shrugged, scowling. "Who knows? Are you hungry?" He changed the subject.

Too weak to pursue a topic he was reluctant to discuss, Cassie let it drop for now. She turned instead to considering his question. Her stomach felt hollow, but the thought of food didn't tempt her much. She remembered quite vividly not being able to keep anything down. "A cup of tea, maybe?" she suggested.

"All right." He turned away, clearly relieved that she wasn't going to harp on his arm. He ambled easily across the room and filled a large copper kettle with water from the tap. Cassie's eyes followed him, taking in all her surroundings for the first time. The cabin wasn't large, all knotty pine and braided rugs, the brick fireplace with its raised hearth at one end near the kitchen area where Brendan was setting the kettle on the huge white old-fashioned stove. Beyond him, through blue-and-white gingham curtained windows, she saw the heavy pine forest filtering the sunlight. Used to the precise landscaping of her own garden, she lay back, pleased and vaguely comforted by the differences here, where nature, not man, dictated the surroundings. "Rest," Gene had commanded. She doubted if Brendan could have found a place more conducive to it if he had tried.

Brendan was carefully laying a tray with cups, saucers and napkins, his attention to detail bordering on the fanatic, and she had a faint suspicion that he was, however odd it might strike her, oddly nervous. Watching him made her feel warm and slightly muzzy, though she wasn't at all sure why. He carried the tray over to her bedside, setting it on the sturdy pine nightstand, and poured out two cups of herbal tea, loading hers with sugar over her protests.

"It's good for you. Gives you strength," he insisted, pressing it into her hands.

"I'm the doctor," she mumbled, scowling at the dark, almond-scented liquid swirling in the blue willow cup she held. But she had never felt less doctorlike. Her body was limp, like a rag doll's, and she turned her head so that her cheek lay against the coolness of the crisp cotton pillowcase while she studied with slow thoroughess the length of jeans-clad thigh at her eye level. The fabric was soft from washing and faded with use. Her fingers itched to touch it, to run down from the faded zipper placket to the well-worn knee and—

"Drink your tea before it gets cold." Brendan's voice broke sharply into her reverie, and as she lifted her eyes to look at him, he scowled and took a hasty gulp of the scalding liquid, moving away quickly as he did so to stand at the far end of the bed.

Cassie made a face but obediently sipped the tea, annoyed that her stomach didn't rebel at its sweet, cloying taste—her taste buds certainly did. But her sips won Brendan's approval apparently, for he smiled at her again, the same tender, heart-jerking smile that he had bestowed on her when she first awakened.

Cassie smiled back, basking in his approval, suddenly willing to drink the whole ghastly cupful if he would just keep looking at her like that. She curled her toes against the soft cotton sheets, feeling a contentment steal over her like that of a cat before a hearth. "You're very good to me, Brendan," she murmured through a yawn, which she tried to stifle against the back of her hand. Her eyes closed heavily, and her hand relaxed. The teacup rattled in its saucer. Brendan's hand closed on it at once, lifting it out of her hand and setting it on the tray. Then he fluffed her pillows and straightened the quilt over her just as her mother had when Cassie was a child. She looked up at him, feeling about seven years old, cosseted and cared for once again.

"Thank you," she muttered.

Brendan's eyes flickered over her, and he sucked in his breath sharply. Then, with a barely discernible hesitancy, he patted her cheek. The warm, comfortable feeling grew within her, spreading to encompass all her limbs, bathing her whole being in a rosy glow. Brendan had done all this for her, had cared for her, had made her feel this way. Tears pricked behind her eyelids. She opened them slightly, seeing the dark hairs on the back of his hand as it lay on the quilt. They intrigued her, attracted her, and her own hand stole out from beneath the quilt and gently touched them, tracing their pattern against his smooth tanned skin.

His hand jerked slightly, then steadied, and he said hoarsely, "Sleep again, Cass." His voice was gentle and persuasive, his skin warm to her trembling touch. She didn't need much persuasion. She slept.

By the time she opened her eyes again, the sun had shifted. Her bed lay in the shadows now, but in the kitchen bathed in sunlight, Brendan bent over the wide plank table, the sleeves of the madras plaid shirt he now wore rolled back to his elbows as he kneaded a heavy mound of dough. Cassie blinked, then blinked again. Brendan? Making bread? She lay perfectly still, enchanted with the sight, almost afraid that if she moved, stretched, even breathed, he would vanish.

He didn't look her way, his attention focused entirely on the motion of his hands and arms as they plied the dough, pushing and pulling rhythmically in time with the steady pounding of the surf. From her warm cocoon under the quilt, she enjoyed the luxury of tracing his profile—the fall of dark hair over his forehead, the proud nose, the jutting brush of his mustache over his sensual mouth, the stubborn chin. Until then she had always stolen her glances at him, sneaking them furtively, quickly, not really daring to linger and appreciate. But now—now she had the time.

Now she could contemplate and appreciate Brendan Craig, the man he was as well as the boy he had been. His face, she decided, had hardened, was more mature, the tiny lines that fanned out from his eyes and the faint shadow of beard on his cheek adding character to a look that was still, she had to admit, endearingly boyish. And the body? Her eyes wandered lower, perusing at leisure the flour-dusted shirt, tails hanging over the snug faded jeans that clothed the lean muscular power of his thighs. A boy's body it was not! She smiled, watching him. He could even knead bread dough with the economical grace of an athlete. Trust Brendan to find good muscle therapy in a household chore.

The fire crackled and snapped as a log rolled off the pile, and Brendan left his kneading long enough to poke it back into the blaze. He stretched, his shoulder muscles flexing as he lifted his hands over his head. Then, as Cassie watched, he kneaded the muscles of his left forearm with his right hand. She sucked in her breath quickly, and Brendan looked up.

"Ah, you're awake." His mouth lifted at a corner, almost hiding his smile behind his mustache, and Cassie stretched, too, his gaze making her aware of the smooth line of her body beneath the quilt and the tingling warmth stirring deep within her.

"At last," she agreed, easing herself up, conscious for the first time that she wasn't wearing any of her sheer feminine gowns, but rather one of Brendan's shirts. She tugged it together over her breasts, fumbling to fasten the buttons, though she had no doubt he had seen it all before when he was putting her into it. A flush crept up her neck that she tried gamely to ignore. Instead, she said, "Does your arm hurt?"

Brendan's mouth twisted ironically. "You are better," he pronounced. "Every inch the doctor again." His eyes were slightly desperate, Cassie thought.

"Not every inch." Her voice was soft. She didn't know if she had meant it to sound as seductive as it did, but Brendan obviously heard it that way. He stuffed flour-smudged hands into his pockets and rocked back and forth on his heels. Her eyes traveled down to his well-worn moccasins, then slowly back up to meet his eyes, which had obviously been doing the same to her. "Brendan?"

She wasn't sure what she was asking, but Brendan apparently had no doubt. He seemed to be engaged in internal warfare over it at that very moment. She could see the turmoil in his face. Finally, he expelled a short, harsh breath and said abruptly, "I've got to get back to the damned bread."

From that point on, the warfare was external; the enemy was the dough he pummeled, and Cassie witnessed it all. Whether Brendan's arm hurt before or not, she knew it would by the time he had finished pulverizing the lump on the table. The battle was long and furious, ending when he slapped the dough into a waiting bowl of glazed blue pottery, draped a dish towel over it and set in on the counter in the afternoon sun. Then, his demons exorcised, he wiped his hands on the back of his jeans and said, "How about another cup of tea?"

Cassie, who had been mesmerized by the sight of him attacking the bread, jerked back to consciousness at the thought of gagging down another cup of the sweet almond liquid and hastily shook her head. "No, thanks." She swung her feet over the side of the bed and dangled them, contemplating the distance to the floor. "How about if I get up for a while."

"Are you sure you feel up to it?" he asked, concern written on his face.

"I'm sure." She stood carefully, her toes curling into the nubby braid of the rag rug as she reorientated herself to being vertical again. "The bathroom?" she ventured, sure she must have used it before but obviously not without help and not without forgetting.

Brendan's strong arm went around her, holding her against him as she tottered forward. "This way." Her shoulder pressed against his rib cage, and she could feel the quickening beat of his heart. He helped her to the bathroom and hovered outside till she finished, then practically carried her back to bed. Her head spun dizzily from just that little bit of exertion, and she clung to him gratefully, in the back of her mind wondering how she ever would have coped without him. He tucked the sheet and quilt around her, then smoothed them gently, his fingers lingering momentarily over the swell of her breasts beneath the faded quilt.

"Okay now?" His voice was gentle, almost paternal, and Cassie blinked, smiling gratefully at him and then catching his hand in hers.

"Why are you bothering with all this?"

He stopped, his body still bent over her as he frowned, a line of puzzlement etched between his dark brows.

"Taking care of me like this, I mean," she persisted. "You don't have to, you know, Bren."

"I want to," he said simply.

He wanted to care for her. It sounded so simple, yet it came close to being mind shattering. She contemplated his words, turning them over in her head, worrying them like a dog with a bone. The idea, however palatable, was completely foreign to her.

"No one ever has before," she told him. Besides her parents, of course.

He had been watching the fire, not looking at her, but when she said that, he turned and sank down on the edge of her bed, his hip nudging her thigh, so that she moved over to make room for him. His eyes locked with hers.

"Not even Mike?" The question dropped like a tennis ball in her court, waiting for her answer. Brendan leaned forward, his forearms resting on his thighs, his hands dangling between his knees in a posture of relaxation. But his body was taut and his eyes intent, and his gaze met hers.

"No." She plucked nervously at the sheet. How could she begin to explain about Michael? Brendan shifted his weight, turning so that he almost faced her, one knee drawn up on the bed. Deliberately, he lifted her hand and held it gently in his so that her fingertips brushed the soft denim covering his thigh.

"Tell me."

Tell him. Just like that. She groped for words, unable to believe that a man like Brendan, a man so in love with life and the sheer joy of the moment, could ever begin to understand Michael. "I—I'll try." His fingers squeezed hers, and involuntarily she squeezed back.

"Michael and I met in college. We were both premed. He was the only one who could ever beat me on tests." She drifted against the pillows, remembering, searching for the words that would make their relationship comprehensible, avoiding Brendan's gaze. "He was the only person I knew who had more goals than I did. It seemed natural that we should go around together. A meeting of minds, if you like." She gave him a faint smile then, which he didn't return. His face was expressionless. She doubted he understood her at all. "We encouraged each other. We shared the same desires. We thought marriage was an excellent way of combining forces." She gave a little shrug, knowing how passionless it sounded. "So we got married and helped keep each other awake during our internships and our residencies. And we had the boys and our practices and our goals, and then—" she waved her hand in the air "—he was gone."

Her voice cracked, and she blinked, swallowing back the lump in her throat she always felt when she confronted the fact of Michael's life being so abruptly snuffed out. "Maybe," she said, forcing out words she had never articulated before, "maybe it would have been different for us if he had just been hurt, not killed. Maybe I would have seen him vulnerable for the first time. Maybe we could have found something in that together. And maybe I would have learned how to be vulnerable with him. But as it was..." Her words stumbled, and tears stung at the backs of her eyes. She blinked them back, her gaze drawn to Brendan's, searching for something—she wasn't sure what; understanding, perhaps?—in his velvety blue eyes. The fire popped and spattered, the flames flickering, their orange glow highlighting the dark hair that framed his face. He sat motionless, his body taut with a tension she hadn't even recognized until she finished speaking and felt his fingers tighten on hers.

"Did you love him?" His voice was raw.

Love him? Love Michael? For years she thought she had. She *liked* Michael, respected him. But *loved*? Love suddenly seemed much more than what she had felt—tenderness, joy, desire, longing, care, all wrapped up together. Feelings that soared and mingled, not merged and plodded. Feelings very much like those she had for Brendan.

The tears welled, then spilled, and she rubbed her eyes ineffectually on the corner of the sheet, overwhelmed at the turn of her thoughts. A sob caught her unawares, and her breasts heaved as she tried to choke it down. "Poor Mike." Her voice wavered and fell. "He deserved so much more than that." She squeezed her eyes shut, and her fingers clenched hard on Brendan's hand.

"So do you," she heard him whisper, and his breath was warm on her forehead. Then soft lips and a downy mustache brushed along her brow and dropped to touch her cheek with the same feather-light caress. "You deserve to be cherished," he went on, his mouth drifting down her cheek, seeking her lips. "To be loved." Then his lips found hers, teasing them lightly, his mustache tickling her nose. There were no more words between them then, only movements. Touches of tenderness, caring, love.

He pulled back for a moment, just long enough to strip off his shirt, dropping it lightly on the quilt before turning again to take her in his arms. And Cassie reached for him, her hands smoothing down the muscled firmness of his back, loving the satiny feel of his skin, breathing in the warm musk of his neck, the mingling of bread dough, almonds and something simply Brendan. His weight pressed her back into the downy softness of the mattress, one hand threading through her curls while the other sought her breast, stroking its burgeoning fullness so that she moaned and her fingers dug into his back.

"Ah, Cass." The words were a breath, no more. A sigh, an ache. He reached down and fumbled with the snap of his jeans, cursed, fumbled some more. Cassie kissed his ear, then nipped gently at its sensitive lobe, delighted to hear his moaned response. Her hands slipped between them, stilling his, then undoing the snap and releasing the zipper herself with an ease that might have looked practiced but was, in fact, beginner's luck. The fires that were licking through her drove her closer to him, and she heard his breathing quicken, too, as he shrugged the jeans off, then slid naked under the quilt beside her, his hands molding her breasts, stroking downward along the curve of her hips, leaving a trail of flames that made her shudder and press against him. Then his arms slid around her, tightening convulsively, branding her with his need. Cassie's foot slid along his calf, smoothing the rough hairs as it glided down, ruffling them on the journey toward his thigh.

"Mmm." His lips brushed her ear, nuzzled. His tongue touched delicately, then probed deeper. Shivers ran down her spine, and she laughed. Brendan pulled back slightly, his navy velvet eyes caressing hers, the planes of his face softened in the shadowy fire glow of late afternoon. Cassie lifted her hand and stroked his cheek, her fingers lingering on the line of his jaw. How strong it was. A tender smile touched his lips, and he caught her hand, bringing it to touch his mouth, planting a sweet, lingering kiss in her palm.

In her mind Cassie had always imagined Brendan as a

fiery lover, intense, passionate, demanding. But nothing she had dreamed of compared with the reality. She saw nothing of fire in him; he made no demands. But the intensity was there as well as the passion—leashed, controlled, and all the more apparent for being so. She saw nothing that made her believe he could not be fiery or demanding if the occasion required it; but in addition she found a tenderness in him that made her want once more to weep.

He never asked, he only gave, bringing to her a sweetness, a gentleness, that at first lulled and soothed her as it warmed. Then, gradually, with every light touch, every smooth caress, he gave her such pleasure, delighted and loved her so well, that she could stand no more and drew him to her, almost frantic in her need to know him completely, to share with him the love that must have, she was sure, been growing for years.

"Now, Brendan!" Her voice was urgent, her arms clenched him, her legs wrapped his, wanting to share with him the pleasure he had been so willingly giving her.

He fitted his body to hers, smoothly, easily, their movements meshing with a timeless familiarity. Cassie's hands stroked his back; her lips tasted the damp flesh of his shoulder. She moved sinuously beneath him, slowly at first, then more quickly as she felt his body tense. This was what love felt like, she decided. Not some quick groping or clinical explorations sanctioned by a marriage license but the warmth and tender joy of total giving, the merging of one body and soul with another, two hearts becoming one.

Spent, they lay in each other's arms, hearts slowing, hands gently stroking, reluctant to stop touching, to move apart and become separate once more. Brendan laid his damp cheek against hers, and she reached up to thread her fingers in his hair, loving its silky softness. The fire crackled and popped, then settled into gently glowing embers, its warmth radiating throughout the room, reflecting the sheen of perspiration on Brendan's back and the contentment in Cassie's heart.

"My love," she whispered in his ear. "Oh, my love." And then, once more, she slept.

THE DULL ACHE in his elbow woke him. Brendan shifted against the soft warm curves of Cassie's body, easing his arm out from beneath her and stretching it reluctantly in the evening air. The fire had nearly died, leaving the room lit only by the fading summer sun. Brendan rolled onto his back, flexing the muscles in his arm, grimacing at the soreness as he made a fist and released it. He'd been a fool to attack the bread that way. But it was that or attack Cassie! He wanted her so badly, too badly—and when she looked at him that way, with her heart in her eyes... Damn. He squeezed his eyes shut, rubbing his arm. It was only muscles, he told himself. That was a good sign. They would come around. It was just part of getting in shape again, like spring training in the middle of summer. He had to get in shape again, had to pitch again. What else, after all, did he have to offer her?

Her words of love—warm comfort while he slept with her curled in his arms—were cold taunts now. They simply pointed out to him how far he had to go, how little he had to offer. Cassie was a successful woman, accomplished, professional, for all that she was at the moment almost totally dependent on him. The dependence wouldn't last, and he knew it. If he was going to keep that love she had whispered, he would have to be just as much of a success as she was. He clenched and unclenched his fist, twisted his arm, palm down, palm up. No, not up, but better. He was getting more range of motion. Yes, of course he was.

Slowly, without waking Cassie, he slid out of the warm coziness of their bed, shivering in the coolness as he tugged on his jeans and buttoned up the madras shirt. Nine-tenths of him didn't want to leave at all.

The ache in his loins, which rivaled the one in his arm, was growing again. The difference was that he knew how to assuage the former. All he had to do was wake Cassie, turn her in his arms and find again in her the warm loving passion they had celebrated just a couple of hours earlier.

And then what, he asked himself, shoving his feet into his moccasins and going to rebuild the fire. Then he'd want her again. And again. But he knew, as well, that he would want more than that—more than just their lovemaking, however impassioned. He wanted all of Cassie, now and forever. He sighed. And the only way he had any right to ask it of her was to be able to offer her himself whole and successful, too. Which meant, he thought with a grimace as he punched down the bread dough that had long before escaped the confines of the bowl, kneading and flexing and anything else that would strengthen his arm. Then he would do some general warm-up exercises, then run on the beach, then... *Don't overdo it, fella,* he cautioned himself as he shoved his fist into the spongy mass of dough. *Just take it one step at a time.*

Two miles down the rock-and-driftwood-strewn beach and two miles back were more steps than Brendan wanted to take. He was loath to leave Cassie even though he doubted she would wake again soon. He just liked sitting by the fire, watching her. But it was a luxury he couldn't afford, not if he wanted eventually to make her part of his life for good. So he did his four-mile run, and by the time he got back, the bread was ready to go into the oven. He plunked the bread pans in, heaved another log onto the fire and changed into a pair of sweats all without even allowing himself to glance at Cassie. If he did, he knew he would abandon all his good intentions and crawl right back into bed beside her. He had tortured himself all the way down the beach and back with memories of her tormenting fingers, her soft moans and cries of pleasure, his own overwhelming need, which found satisfaction only in her. He was incredibly out of breath when he reached the wide front porch on his return, and he was quite sure that most of his shortness of breath had nothing to do with running four miles at all.

He dropped down onto the braided oval rug before the fire and sat with his legs spread, linking his fingers behind his head as he bent his torso to touch each elbow to the opposite knee in turn. Fifty of those, then sit-ups. No push-ups yet. His arm wouldn't support his weight. Sweat trickled down his back, and he pushed damp hair off his face. The smell of baking bread filled the room, seducing him with its homey comfort. His eyes strayed to the high iron bed. One of Cassie's bare feet poked out from beneath the quilt.

He would just cover it up, Brendan thought, rising slowly to his feet, feeling the ache of every muscle in his body, grateful that he did but wishing that he felt the ones of a purely masculine nature far less. He thought that by now he ought to have worn himself out. But no, the fire in his loins still raged unquenched, and the feel of Cassie's soft heel against his fingers as he slid her foot back under the quilt nearly undid him.

It was nine o'clock before the bread came out. He ate a chunk of it, still hot from the oven and dripping with butter, letting it assuage one of his hungers. But the other grew, consuming him, so that he licked the butter from his fingers, wrapped the bread in plastic bags, stoked the fire, stripped off his clothes and practically flung himself into the bed.

Once there, he didn't know how he could have held off so long. The sagging bedsprings combined with Cassie's weight caused him to roll immediately to the center of the bed where, still sleeping, she stretched, almost purring, as she welcomed him into her arms.

Sweet torture, he thought, his hands gliding down her body, molding it against his, gently slipping his knee between hers. Cassie's arms tightened around him, drawing him against her so that her warmth pressed intimately on the heat of his desire. Unable to stop himself, Brendan arched his hips, needing to feel the pressure, the delicious tension that was growing—had been growing all afternoon—deep inside him.

Cassie's hands slid down his back, over his hips to cup his buttocks, holding him against her as she opened her eyes. "Hello again." Her voice was a sleepy, amused whisper. "I missed you."

Brendan's eyes widened momentarily. Had she been watching his display of olympian self-denial all evening? Did she realize that all that exertion was an effort not to do now exactly what he was doing? "Umm, are you hungry?" he stammered.

"Yes."

Her fingers squeezed his buttocks, and she rocked her hips against his, leaving him no question about what it was she hungered for. His heart quickened. The bread could wait. He rolled over onto her, pressing her back into the feathery mattress while his mouth sought hers, his kiss hungry and demanding, a witness to the desire he had pent up all afternoon. Cassie's hands roved their way up the length of his spine, then kneaded his shoulders and finally caught him by the hair, tugging him back breathless.

"My turn," she told him simply, and placed her hands against his chest, pushing him back.

Bemused, Brendan allowed it, dropping off her and letting her arrange him alongside of her, not needing to direct the proceedings this time, content now to accept what she gave. And how she gave—my God! He shivered with pleasure at the feel of her hands on him, stroking down his arms, drawing delicious circles on his chest, making forays down to his navel. He watched her, marveling at her intense concentration. She pushed the quilt down to the foot of the bed, then knelt between his knees, looking for all the world like the goddess of fire, the golden sheen of her skin and the ginger of her curls heightened by the flicker of flames behind her. Brendan swallowed hard. His fantasies, his dreams, had never come close to this. He had imagined her an ardent, active lover, but the trail of silken fire she left as her fingers traveled across his abdomen, then down his thighs, then back up, circling, hovering, coming ever closer to the center of his desire, made his heart pound and his jaw clench. He arched his hips, willing her to touch him where he burned, where he needed to feel her hands.

Cassie smiled, a witch's smile, then bent to kiss him, her tongue circling his navel with a warm, wet heat that sent shivers of longing through him. Lifting her eyes to meet his, she whispered, "I dreamed of this years ago, but the reality is even better."

"Cass!" It was a plea, a groan. He clenched his fists around bunches of the sheet, trying to fathom what she said. Years ago? When she had looked down her nose at him? When she had ignored him on the beach, in class? When... But rational thought escaped him. The sensations she was creating were enveloping him, and in a tiny corner of his brain he realized that for once his arm seemed unimportant, insignificant, and scarcely hurt at all. Then her fingers found him, stroking him while she kissed the sensitive skin of his inner thighs.

"Cassie!" He needed her, now. He sat up, and she lifted her head, then moved upward so that she straddled him, settling herself onto him.

"This time I want to give to you, Bren," she murmured, her hands brushing over his chest as she began to move. His fingers dug into her hips, clenching the soft flesh as she moved rhythmically, slowly at first, then more quickly, a look of rapture growing on her face.

Brendan bit his lip, lifting his hips to meet her, thrusting against her. She was so warm, so beautiful, so giving, so... He felt it building, but nothing prepared him for the force of the feelings that rocked him when the explosive moment arrived. He twisted on the mattress, consumed by her love for him, his fingers grabbing at her, scoring her delicate skin, at the same time that she cried out and collapsed against his chest, her breasts heaving with exertion, as if she had run a marathon at least.

"Are you all right?" His voice shook as he stroked her damp back, concerned that she might have overdone.

He heard a muffled giggle against his chest. "Is that what you're supposed to say?" she asked him, lifting her head to let him see amused eyes glinting in a still-flushed face. She leaned forward and kissed him on the end of the nose. "I am happy to report, Mr. Craig, that I have never felt better in my life."

Brendan grinned, hugging her hard against his chest. "Neither have I," he rasped, an odd catch in his throat. The next day, when he was sane again and thinking how questionable their future together was, he wouldn't be, but he wasn't going to dwell on it tonight.

THE BREAD was heavenly, food for the gods, Cassie decided as she cut herself another hunk, slathered it with butter and cradled it in her palms while she sat at the table watching the sunlight play across Brendan's sprawled form on their love-rumpled bed. She took another bite and washed it down with some freshly perked coffee, a far, far better form of liquid refreshment than that wretched almond tea that Brendan had foisted on her the previous day. But she smiled; this morning she could forgive him anything. After the night before, the bread wasn't the only thing that smacked of a touch of heaven. What she and Brendan had shared was so beautiful that she felt she must be living in a dream. And not just what had happened in bed, either. Everything, from the moment he had come to live with her, seemed magical somehow.

Don't exaggerate, she admonished herself. But truly she didn't feel that she was. What Brendan had given her in terms of insight, in terms of love, could scarcely be measured. With Michael she had felt challenged, as if he were stretching her, testing her to her limits professionally. But with Brendan she felt complete, as if she had found the other half, the complementary opposite that would fill out her life. She sighed and stretched languorously, her eyes seeking once again the slumbering masculine form on the bed. His gentleness that first time still had the power to astonish her. How could he have known that she needed confidence, a slow stoking of the fires that had been building relentlessly within her? There were hidden depths of understanding in him that she had never suspected. He had given her a gift of love beyond price, and she wanted to give to him in return. That was what their second loving had been. But it wasn't enough. She wanted to give him a future.

Another word for marriage, she asked herself, taking another swig of coffee. It was what she wanted herself. She could admit that now, at least in the privacy of her own heart. But was it what Brendan wanted? She didn't know; he hadn't said. But she knew one thing he did want—he wanted to pitch again. And if anyone alive could help him achieve that, she could.

"We'll do it, Brendan," she promised the sleeping man. "We will."

But at the moment Brendan didn't look capable of doing anything other than catching up on his rest. The poor man must have been exhausted from caring for her almost nonstop for three days. Cassie got up and went to stand beside the bed, her eyes following the line of his shoulder, the curve of his hip, loving him. Then, taking pity on him, she bent to kiss him chastely on the forehead, deciding that while she might like nothing better than to join him beneath the rumpled quilt, she would go for a walk on the beach instead.

He had packed an odd assortment of her clothes. But from the tumbled heap in the suitcase she rooted out a pair of faded brown corduroy jeans and a royal-blue UCLA sweat shirt older than Keith. She didn't remember having worn it since her undergraduate days, but she put it on quite happily now, luxuriating in the soft baggy folds, so unlike the stiffly tailored dresses and suits she usually wore. She felt younger, more carefree, less burdened by responsibility than she ever had in her life. Which was strange, she thought, because in another way, by accepting responsibility for helping Brendan with his future, she had committed herself to another human being and his happiness in a way she never had before. Not even with Michael or the boys. Humming softly, contemplating this, she folded the rest of the clothes that Brendan had hastily packed, sorting his from hers, brushing fingertips over the soft wool of his Black Watch-plaid shirt and the worn nap of his navy cord jeans. The bed creaked, and she looked over at him hopefully, but he had only flopped over onto his stomach, hugging her pillow tightly to his chest. A wave of love and longing more powerful than the surf just beyond the cabin walls crashed over her.

"I love you, Brendan," she murmured, trying the words out in the bright light of day, tasting them on her tongue, rolling them around, exploring their nuances, probing the meaning. She smiled. Yes, they sounded right. They sounded good. She blew him a kiss, which he received unaware, his dark, ruffled head turned toward the wall. "I love you," she repeated with satisfaction, and went out into the sunlight for a walk.

The cabin sat on a bluff overlooking the Pacific. Cassie followed a well-worn trail down to the edge of the cliff, and finding a path, scrambled down it until she was standing on an expanse of white sand beach entirely deserted except for herself and a dozen or so sea gulls. Her legs felt a bit unsteady, from her illness probably, but she decided that a short walk wouldn't do her any harm. Her surroundings intrigued and enchanted her, as totally unexpected in her life as Brendan was. Used to the sterile artificiality of hospitals, she felt all her senses assaulted at once by the completely natural environment. The smell of sea and tar; the brisk cool wind, the salt spray, jarred her, shaking her awake, making her more aware than ever—if that was possible—of her feelings, of the experience of loving that she had just shared. *Oh, Brendan, you are good to me,* she thought, then pressed her lips together tightly and closed her eyes, praying, *Let me be good to you.*

When she clambered back up the hill from the beach, she found him awake and sitting on a large rock outcropping at the top of the bluff. He looked sleepy, rumpled and infinitely dear in his gray sweat suit, one leg thrust out in front of him, the other drawn up so that his chin could rest on it while his arms loosely clasped his knee. Smote by a momentary awkward shyness, she stopped a few feet from him, wondering what one said to the man who made life worth living, whose very presence brought her joy that she had never experienced before. He didn't speak, just regarded her with a tenderness that warmed her in his soft blue eyes.

"Hi."

"Hi, yourself." He held out his hand to her then, and she took it, her thumb rubbing over his knuckles as she dropped down onto the rock beside him. He pulled her close, draping his arm around her shoulders and turning his head so that his warm breath fanned her ear for just a moment before she felt his lips touch her temple. Her heart quickened at his kiss.

"I didn't just dream it, then?" she asked, and dared to slant him a teasing glance.

Brendan squeezed her against him. "If you did, I think we dream along the same lines," he growled.

Cassie laughed but then gently drew back. "If you start that now, you know where we'll end up!" She rose to her feet and brushed off the seat of her jeans, scattering pine needles and blowing a cloud of dust in his face.

"Wretch!" Brendan scrambled up after her, grabbing her hand as she headed up the path toward the cabin in the woods. "And what's wrong with where we'll end up?"

"Nothing," she assured him, smiling as she towed him after her up the hill. "Absolutely nothing. I just want to make sure you have a square meal before you embark on any more strenuous exercise. I wouldn't want you collapsing on me!"

"Literally?" Brendan teased.

Cassie flushed but met his teasing with a grin that just showed, she thought, how far she had come. God, how she loved him. "Sit," she commanded, and steered him toward a spindle-backed chair pulled up to the broad pine plank table. "And eat. Then, after you've done, we'll discuss all the hedonistic activities you like."

Obediently, Brendan sat, hacking off a large chunk of his home-baked bread while Cassie poured him some coffee and cracked two eggs into the cast-iron skillet on the stove. "All right," he told her with a grin that sent shivers of anticipation down her spine, "but as far as hedonistic activities go, it isn't just discussing them that I've got in mind!"

Chapter Ten

It wasn't only *discussing* hedonistic activities that Cassie had on her mind, either, and she discovered to her pleasure that as the week went on, they had plenty of time for both discussion and practice. They also spent hours wandering hand in hand along the narrow hard-packed sand beach and exploring the forested slopes that descended nearly to its edge. In the mornings she helped Brendan with a regular regimen of exercises that would increase his range of motion and develop his strength and endurance again. In the afternoon they frolicked in the chilly surf, building sand castles and gathering shells and driftwood, and in the evening more often than not they ended up in bed long before the sun disappeared beyond the horizon. The weather behaved admirably, providing only a mist that burned off before midday and drifted in again around nightfall, shrouding the cabin in a lightly swirling fog that lent a further aura of unreality to an idyllic time. It was almost a Garden of Eden, Cassie decided. There were no real worries, no deadlines or demands, no shame. All it lacked, she thought as she lay stretched out on the bed and watched as Brendan worked his way through his second set of general calisthenics of the afternoon, was a serpent.

"You never did tell me," she remarked idly as his head dropped forward toward his left knee and his fingers reached to touch his toes, "how you just happened to have this cozy little retreat up your sleeve."

Brendan grunted, his head bobbing up just long enough to scowl at her before plunging toward his knee again.

"I must say," she went on as if he had answered her, "you are a man of many talents." She allowed him a seductive smile and shifted on the quilt, displaying a nice expanse of golden brown thigh below the hemline of her yellow corduroy shorts. She had never felt more like Eve. The experience was positively heady.

Brendan glared at her, his face red with exertion, his breath coming faster. Then, wordlessly, he spun around on the floor so that she was treated to a view of his bare back, dipping and bending, and the pale line of flesh at the hollow of his spine where his sweat pants slid below the mark of his tan. Cassie felt her own pulses begin to race and thought ruefully that, however inadvertent on his part it was at the moment, this seduction was a two-way street. She sat up, wrapping her arms loosely around her drawn-up legs, and watched Brendan, entranced by the supple movements of the muscles of his back, wanting to smooth her hands down the length of his spine for reasons that were definitely not medical. She had ceased to look at him professionally long, long ago. Now she saw him as "the man in her life." She hoped, especially after what they had been sharing that week, that she was the woman in his. But she didn't know. Commitment, marriage, permanence—all three were words that had never been mentioned. At first she was content with the loving; she had thought it was enough. Now? Now she was worried. Where did they go from there?

At last he stopped, his back heaving as he slumped over, resting his hands on his thighs. Then, slowly, he turned to meet her eyes, desire heating his gaze, a wry grin twisting his mouth and turning up a corner of the mustache. "You're driving me crazy, lady."

"Me?" Cassie grinned, stretching luxuriously, feeling the pull of well-used muscles in her own arms and legs. "Surely not." She batted her eyelashes at him with an effect that was more laughable than seductive, but Brendan took the bait, springing to his feet with a disgusting show of energy for a man who ought to be dropping in his tracks from sheer exhaustion.

"Do that again," he demanded, advancing on her, a pantherish glint in laughing blue eyes.

"Do what?"

"That enticing catlike stretch, that blatant come-on with those big green eyes." He was just inches away from her now, his bare midriff on a level with her eyes, perspiration sliding down freely and dampening the dark line of hair that disappeared beneath the waistband of his sweat pants. Her eyes tracked lower, finding exactly what she expected, then lifted to meet his with an impish smile.

"You can't possibly have the energy left," she chided, her fingers extending to brush suggestively against the front of his sweats as she shook her head.

"No?" There was laughter in his voice.

"Of course not."

Then a pair of strong hands bore her backward, and Brendan crashed on top of her, nearly leveling the bed. "Wanta bet?" His fingers were busily unbuttoning her shirt, his mouth covering hers in a mind-blowing kiss, and Cassie met his demands with equal ones of her own. Her fingers were quick and sure as she tugged at the drawstring of his pants. Amazing what all that practice can do, she thought, smothering a giggle against his mustache, which Brendan heard, anyway, and turned to his advantage by pulling her shirt off and tickling her ferociously.

"No fair!" Cassie shrieked, batting at his hands, stifling gasps of laughter. "Brendan!"

He paused just long enough to unbutton her shorts and slide the zipper down. "What?" he mumbled, his mind clearly not on conversation.

She caught his hands as they grasped the waistband of her shorts. "How *did* you get this cabin?" Maybe, she thought, he owned it as a retreat, a hideaway from fame and fortune. Though she had to admit that she had never seen Brendan when he had retreated from something he couldn't handle, not even his accident. Still, he had avoided her question about ownership often enough.

"A friend," he mumbled, dropping his gaze, intent on relieving her of her shorts.

"Do I know him?"

Brendan sighed heavily and rolled onto his side, one hand still stroking her body but the other clenching the quilt in a tight grasp. "Her," he corrected, his voice flat. "The cabin belongs to Susan."

Cassie wished she had never asked. And her feelings obviously showed on her face, because Brendan sucked in his breath sharply and slammed his hand against the feather pillow. "Damn it, Cass," he exploded. "That's why I didn't tell you! I knew you'd act this way!"

"What way?"

"Go all defensive on me. Pull your uppity teenager act again!" He was glaring at her now, his dark brows drawn down.

"I never—"

Brendan said a very rude word. "You should see yourself," he said scathingly. "Listen to me. I don't give a damn about Susan Rivers except as a friend. I've never made love to her, and I won't have you impersonating a glacier every time I mention her name. You forgot your damned insecurities all week! You can forget them now, too!" Eyes flashing fire, he pinned her to the mattress, throwing one thigh across her legs to anchor her while he plundered her lips with his mouth. She stared at him, eyes wide with astonishment at his outburst; then she was overpowered by the urgent demands his body made on hers. His questing hands banished her shorts, then sent his sweat pants following them to the floor. His words "I've never made love to her..." echoed in Cassie's ears, calming her and seducing her simultaneously until her resistance gave way and she opened her mouth to his kiss, opened her body to his need, embracing it with one of her own.

This Brendan was the powerful fiery lover she had expected, taking charge, making sweet demands that brought both of them infinite pleasure. And the pleasure was all the sweeter because she believed in the exclusivity of his love. That week he had given himself to her body and soul, his anger at her unwitting response to finding out about Susan's ownership of the cabin only reinforcing what in her mind she already knew. If he belonged to anyone, Brendan belonged to her. In her mind, then, Susan was transformed from serpent into benevolent benefactor. Cassie forgave her both her beauty and her charm. What did they matter when she knew she was loved? She could feel his love in every graceful, athletic movement Brendan's body made. And she loved him back, rising to meet his demands, cherishing both his gentleness and his passion, his impulse and his control.

Minutes—or aeons—later, when her pounding heart slowed and she opened her eyes, she was amazed to see the same Oregon sunshine and the blue jay on the windowsill calmly observing it all.

"I love you, Bren," she whispered. "I will love you forever."

He lifted his head off her breasts, his eyes dark with an emotion she couldn't read beneath the damp fringe of hair that fell over his brow. "Ah, Cass," he murmured. "I love you, too. I—" Their eyes locked for a moment, and she witnessed in his a struggle she didn't understand. Then his gaze dropped, and a moment later she felt his head resting against her breasts again as his arms came around her to hold her tight.

A tiny hurt pricked at her; an insecurity stabbed. She felt the tension grow in him and a restless unnamed anxiety spring up beneath the gentle stroke of her hands. It should be simple, she told herself. *I love him, he loves me.* What, then, was holding him back?

BRENDAN KNEW very well what was holding him back. He loved her deeply, and he wanted to give to her as much as she was giving him. He wanted to bring to their relationship, to their marriage: yes, he even dared himself to use the word; it challenged him somehow—what she brought—a career, a future, success. And until it was within reach, he was going to bide his time. If he couldn't offer that, he couldn't offer marriage. It was as simple and as painful as that.

The previous day, when they had made love in the afternoon, after he had told her that Susan owned the cabin, he had almost weakened, had almost asked her to be his wife. It was so tempting, so terribly tempting—not just because their loving had been so magnificent, so right, but because she had believed him, had trusted him about Susan. If she hadn't, he wouldn't have known the depth of her trust and her love.

So now you know, buddy, he chided himself, staring at the wood-beamed ceiling. *So what are you going to do about it?* He shifted uneasily on the bed, turning so that he could look at the woman curled next to him in the early-morning light. The first glint of sunlight filtered through the mist and the trees, catching soft tendrils of her hair and burnishing them red-gold. His hand lifted to settle among the curls, twisting one gently around his finger as he recalled a childhood itch to tug them that seemed to have come back to haunt him after all these years. "Marigold," he whispered into the morning stillness, and he smiled, remembering.

There had been row upon row of starched and prissy little girls in his early years, every one of whom had looked down her nose at him or shrieked and run to tell her mother of his latest indiscretion. Only Cassie had stood her ground, sicced her dog on him, coveted his tarantula, punched him back. He might be able to annoy her with his teasing, make her blush and clam up with his taunting remarks, but he could never cow her, never dissuade her from her almightly goals or defeat her fierce, strong spirit. And his childhood attraction, for all that it had been tempered by fear of her powerful drive and indomitable will, had proved right. He leaned over and kissed her nose lightly. Cassie sniffled in her sleep and swatted at him as if he were a pesky fly. His throat tightened, and he swallowed to relieve his tension.

"I want to marry you, Cass," he said softly to her sleeping figure. All the questions he had had about whether she was really the woman of his dreams or just the fantasy he remembered from his childhood had been more than adequately answered. The question now was whether he was the man of hers. Ironically, he realized that before the accident he wouldn't have had any doubts. Then he had been strong, whole, capable, successful. Since then, all of those things had been thrown into question. Yet it had been the accident that had brought Cassie back into his life. He sighed and stretched. His arm felt better. Every day he had greater extension, wider range of motion. The exercises he did alone and the ones she did with him all helped. He ought to feel confident, positive. He turned his wrist, wriggled his fingers, flexed his elbow. Not bad. Promising, in fact.

Suddenly, he needed more than promise, more than just hints. Sitting up, he eased himself out of bed and pulled on his jeans, then tugged a burgundy-and-navy rugby shirt over his head. Stuffing his feet into his moccasins, he hurried out to the car and extracted his Oregon map from the glove compartment. It probably wouldn't take more than three hours to drive to Eugene. If he left now, he could be back by midafternoon. Maybe, just maybe, with enough confidence to pop the question.

He chewed on the eraser of his pencil, trying to formulate a note for Cassie. That she would be annoyed was a foregone conclusion. "*I'm* your doctor," he could hear her saying. "If anyone should be there, I should." But he couldn't take Cassie, because she wasn't only his doctor. She was the reason he needed to know. And if the results weren't good, he could deal with that better if she wasn't around. He started to write, then scribbled out the words and began again. Finally, in desperation, he wrote, "I've gone to town for the mail and some food. See you this afternoon." At least then she wouldn't worry.

He did enough of that himself. All the way on the twisting highway along the coast and through the coast mountains to Eugene he tried to relax, to put his mission out of his mind. But his fingers flexed unconsciously, his arm tensed, his elbow ached. He called the head trainer from Coos Bay and received a warm welcome. "We'll be expecting you," the man had said. "Just ask any student for directions."

Brendan did, with mixed results. He happened to ask a Mustang fan, one who identified him immediately as Lefty Craig and who escorted him personally to the trainer's door. That was the plus. On the minus side, the boy was so impressed, so enthused by the presence of his pitching idol, so concerned about the outcome of the tests in the trainer's office, that the butterflies in Brendan's stomach seemed to increase geometrically in proportion to each solicitous comment the student made.

"You will be throwing again soon?" the boy asked, his eyes drifting down to Brendan's arm as if it held all the answers.

Brendan thought he wasn't too far wrong. "I hope so,' he said, edging toward the trainer's open door. "That's what I'm trying to find out."

The boy grinned and pumped Brendan's hand enthusiastically. "Good luck to you then, Lefty. I hope you win again this year."

No more than I do, Brendan thought, forcing a smile he didn't feel. "Thanks for your help." Then he turned and went into the office to meet his fate.

It was kinder than he had hoped.

"Your left arm is not quite working at sixty percent of your right yet," the trainer told him. "But it won't be long." He smiled encouragingly and clapped Brendan on the shoulder. "I would think that if you don't have any pain and you have the range of motion for it, a little gentle playing catch wouldn't hurt."

Brendan stared at the graph in the man's hand, then at the percentages listed, which showed a comparison between the extension and flexion of his right and left arms, scarcely daring to believe his ears. "You mean it?" he mumbled. But it was right there in black and white, as well. Not quite sixty percent, which was what Cassie and the Mustang trainer had told him that he ought to measure before he started to throw again. But it was close. And ahead of schedule! Cassie had predicted that it would take him four weeks to attain that level after he got the cast off. But it had been only two, and barely that.

"Hallelujah," he muttered, a grin dawning on his face. He patted the Cybex machine as if it had been responsible for the results instead of just the means of measuring them. "Hallelujah!" He wiped damp palms on his jeans-clad thighs and grinned delightedly at the trainer.

"You don't know how I appreciate your taking the time to run these tests for me," he said. The man couldn't—no one could. Of course they all knew how it would matter to Lefty Craig, the pitcher. But no one knew about Cassie and how much the rest of his life hinged on those results, too.

"Glad we could help you out," the trainer said, returning his grin and handing Brendan the sheaf of papers that validated his tests. "Just don't overdo things. You've still got a long way to go."

"But I'll get there," Brendan vowed as he drove away from the university and headed for a jeweler's shop in downtown Eugene. "It's only a matter of time."

THE SHEET BESIDE HER was already cool when Cassie awoke. Stretching leisurely, she glanced around the cabin, expecting to see Brendan at the table eating breakfast or sprawled on the floor doing some of his interminable exercises. In fact, he was nowhere around.

Her brow furrowed, and she sat up, craning her neck to see if he was outside on the front porch. He wasn't.

She frowned. Well, maybe he had gone for a run. But that wasn't his usual practice. When they ran, they ran together. Since they had arrived, they had been almost inseparable. Where she was, Brendan was. But that morning there was no off-key whistling, no groans of exertion or thump-thump of rhythmically exercising legs and feet. Feeling strangely bereft, she got out of bed and gathered up a sweat shirt and a pair of jeans to wear. A whiff of Brendan's after-shave assailed her from the sweat shirt she held, and pressing it possessively against her breasts, she headed for the shower. A long, luxuriously hot shower sounded marvelous right now. And, she thought with a wicked smile, if she dallied long enough, Brendan might come back in time to join her.

Twenty minutes later, when the hot water was running out and she was dangerously close to turning into a prune before her very eyes, she wrenched the faucet off and grabbed the scratchy towel, rubbing her body with it briskly, shivering and increasingly annoyed. Where the hell was he?

You don't own him, her annoying little inner voice reminded her.

She scowled at herself in the steamy mirror. "I know that," she said aloud to the long, sad face that stared mistily back at her. "I just miss him, that's all." Would it be like this when he had tired of their paradise and gone back to the real world, she wondered. When she was left alone again?

"Stop it." Her voice was firm, loud, startling almost. "Don't think that way. He's not like that. He loves you." And she squashed her insecurities down and shut the lid on them. He did love her. He did! All the same, she wished that he would come back.

She found his note only minutes later. Feeling more puzzled than mollified, she cut a chunk of his homemade bread and dropped another log on the fire. He could have waited. For that matter, he could have awakened her. It wasn't as if she were dropping from exhaustion anymore. She wouldn't have minded a trip into town, too. They had only gone in once in the nearly two weeks they had been here, and a little civilization might have done their relationship good, allowed them to perceive themselves as a couple in the world at large.

Unless Brendan didn't want to see himself that way. Damn. She stomped over to the window and scowled at the empty clearing where their rental car was normally parked. Well, he would be back soon enough. It didn't take more than half an hour to drive there. She scowled at the note again, rereading it. What did he mean, "See you this afternoon"? It was just past nine now. He could have gone and come back by the time she had eaten her breakfast and taken that interminable shower.

"He probably just needed a little space," she said to the blue jay, which seemed to have taken up residence in a corner of the porch rafters and which she could see peering down at her from the nest tucked under the beam.

The blue jay didn't answer. Cassie ground her teeth on the tough crust of the bread, pretending it was Brendan she was chewing up. Well, all right, she decided. If he could have space, so could she. There were miles of beach just waiting to be explored. Let him wait for her for a change.

She rooted through the cupboards, finding little and conceding that it was perhaps time to go to the store, before she unearthed enough to put up a lunch to take with her. Then, slinging her windbreaker over her shoulder and clutching the plastic bread sack containing limp carrot sticks and a rather bruised apple that she had found at the proverbial bottom of their barrel, she set off.

There was no way she could stay annoyed for long. The weather simply wouldn't permit it. Uncharacteristically balmy sea breezes lifted her curls and caressed her face; the ocean was almost mirrorlike in its unruffled placidity, and the mixture of salt and pine was heady enough to make her forget, for once, the more intoxicating smells she associated with this interlude with Brendan. She walked several miles, much farther than she had ever gone with him, and scaled some bluffs that gave her such a broad view of the horizon that she wouldn't have been surprised to see Hawaii at the skyline. She wondered about the boys, hoping that things were going as well for them as they had been for her. A phone call to her mother the one time she had gone to town with Brendan had assured her that their impromptu vacation was a complete success. Keith was learning to surf, and Steven and Raymond had become fast friends, shell hunting when the tide was out and playing golf in the afternoons. They would probably be sorry when their interlude in the Pacific was over.

Just like me. Cassie drew up her knees and wrapped her arms around them, contemplating the changes in her life since Brendan had come. It was like a before-and-after commercial. The drab, lifeless woman who had become the enthusiastic, lively person after brief months of contact with him. The only problem was that she had no idea where things went from there. The only thing she knew for sure was that however wonderful paradise was, it wouldn't last forever. In fact, she reflected grimly as she rose and brushed the dirt and pine needles off her jeans and prepared to descend the bluff, it was quite possible that the end—whatever it was—was in sight. When she got back to the cabin, she would find Brendan and ask him.

But Brendan wasn't there. It was close to three, and he still hadn't put in an appearance. For the first time, her annoyance turned to worry.

Had he been in an accident? Had car trouble? All her

years in the emergency room flooded her mind with images she would rather have buried once and for all. She saw blood, broken glass, crumpled metal, disaster. Her stomach lurched, and her heart began to pound. *What could she do?* She was miles from anywhere, without a phone, without neighbors nearby. Her mind spun dizzily with possibilities—for her, none of them feasible; for Brendan, all of them bad.

"Calm down," she commanded herself aloud, forcing herself to sit down on the step and think. "He's a grown man, a responsible one."

The blue jay squawked derisively.

Cassie glared at it. "What do you know?" she demanded.

The bird returned her unblinking stare. She remembered that Brendan had been in an accident before. It was how he'd come back into her life. The thought for once provided no comfort at all. She jumped up, pacing up and down the porch, her fists stuffed in the pockets of her jeans, fuming and worrying. So what if it was unproductive; it felt better to move than to sit and brood.

It was twenty past four when she heard the sound of a car. She had imagined it so many times that she didn't believe it was real until the dove-gray Chrysler rounded the bend and she saw Brendan, upright and unbloodied, at the wheel.

Fury born of the afternoon's agonizing consumed her. Hands on her hips, she stood on the porch and glared at him. "Where the hell have you been?"

A grin lit Brendan's face, and he gave her a wave. Such nonchalance. Such insouciance. She wanted to punch him! "Brendan Peter Craig, where in the name of heaven have you been?"

He hopped out of the car and hauled one lone grocery bag out with him. "Shopping." He hoisted the bag up higher to illustrate his statement.

Alongside her irritation, Cassie felt a sense of foreboding growing. One bag? Just one? So she had been right that afternoon. The idyll was almost over. And then what?

She had no time to speculate, for in seconds Brendan was bounding up the steps, dumping the bag on the porch and swinging her up in his arms. "Miss me?" he asked, the mustache twitching, the eyes teasing.

She dug her fingers into his shirt, tickling his ribs. "Thought you were dead and buried," she babbled. "I wondered what you'd left me in your will. Put me down; you'll hurt your arm."

Provocatively, Brendan let her slide down the front of his shirt and jeans, his hands still holding her close. If he meant to end their paradise, he certainly seemed to want to wring every bit of goodness out of it first. Cassie tried to draw back, instinctively wanting to protect herself, but it was no use. He was too intent, and she wanted him too badly to refuse. The moment his lips touched hers, resistance dissolved. Pure, unadulterated relief at having him back was all she felt. That and a growing need that warmed the blood in her veins and caused her to twine her fingers in the unruly locks of his dark shaggy hair, savoring the very essence of him and praying that she might never have to let him go.

Breathing unsteadily, Brendan drew back. "I should go away more often," he said softly, "if that's the welcome home I get."

Cassie shuddered, remembering all the awful things she had imagined might have happened to him. "No," she said, locking her arms around his waist and holding him tightly. "No. You should never go away at all."

For a split second Brendan's eyes darkened unreadably. Then he bent his head and kissed the tip of her nose. "I'll always be back," he vowed. Then, taking a step backward, he said, "Guess what I got for our last meal."

Cassie's heart plummeted. Even knowing that this was an idyll that would end and that they would have to go back to the "real world" sometime, she still wasn't prepared for the reality of doing so. "Last meal?" she echoed, trailing after Brendan as he lugged the grocery sack into the house.

"The end of a beautiful time in my life." Unperturbed, he set the sack down on the table.

If she had ever heard a eulogy for a relationship, Cassie decided that that was it. She let out a deep breath, not realizing until then that she had been holding it. Brendan scowled at her as though she were the one behaving badly, not he. "You must be looking forward to getting home, then," she ventured.

He turned, his mustache turning up as he grinned over his shoulder. "I'm looking forward to the future, Cass."

"Oh?" That was news. It was different, just as the aura of repressed excitement, the kind of little-boy bounciness that his father was always trying to squelch, was different now.

"I went to Eugene today, Cass. I wanted them to run tests on my arm." His eyes were sparkling, betraying his serious expression, but Cassie was dismayed.

"It's too soon," she protested, twin fists of hope and fear clenching her insides.

Brendan shook his head. "Nope. It looks good. The trainer said I was in better shape than most people with the same injuries. Something about the general condition of my body." He shrugged, but he looked incredibly pleased. "Come on outside," he commanded. "I'll show you." He bounded out the door and down the steps and across the clearing to the car, returning moments later with a fistful of papers that he dumped on the table in front of her. In his other hand he held a baseball, which he was tossing periodically in the air. Cassie's eyes scanned the readouts he had given her, translating the figures into responses, making comparisons, her eyes flickering to his arm and back to the papers again. The smile widened. Obviously, the trainer was right and she had misjudged.

"Well?" Brendan prodded, grinning.

She lifted her eyes to meet his. "Excellent. Congratulations." Then, trying to keep her personal feelings out of her voice, she asked, "And this is why we're going back now?"

He nodded. "It's time."

She didn't reply. Then, with an act of courage that she wouldn't have believed herself capable of three months earlier, she made herself ask the question that mattered the most in her life. "And us? What about what happened here between us?"

Brendan smiled, then reached down and pulled her to her feet, towing her outside. "Play catch with me."

It wasn't the answer she expected. She wasn't sure it was an answer at all. But with Brendan one never knew. She could see now that he was just barely containing his enthusiasm. She wished she felt more like sharing it. By rights, if she weren't so selfish, she would.

"Stand over there," he commanded, pointing her toward the edge of the clearing. She moved into the shade of a towering pine tree about fifteen feet away.

"Don't overdo it," she cautioned.

Brendan grinned. "Yes, doc." He lobbed the ball to her easily. She caught it.

"How's your arm?"

"Fine."

The tosses continued. Five. Eight. Ten of them, all smooth and accurate. "That's enough," Cassie said.

"One more," Brendan countered, beginning to walk toward her. He reached into his pocket and pulled something out, then tossed it to her.

Instinctively, Cassie caught it. A black velvet box lay in the palm of her outstretched hand. "Brendan?" Her voice took flight, leaving only a faint trail of sound.

He stood beside her, his dark head bent as he watched her fumble with the lid. "Open it, Cass."

Fingers shaking, heart slamming, she did. Inside, a diamond solitaire, simple and unadorned, winked at her. She lifted her eyes to meet those of the man she loved.

He grinned. "I figured once I was sure I had a diamond in my future, you deserved one, too. Will you marry me, Cass?"

Cassie laughed, a slightly hysterical laugh that caused Brendan to scowl for an instant before she threw her arms around him. "You had to ask?" she demanded. "You didn't know? Yes, of course I'll marry you, Brendan! A thousand, thousand times yes!"

Chapter Eleven

Books ended there. A proposal, an acceptance, then happily ever after. Cassie knew the formula. She also discovered more quickly than she wanted to that it had nothing whatever to do with real life. Not her life, anyway. Her life took up, the day after they returned, almost exactly where it had left off before she got sick. As soon as she called Gene to tell him she was back, he broke in, saying, "Swell. You sound great. My turn," and proceeded to tell her that he, Lynn and the kids wanted to go to Arrowhead for five days if she didn't mind.

Cassie glanced up to see Brendan churning through his second mile of the day in the pool and shoved a weary hand through her hair. "No, I don't mind," she said. After all, what difference would it make? The minute they had walked in the door the day before, Brendan had given her a quick kiss and disappeared into the den to use the phone, emerging moments later to say, "Ballard's on his way over." Cassie had groaned, wishing for a few more hours respite, but Brendan just laughed.

"I owe him a demonstration, sweetheart," he said easily. "He thinks I've spent the last two weeks doing nothing but working out."

"You did," Cassie replied, recalling all his runs on the beach, all the calisthenics, all the hours of kneading bread and squeezing racket balls. The happier hours, which they spent walking hand in hand, reminiscing about their childhood antics as they lay before the fire and sharing wonderful meals seemed to dim now that she was faced with a Brendan eager to get on with his baseball career. Brendan himself had no second thoughts at all. He slung their suitcases on the counter in the laundry room and began stuffing dirty clothes into the washing machine, whistling happily. Shrugging, Cassie wandered off, drifting aimlessly from room to room, trying to recapture some of the magic she had experienced the past two weeks and feeling, unaccountably, as if she had never been away at all.

She had precisely the same feeling the following afternoon when she took over Gene's rounds at the hospital. The click of her heels on the polished linoleum floor echoed briskly as she moved from room to room, stopping to visit each patient, listening to their worries and checking out their complaints. The sun and surf, the home-baked bread and black-eyed susans, seemed a million miles away. As far away, she thought as she finished and headed for the elevator, as Brendan.

What kind of day had he had, she wondered, and remembered the times he and the boys had been waiting for her as she was leaving. Would he be waiting tonight? She glanced at her watch: 6:45. Maybe. The boys weren't due back from Hawaii until the weekend, but he might have come on his own. Her heart quickened, and she stepped promptly into the elevator as soon as the door opened.

"Hey, welcome back!" Lainie beamed at her, then threw her arms around Cassie, crushing her in an enthusiastic hug. "Guess what!"

One look at Lainie's flushed face, million-dollar smile and left hand gave Cassie the answer. "He asked."

"He did! Called me last week from Pittsburgh and popped the question!"

"Pittsburgh?"

Lainie shrugged. "So it's not romantic," she said blithely. "Maybe that's why—he had nothing else to think about but me!"

"Congratulations! When's the big day?"

"Right after the end of the season. Griff isn't working in the playoffs or the series this year." Lainie grabbed her hand as the elevator opened and towed her down the hall toward her office. "Come have a cup of coffee and I'll give you all the details! And you can tell me about your weeks in the woods with Mr. Wonderful."

Cassie's cheeks flamed, and she tried to pull away, casting a glance around in the hopes of seeing Brendan waiting, but no one was there to save her. "I do have to get home," she protested, but Lainie was having none of it.

"Miss him that much, do you?" she teased, opening her office door and dragging Cassie in.

"Of course not," Cassie insisted, but then, smote by honesty, changed her reply to "Well, yes, but..."

Lainie shut the door, laughing. "Yes," she said, swinging Cassie around. "Yes! Yes! Yes! You do love him, don't you?"

Flushed and expecting the "I told you so" she knew was dangling from the tip of Lainie's tongue, she sighed. "Yes."

"Great! When are you getting married?" Lainie poured two cups of coffee and thrust one into Cassie's hands.

"We haven't decided." Brendan hadn't wanted to set a specific date. All he would say was that he wanted to finish the season first. Cassie guessed she could see why; he had a lot on his mind getting back into shape. But she would have preferred to have married him and helped him get in shape. When she had said so, Brendan had shaken his head. Knowing how stubborn he could be, she acquiesced. "We're in no big hurry," she said now, blowing on her coffee.

Lainie rolled her eyes, obviously amazed at such restraint. "No hurry?" Then she laughed. "Ah, well, you don't still live with Mama and three older brothers. You don't need to hurry, I guess!"

Maybe not, Cassie thought, but she wouldn't have minded. "I'm glad for you and Griff," she said, changing the subject to one she hoped would distract Lainie. Happily, she was right. She was treated to a recitation of Griff's virtues until Lainie realized the time and said, "Heavens, Griff said he'd call tonight. I've got to get home." She grabbed her sweater, waited impatiently for Cassie to gulp the rest of her coffee, and ushered her friend out the door. "Sorry I've gotta run."

"No problem," Cassie assured her. "Brendan will be waiting for me, too." But he wasn't. Not in the car park at least. And when she got home, there were no lights on there, either. Odd.

She opened the front door with her key. "Bren?" Her voice echoed through the spacious but conspicuously empty room. Cassie dropped her purse on the rug next to the Boston fern and kicked off her heels, digging her toes into the thick pile of the carpet. "Brendan!"

The clock in the kitchen chimed eight times as she hurried in, the fading evening sun barely lighting her way through the darkened house. Pausing to flick on the light, she sniffed hopefully for signs of dinner. There were none. Only a single piece of notebook paper tacked onto the refrigerator door with a Snoopy magnet. "Gone to ball park," it said. "See you tonight."

Ball park? Cassie stared at the word as if it were a foreign term. He went to the ball park? Tonight? So much for her fantasies about cozy dinners for two with candles and smiles and the comfort of his arms after a long day in the office and at the hospital. "Damn," she murmured, then flipped on the radio and searched the dial for sounds of the game. Finding it, she paid scant attention while she changed into her royal-blue caftan and then slapped together a grilled cheese sandwich and opened a can of soup. "Cheers," she saluted herself with a glass of tomato juice, feeling ridiculously like crying. "Grow up, Cassandra," she commanded herself. "You have spent the evening alone countless times before this." But it wasn't the same now. And she couldn't change it, either. Sighing, she snapped off the radio, washed the dishes, swam twenty laps, called the boys and then went to bed.

But not to sleep. She lay awake imagining the sounds of the surf, the chirp of cheeky blue jays, the crackle of the cabin fire, Brendan's laughter, his smile, his touch. Mind and body agreed; both wanted him home.

She didn't know how many hours later she finally heard his footsteps in the hall. Holding her breath, she waited, listening as he moved quietly to the bathroom. She heard the shower cut on and lay expectantly, waiting for the moment it would cease. She could visualize him stepping out of the shower, rubbing his graceful athlete's body briskly, toweling his hair. A part of her wanted to get up and do it for him. It was the little things like that, as much as making love, that bound her to him. She had done it in Oregon, sitting on the bed while he sat cross-legged on the floor and leaned his head back against her. She smiled, wishing he would hurry. If he didn't, she would fall asleep again any minute. The day had been grueling. Had every day been like that before Oregon? How had she stood it? She would have to talk to Gene about getting a partner. There was more than enough work to go around. She yawned, her eyes slipping shut.

Hurry up, Brendan, she thought muzzily, rolling over toward the empty side of the bed and reaching out to brush her hand across the pillow where soon she would be able to stroke again the soft thick hair on his head. The door opened to the bathroom. He padded softly down the hall. Drawers opened and shut in his room. She burrowed deeper, yawned again. Come on, Bren....

ALL EVENING LONG she had been on his mind. His command appearance at the ball park hadn't been his idea but Ballard's. Still, he was in no position to argue; in fact, once he got there, he knew in his bones it was the right place to be.

The combined scents of old sweat socks, resin and chewing tobacco hit him the moment Brendan opened the locker-room door. They worked like a shot of adrenaline, and his steps quickened, his apprehension lifting and his smile broadening as he crossed the spotless cement floor.

"Hey, man, good to see you!"

"'Cha comin' back for? Gonna bail us out?"

"How th'arm, Lefty?"

Faces he hadn't seen in a couple of months swarmed before him, grinning and laughing. Hands slapped him on the back. He beamed, nodding his head at their joshing, flexing his arm as a demonstration of his fitness. "Didn't think I'd let you win without me, did you?" he asked. "You know pennant races always bring out the best in me."

He heard Lem Ballard's voice behind him. "You don't know how glad I am to hear that."

Brendan spun around, stiffening, he hoped, imperceptibly. He had felt the brunt of Ballard's unspoken criticism the day before when the Mustangs' owner had come over to watch him toss a ball to Cassie. It was undeserved, and knowing it, he had chalked it up to Ballard not getting his own way during Brendan's convalescence. But it had angered him, and he was perversely glad that Ballard had demanded he show up that night. He'd be only too happy to show him that his weeks under the care of Cassie Hart hadn't been for naught.

In fact, they had been the most significant time in his life. So far. And if he could make a go of this, he reminded himself, the best was yet to come. He would show everyone—Ballard, his teammates, the press and, most of all, Cassie herself.

He had acquitted himself well, he decided on the long drive back to Cassie's after the ball game. In the sixth inning he had got up on the sidelines and played catch with the third-string catcher. It was a lopsided game—the Mustangs leading by six runs—and he had more of an audience than the actual game did. That was what Ballard wanted. "Show me," he had demanded. So with Reed, the trainer, standing by, Brendan had. Twenty lobs—nothing, really—but Ballard had left satisfied, and Brendan, flexing his arm now as he gripped the steering wheel, felt nothing but the usual tiredness. He smiled. And in fifteen minutes he would be seeing Cassie.

He hadn't seen her all day. She was gone when he had got up in the morning. He had found a note by the toaster that said, "Love you. See you tonight." He counted the hours. There had been twenty-three since he had fallen asleep with her curled in his arms. It felt like twenty-three years.

The house was dark when he drove up. God, she couldn't have gone to sleep! Not when he'd been waiting all day! But he couldn't really blame her if she had. It *was* after midnight, and she had been on the go since six. He grimaced, thinking about it. She had fallen right back into the same schedule she'd had before she got sick. Shaking his head, he climbed out of the car and fished in his pocket for his house key. She had said that she and Gene would be looking for a partner. He hoped so. He'd have to remind her of it. If she was awake.

She wasn't. The house was like a tomb. There was no light under her door. Depressed, he opted for a long, cool shower. It was all too clear that there would be no other satisfaction forthcoming. Damn. He rubbed a hand through his hair and scowled into the mirror as he flicked on the cold water. It wasn't the lovemaking per se he was missing, though God knew that was fantastic. It was the closeness he had been looking forward to—telling her about the game, listening to her, holding her in his arms.

He wondered, after he had finished showering, if he even ought to bother her at all. Maybe he should go back to his own bed, though he hadn't slept alone since they had gone to Oregon. He stood by the bed just looking down at her. This was a Cassie he had only recently come to know—a vulnerable, defenseless one. A lump grew in his throat as he saw her lying there, her face toward the empty side of the bed, her lips slightly parted, her hand stretched out against the pillow as if to touch him. He sighed. So much for the efficacy of the cool shower. Obviously it only worked if you kept your thoughts one hundred percent pure thereafter. Brendan's thoughts were far from pure and his resolve nonexistent. Whether she knew he was there or not, he needed to be with her.

Carefully, edging in so as not to wake her, he lifted the sheet and slid his long body into the bed beside her. Mumbling, Cassie shifted, her hip moving toward him and her arm going around him as she drew him against her warm body. For a moment he peered into her face, hoping against hope that her actions meant she was awake. But they were automatic. He might as well have been her pillow, he thought dismally as he drew in the scent of soft, daisy-fresh curls and brushed his lips over the smooth skin of her forehead. Then, reluctantly, he willed himself to relax.

Yeah, sure, he thought as he hugged her against his chest. But he really couldn't complain. At least he had her in his arms. He would take what he could get. There would be time after the season ended for more of what they had shared in Oregon. Now he, too, needed a good night's sleep so that tomorrow he could continue his training. Tonight he had heard the cheers of the crowd again, felt the smooth leather and the ridged seams of the baseball, tasted again the victories that up until three months before had been his almost as a matter of course.

A sense of need, of anticipation, grew within him. It had nothing to do with Cassie, only with his career. In his mind it was the last of the ninth, and he was pitching to the Phillies. His fast ball was steaming, his change-up dropping and catching the inside corner of the plate. In quick succession he managed to retire the hitters on a pop fly to short, a high chopper down the first-base line and a called strikeout. He drew a deep breath as he heard the cheers, and in his mind's eye he saw the bouncy marigold curls of the woman running to meet him and throw her arms around him as he stepped off the mound.

"WHAT DO YOU MEAN, 'How's Brendan?'" Cassie demanded irritably as she and Gene walked down the corridor of the hospital. "How would I know? *I* never see him. He's alseep when I get up. He's at the ball park when I get home. Ask Lem Ballard. You'd think *he* was engaged to Bren!" She knew she sounded spiteful, but she couldn't help it. In the week they had been home she had seen him awake a total of thirty-seven minutes, give or take a second or two. If she and Michael had passed each other in the corridors of the hospital, she and Brendan didn't even do that! The difference was that with Michael she hadn't believed another sort of existence was possible. She knew that with Brendan it was. If only it weren't for his damned baseball!

"It was a lot simpler when he was recuperating," she told Gene grumpily. "Now he's gone all the time."

Gene shrugged. "It's his job, you know. He probably says the same about you. Want a cup of coffee or a Coke before we head over to the office?"

"Coke would be fine. I don't know how he could think that. You can hardly compare the two. My *kids* play baseball, for heaven's sake!"

Gene grabbed two bottles out of the refrigerator in the doctors' lounge and popped the tops off, handing her one. "But they don't get paid for it."

Cassie sighed. "You're right, I suppose." But she couldn't help thinking that she had a point, too. They really didn't need him to go out there and throw baseballs, did they? She made more than enough money to support them all just fine. And when he was home in the evenings, at least she got to see him.

"Cheer up," Gene counseled her. "It's just prenuptial nerves. And things will ease up around here once we get another partner, too. Then you'll have more time. You can tell him that."

"I will," Cassie said, "if I ever see him."

She didn't, though, until the weekend when he wandered out into the kitchen just as she was cleaning up her breakfast dishes and preparing to go to the airport and pick up her mother and the boys. Then he surveyed her with his typical early-morning bleariness, though it was well past ten, and mumbled, "What are you doing here?"

In retrospect, she thought he must have meant it facetiously, being under just as much time pressure as she was, though on a slightly different clock. At the moment, however, it was the absolutely wrong thing to say. "I live here, you know," she answered, bristling. "Isn't it nice you've decided to get up and join the human race?"

"Isn't it?" he retorted sarcastically. "And for once you're not out saving it!"

Cassie stared, shocked. "My job is important!"

Brendan rubbed his hands across his face as if he were a fighter trying to recover from a hard punch. Then he sighed and hooked his thumbs into the belt loops of his jeans. Crossing the room, he leaned against the counter and regarded her solemnly through sleepy eyes. "I know it, Cass." His voice was quiet, conciliatory, hurt almost. "I know. It's just that... Damn it, have you and Gene found any candidates for the partnership yet?"

"A couple," she said almost absently, still trying to pick out the nuances in his tone. "There are a couple of guys in the Bay Area he's contacted. One of them might work out. He said to tell you so."

Brendan smiled wanly. "I hope so." Easing away from the counter, he went to stand behind her chair, resting his hands lightly on her shoulders, then bending over to nuzzle in the springy curls of her hair. "I'm sorry, Cass. I didn't mean to snap at you. It's just that I miss you."

"No more than I miss you," she told him, turning in the chair to plant kisses on his bare chest. She felt a shiver of pleasure run through him, and he tilted her head up so that his lips could meet hers.

"How about a little loving before breakfast?" he asked, a plaintive look on his face.

Cassie looked at him, then at the kitchen clock, then at Brendan again, her longing for him mixed with dismay. "I have to pick up Mom and the boys in less than an hour."

Brendan looked momentarily horrified. "Today? They're coming home now?"

"I left you a note," Cassie reminded him. She had, and she had called him on the telephone. She had begun to forget what it was like to communicate with him face-to-face.

Brendan sighed. "So you did." Grimacing, he stuffed his hands in the pockets of his jeans, then shrugged. "How about a kiss, then?" he asked with a rueful grin. "To tide me over, so to speak."

Till when, Cassie wanted to ask. But she wasn't sure she could say it without sounding even more sarcastic than she felt, and the last thing she wanted now was to provoke another skirmish with him. It was all too obvious they were both edgy. She felt as if he were slipping away from her even though intellectually she knew he was very likely just as committed as ever. Still, she couldn't help saying, "We could always get married now."

Brendan's grimace turned to a scowl. "What good would that do? We'd still never see each other. Besides, I said I wanted to finish the season first. I can't devote time to marriage right now."

No kidding, Cassie thought. But she had seen his stubborn look before, mostly when he was a child and on the losing side of an argument with his father. She could understand Hamilton Craig's feelings of despair about his son. *Obstinate* didn't even begin to describe it. "I suppose you're right," she said, less graciously than she might have. "Finish the season, then." She turned her back, leaving the room to go to the bedroom and dress. Before she got five steps, warm, rough palms settled on her shoulders, caressing her through the thin cotton of her shift.

"I want to, Cass. You know I do," he said into her ear. "But I want the time to be right."

Cassie thought the time *was* right. She didn't understand Brendan's reluctance. She shook him off, confused and irritated.

"We'll make it, Cass," he said. "It's only five more weeks."

But five weeks might as well be five years, Cassie thought before even one of them was over. Elsa and Raymond and the boys were scarcely off the plane before her mother announced that she and Raymond were getting married. Cassie felt a twinge of jealousy, though she tried to mask it. Her mother was so obviously pleased that Cassie couldn't help but be happy for her, even though, as the days went on, it seemed that Elsa was having more of a proper courtship and engagement period than she! Raymond took her to dinner, to the movies, for walks on the beach; they made plans for their wedding that put Cassie's minimal thought in that direction to shame. *I would do more,* she thought, *if I could ever see Brendan long enough to talk about it*. But she was incredibly busy at the office, was called out on emergencies three times, and the few evenings she did manage to get home, Brendan, of course, was at the ball park. The only time she saw him awake that week was the night she, Elsa, Raymond and the boys went to a game. And that was almost worse than not seeing him at all.

For one thing, he looked gorgeous in his uniform. Cassie hadn't been to a baseball game since everything was wool and baggy. She got the shock of her life when she identified that singularly attractive man with the wicked-looking mustache above his lip and the red number 15 on the back of his snug, form-fitting shirt as the same man she had seen asleep with his pillow crushed in his arms when she had left the bedroom at six that morning.

"Such a man," Elsa crooned, as unabashed as ever when displaying her opinion. "I just knew he was right for you, Cassie, dear! I just knew!"

Embarrassed at the number of heads that turned to stare at her, Cassie ducked her head and muttered, "Shush!"

But Elsa was right. Everything about Brendan was perfectly right—except that he was a hundred yards away. She kept her eyes glued to him all evening, not noticing who hit home runs and who struck out. The boys took care of noticing that. She spent her time watching him tilt back on his chair in the bullpen, toss the ball up in the air like a juggler or wipe his palms on the sides of his tight uniform pants. She was mesmerized just looking at him, marveling at how at home he seemed there. It was a side of him she hadn't really thought much about, but it took her aback for a moment. Suddenly, she could imagine just a bit how much all this mattered to him. Right now it even mattered to her. She wondered how she'd feel if he ever got into a game. It was bad enough just sitting there watching him on the sidelines, worrying about him, without everyone else doing it, too. Especially when it mattered.

Of course, thank heavens that wasn't an issue at the moment. He still had a ways to go before he would be ready to pitch in a game. Just how much more time it would take, she wasn't sure. He was entirely in the hands of his trainer now. Her job was finished, unless, God forbid, he broke something else. A split second's wish that he would so that they could have some time together as they had had before was followed by several minutes of guilt. "It was his job," she remembered Gene telling her. But right now it seemed to be the main thing that was coming between them.

They all waited for Brendan afterward, the boys hopping around the parking lot like hyperactive jackrabbits, Elsa proclaiming future greatness for her prospective son-in-law and Raymond recounting the game play-by-play so that Cassie couldn't have missed it even if she had tried. It was more than a half an hour later when Brendan finally emerged from the locker room. He was carrying a duffel bag and laughing, saying something over his shoulder to the two people who followed him out. One, a monster of a man, one of his fellow pitchers whose name she couldn't recall, was tamping down the tobacco in his pipe; the other, Susan, was slinging a rosy cotton shawl around her shoulders. Cassie gaped.

"Ah, you waited. Good." Brendan slung his arm around her shoulders, the weight of his duffel bag causing her to sink somewhat, but not as much as the sight of Susan.

"You—" she gabbled. "She—she came out of—" But of course she had. Obviously a liberated reporter, Susan would have had no qualms about poking around the locker room in search of a good story. Why Cassie felt so shocked, she had no idea. Except that if she, as a doctor, saw men as patients, it was always a very *sexless* proceeding. She couldn't imagine Susan in the same sentence with that word.

"See you around, Sue," Brendan said with a nod of his head as he reached down and tipped Cassie's head up, shutting her mouth with his finger and planting a kiss on her lips. "Let's go home, beautiful lady," he murmured in her ear, and suddenly Cassie didn't care if Susan saw the entire starting lineup stark naked as long as Brendan's lips and love belonged to her.

She slipped her arm around him and walked by his side to the car, Keith on her other side, Steve hanging on to Brendan's free arm. A family, she thought. Well, almost.

Over the next few days the closest she came to thinking of Brendan in terms of family was listening to Elsa's plans for him in her wedding. Raymond's son was going to be best man and Cassie the matron of honor. Brendan—so he wouldn't feel left out, Elsa said—would be the usher. It was her mother's way, Cassie realized, of getting him into a tuxedo. Brendan, not being home of course, was not consulted. Cassie simply threw up her hands and agreed. One did not argue with Elsa—not about things like that, at any rate.

"You'll tell Brendan, won't you?" Elsa said one evening after dinner when she and Cassie were clearing the table.

"When I see him," Cassie promised. *If* seemed the more likely word to use at the moment. She hadn't seen him awake since that night at the ball park. She was beginning to wonder why he was even bothering to stay at her house anymore. Elsa seemed to accept it as a matter of course—*she* would, Cassie thought, since she had had no compunctions about spending the summer with Raymond—but Cassie wondered what other people thought—Susan, for instance, or Lem Ballard. On the other hand, nights were the only thing they had together anymore. If he weren't there for her to look at in the mornings, she might never see him at all save for brief glimpses of the bullpen on television when she had a few spare minutes to catch a game. And that was almost less satisfactory than not seeing him at all. Tonight, she decided, she would stay awake and talk to him. They might not have the hours for each other they had had in Oregon, and they might even be too tired to make love, but at least they could smile at each other and share a few words.

She was already yawning when she bid Elsa and the boys good-night and settled into the corner of the couch in the den, hoping that the old Cary Grant-Grace Kelly movie would be enough to keep her awake. It wasn't. One minute Cary was running along the rooftops above the Mediterranean, and the next Cassie felt strong arms lifting her.

"Wha—" She floundered, her arms going out to grab for support.

"Shh." It was Brendan's voice, warm and amused. His arms shifted her weight as he carried her down the hallway to the bedroom.

Sleepily, Cassie smiled up at him, loving his silky mustache and the pattern of tiny laugh lines at the corners of his eyes. Languidly, she stretched and threaded her fingers through his hair. "Imagine meeting you here."

Brendan chuckled, easing open the door to the bedroom with his foot and depositing her in the center of the bed. "Imagine meeting me anywhere. I thought maybe we weren't inhabiting the same planet anymore—at the same time, that is. Were you waiting up for me?" His hands were stripping off her robe and sending shivers of longing through her as they smoothed down the length of her arms. She felt as if she hadn't seen him in years, aeons. His mere touch caused her to tremble.

"Mmm, yes. I missed you." She lay back and watched as he pulled his shirt over his head, unzipped his jeans and stepped out of them. Seconds later, he lay beside her on the bed, and she nestled eagerly against the length of him, supremely aware that her thin nightgown was the only thing separating her from his nakedness. Even that was too much. Her arms stole around him, stroking down the length of his spine, reveling in the response of the smooth muscles of his back under the caress of her palm. It was a miracle, she thought now. A homecoming. She arched against him, needing him.

Brendan's breathing was rough and quick, his hands and mouth demanding. With incredible haste he stripped off her gown and panties, settling himself between her thighs with a sureness that she knew she equaled. Her body was ready for him, eager even; her hands moved between them to bring them together. Then, united, they fanned the flames that roared between them, white hot and consuming.

"God, Cass, I love you," he groaned, surging inside her one last time, his voice wavering from a sob to an almost-exultant laugh. Then she, too, reached a peak she had never scaled before and found a vista of heaven in his arms. She hugged him tightly, wanting never to have to let him go, tears pricking beneath her eyelids, so moved did she feel by their love.

"So much for talking," she said softly, nuzzling her nose against his stubbled cheek.

"Talking?"

"That's what I was waiting up for," she told him, smiling.

"Wanta talk some more?" he asked, and she saw his grin glint beneath his mustache.

Cassie yawned. "I'd love to, but I might fall asleep."

Brendan leaned over and kissed her nose. "I bet I could keep you awake."

She wrapped her arms around his neck. "You probably could," she agreed, remembering times in Oregon when he had brought her to ecstasy again and again. "But I have to be up at five-thirty. I'm doing surgery before seven."

Brendan's grin disappeared. Then he shrugged philosophically. "Oh, well, we might wake your mother and the boys, anyway," he said. "I'm surprised she hasn't taken exception to my staying here."

Cassie shook her head. "Not *my* mother. She thinks you're great. Anyway, it's not as if you were seducing me. If she thought there was nothing but sex between us, she'd be frantic. Making love is different. She's a total romantic. For thirty-two years I've been a disappointment to her. Now that I'm finally living up to her expectations, she's on cloud nine. In fact, the only thing she's looking forward to as much as our wedding is her own. And," she teased, "I think the main reason for that is she wants to see you decked out in a tux."

Brendan's body went still under her hands. "I've

been meaning to talk to you about that," he said slowly. One hand came up to close over hers, holding it steady above his heart against the warmth of his chest. She felt the steady beat beneath their entwined fingers.

"Don't tell me you're allergic to tuxedos," she said lightly, letting her eyes rove down the length of his body, then back up, imagining how he would look in one. Then she met his gaze, expecting to see an answering light of humor in his eyes.

Brendan wasn't smiling. "I can't go to her wedding," he said, his voice apologetic but calm. "I'm going to be with the team on the road."

Chapter Twelve

"I wish you'd quit," she told his sleeping form when she dragged herself out of bed the next morning. "It would be so much easier." They still wouldn't have as much time for each other as normal couples had because of the nature of her job, but at least they would have something. The road trip was the last straw. It was insane not to have realized before that he might go away for weeks at a time, but since he had come back into her life, she had grown used to thinking of things day by day. "That'll teach you," she muttered to herself as she splashed cold water on her face and tried to wash the sleep out of her eyes. Now she had to confront the prospect of twelve days without even a glimpse of him. Added to his almost-complete absence from her life since they had returned, it put her in a strangling mood. She rubbed her face briskly with the soft towel and stalked back into the bedroom, banging the drawers with more than necessary fervor as she dressed for work. He couldn't pitch forever; even he knew that. So why didn't he just pack it in now, give them a chance to spend some time together?

She glared at him. He snored. There was no way she was going to be able to say any of that to him. Every time she even mentioned pitching or his arm, he got stiff-jawed and obstinate. Talking to him then was about as useful as convincing her mother that a woman could live without a man. Sighing, she pulled a creamy cotton knit top over her head, tucking it into the waistband of her mint-green skirt. It was a cool, refreshing combination, one that usually encouraged her power of positive thinking and lifted her spirits. She could use that. Right now they couldn't get much lower. Even staring long and hard at the diamond on her finger depressed her; it only reminded her of the other diamond in Brendan's life. At the moment she didn't want to think about that. She sat down on the edge of the bed to pull her panty hose on and was just standing up to wriggle them over her hips when an arm snaked out and wrapped around her. "Brendan!"

He grinned at her sleepily. Then, when she tried to pull away, his arm tightened, and he hauled her down on the bed on top of him. "Temptress," he growled, his whiskery chin rubbing against her cheek. "Walking around here half-dressed."

"You were asleep," Cassie protested, struggling in his arms, half wishing she could simply acquiesce to his demands. He felt so good—so warm and cuddly and sleepy. "I'm trying to get dressed!"

"So get *un*dressed." His fingers were slipping inside the waistband of her panty hose. "You were the one who woke me up by sitting down there."

"I can see now I should have let sleeping jocks lie," Cassie told him, smiling as she shoved him back against the pillow, pushing herself up and straightening her blouse, then dipping her head to kiss the tip of his nose before dancing back out of reach.

Brendan moaned, his frustration obvious. "Just a few minutes of hugging?" he suggested with little-boy hopefulness.

The ever-diligent digital clock said 6:03, and Cassie sighed and shook her head. "I can't. I have surgery, remember. I'm sorry." She was, desperately. But what could she do, after all? It was her job.

Brendan scowled, then raised up and leaned back against his elbows so that his chest was exposed above the sheet, still tangled about his waist. "I know," he said, but there was more than a hint of exasperation in his voice. He thumped his fist down on the mattress. "But damn it, if just once—" Then he sighed, knowing as well as she did that they had covered this territory before. He shook his head and waved her out the door. "Go on, Cass. I understand."

But he didn't look as if he did. Not really. "What about tonight, then?" Cassie groped for a compromise. "I can be home by six-thirty."

Brendan shook his head glumly. "I have to be at the park by then."

The clock said 6:07. Cassie stuffed her feet into the open-toed sandals and wobbled as she tried to come up with another idea. She couldn't. "Well, um, wake me when you get home, then," she suggested.

"If I do, you'll be exhausted again."

That was true enough. The previous night's sleep had been no more than a catnap. But a little time with Brendan was worth a year of catnaps—if only she didn't have to be so alert for her work! Damn. "I know," she acknowledged, shrugging awkwardly. "I'll see you. All right?"

"Right." He looked pensive for a moment, then smiled his quicksilver smile.

She would die for that smile. But the clock said 6:09, and if she didn't leave that instant, she was going to be more than a little late. Helplessly, she gave him a quick little wave and blew him a kiss, then dashed for the door. He wasn't going to leave until Friday morning. That gave them three days. Surely with concerted effort they ought to be able to claim twenty minutes or so of that time for themselves, she thought wryly. *I'll see him tonight,* she promised herself as she grabbed a granola bar and an apple on her sprint through the kitchen. *We'll have that at least.*

BUT SHE WAS WRONG. He found a note when he got in at midnight after having nailed down his second speeding ticket in two weeks trying to hurry home to her. The note said, "Accident. Called to hospital. Doesn't look good. Love you. Cass."

He drank a glass of Seven-Up and popped some popcorn, read the rest of the new Ludlum book until 3:00 A.M., then got up and checked her room to see if she had crept in when he wasn't listening—an impossibility, of course. She hadn't. He fell asleep at four on the couch. He never heard her come home. He had an appointment with the trainer for another set of Cybex tests in the morning, a last-minute check before the upcoming road trip. He was gone until noon. When he got home, she had already left again.

The rest of the week went the same way. If he saw her marigold curls on the pillow when he tiptoed in at night, he counted himself blessed. He never woke her again. He had only to look at the dark shadows beneath her eyes and the lines of strain that never quite disappeared from her face even in sleep to know that she needed every bit of rest she could get. The only positive thing in his life right now was his arm. All his tests were good. The trainer was pleased. Ballard was, of course, ecstatic. Almost as thrilled as Brendan himself. But he had worked for it, he reminded himself. He had put in long, hard hours getting in shape again, throwing and throwing more.

"You'll be our secret weapon," Ballard chortled. "We'll knock 'em dead."

Brendan hoped so. The road trip would be his proving ground, a make-or-break journey for him and for the rest of the team. They had a pennant race to win; he had a career to renew. And he felt good, confident, his spirits buoyed by Reed, the trainer's, optimism.

"A little pain or stiffness is natural," he had assured Brendan. "Your tests are great."

Well, he was glad they were, because nothing else in his life at the moment could even be remotely construed as "great." He and Cassie, for all that they had declared their love, seemed to be passing like the proverbial ships in the night. He was frustrated, annoyed, and he needed something going well. If he could pitch well, that would help. For one thing, he would feel better able to deal with Cassie on her own level. She was every inch the professional again now that their Oregon interlude was a thing of the past. It was all too clear to him that he had to be professional and competent, also.

The first five days on the road were the longest of his life. He was ready to pitch now, dying to, in fact, but he never got into a game. How could he prove that he was well, whole and capable, if they never let him pitch?

Twice he warmed up in the bullpen for about half an inning each time, but he only managed to tire his arm. He never got in the game to see if he could get anybody out. Sitting on the sidelines was the worst because his mind was filled with Cassie. He spent hours trying to pinpoint where she was and what she was doing at that very moment. He envisioned Elsa and Raymond's entire wedding, wishing he were there even if he did have to wear a tuxedo. It would have been worth the discomfort of it just to see Cassie in the pale blue silk dress she had chosen to wear. She had tried it on for him once, and he had said, "I didn't think matrons of honor were supposed to be so sexy," and she had laughed, but he wasn't entirely kidding. The surge of desire he felt surprised him. Even now, three days and two thousand miles from the event, he could still feel that same need for her. There was nothing in the bullpen that could take his mind off her, and he needed something just then. He had seven more days until the return flight to L.A. At the rate he was going, he'd be a basket case by then.

"Skip wants you up, Lefty."

All four legs of his folding chair hit the ground at once. "Now?"

The catcher who had answered the bullpen phone rolled his eyes and drawled, "Naw, next Easter."

"I'm up." Brendan stripped off his jacket and strode quickly to the rubber, shaking his arm, loosening it with a few elementary range-of-motion exercises. He had been up the day before briefly, and his arm still felt a bit tight. A glance at the scoreboard told him the Mustangs were leading by only one run. But the starter, Banks, was in big trouble. Brendan could see him dropping his shoulder with every pitch. Closing his mind to Banks's problems, he took a grip on the ball and considered his own.

"Lookin' good," the coach said after watching him a few minutes. "How's it feel?"

Tight, Brendan thought. But it would work itself out. It had to. "Fine," he replied. He couldn't take another exercise in futility. He had to pitch this time. If Banks blew it, he could save the game. He knew he could.

"You're in, then."

At last. Finally, a chance to prove himself. He might not be the great surgeon that Cassie was, but he did have his talents. It was a situation he could succeed in, a place he could win. Apparently, the crowd thought so, too. The screaming got louder as he reached the mound. He doffed his cap to them all. He was at home there, in control. It was where he belonged.

He took his warm-up pitches. Damn, what was wrong with his elbow? The tightness persisted. He shook his arm, irritated, trying to shake it out. Then, flexing his shoulder and elbow, he gripped the baseball, turning to face the runner on first. For a split second he stared at the base runner, then fired the ball to the plate. Ball one. Brendan scowled, straightening his arm. Relax, he told it. Hang loose. Win it for Banks. Banks nothing. *Win it for Cassie. And for me!*

He kicked the rubber, went to the stretch and pitched. Ball two. Come on, put it in there. Damn fool couldn't hit a grapefruit. He drew a deep breath. Ball three. Brendan wiped his palm across his forehead. How could he have worked up a sweat so fast? Chewing on his lip, he contemplated the runner again, then the batter poised at the plate. Sucking in his breath, he drew back and fired. His elbow resisted. Ball four.

Come on, Craig! The inner voice of panic was his own now. The boos he had heard when the home team feared him had now turned to cheers as the batter trotted down the line to first. Brendan frowned and looked in at the catcher for a sign. Nodding, he toed the rubber. He was working from a full windup now with the bases loaded. The better to fan you with, he thought as he delivered the ball.

Since his wrist had snapped on the rain-slick highway four months before, Brendan didn't think he had heard such a sickening sound. Solid wood on a small white ball. He didn't even turn around to see how far over the fence it went.

A grand-slam home run. The three to two victory he was supposed to be saving for Banks had turned into a six to three loss of his own. And his arm! Good God, what was wrong with his arm? Bowing his head, he gritted his teeth against the ache in it.

"Bring in Travis! What's the matter with you?" Dale Holt, the red-faced manager strode to the mound, his expression harried as he sent a stream of tobacco juice toward Brendan's feet.

What was wrong? Who knew? But there wasn't time to find out any more that night. Holt had obviously had enough of "Ballard's secret weapon." Mick Travis was already in the golf cart on his way in from the bullpen.

"Have a shower," Holt said, dismissing Brendan. Sticking his glove under his arm, Brendan walked off deliberately, closing his ears to the noise of the crowd.

"What the hell happened out there?" Jeremiah Reed demanded as he tossed Brendan his warm-up jacket and jostled him through the dugout and into the tunnel to the dressing rooms. "Your arm looked all right. Nerves?"

"Probably." Brendan didn't want to think about it. He felt sick. Reed held the door for him, then waited while Brendan stripped down to his uniform pants.

"Let's have a look, then," he said, reaching for the arm. But if Brendan had expected the dawning of knowledge on Reed's face after several minutes of twisting and turning, flexing and extending Brendan's arm, he was disappointed.

"Did it hurt when you were pitching?" Reed asked finally as he set an ice bucket on the examining table where Brendan sat and thrust the arm into it.

"Some. I thought you said that was normal." The ice felt wonderful, deadening his nerves. He wished it would deaden his emotions, as well.

"It could be," Reed hedged. Brendan's throat tightened even further. The clubhouse phone rang. Ballard, no doubt, wondering what happened. He wasn't the only one, Brendan thought. Pray to God it was just a fluke. He shifted his arm in the ice bucket while Reed went to answer the phone.

"For you." He held it out to Brendan.

Steeling himself, Brendan took it, cradling it against his bare shoulder. "Craig here."

"Are you all right?" Cassie's voice contained all the fears he felt.

Brendan almost dropped the receiver. She had been watching? She saw him get bombed? God in heaven! "Cassie?" he croaked, his mind as numb as his arm, his emotions raw.

"Are you okay?" she asked again.

"Yes. Yeah, sure I am." He could barely get the lie past the lump in his throat. "You saw it?"

"Yes. Oh, Bren! I'm sorry." She sounded as if she might cry.

Don't, he thought wildly, or he might, too.

"It's okay," she went on rapidly. "The first time back doesn't mean anything. Gene says you're probably just stiff. You'll succeed. I know you will."

Brendan thought he heard a note of desperation in her voice, but it could have been projection. "Sure," he mumbled.

"We've got lots of confidence in you."

"Yeah?" He knew he wasn't speaking above a whisper. *What if your confidence is misplaced,* he wanted to ask. *What then? What if I don't succeed? What if I bomb them all?* "I hope you're right," he said.

"C'mon," Reed prodded him. "I wanta take another look at that arm."

"I gotta go, Cass," he said. Why had she called now, for God's sake? He hadn't been able to reach her in five days. And now she had called at the lowest moment in his life! So much for being on a par with her. He wanted to die and said so.

"Tomorrow," Reed promised. "Tonight I gotta see this arm."

TOMORROW, Brendan decided as he lay awake all night feeling every single muscle, sinew and bone in his arm, was a long time coming. He had considered drowning his sorrows and miseries in the Jack Daniel's whiskey that his roommate, Greg Bucholz, was downing in the hotel bar. But there were times when booze helped and times when a clear head was a necessity. He watched the lonely flicker of the neon sign on the building across the street and thought that this was one of the clearheaded ones. He needed to think, to figure out what in God's name he was going to do now.

It wasn't just that he had bombed. God knew he had bombed before on several occasions. Once, in San Diego, Holt had left him in while he gave up *nine* earned runs. That had been embarrassing in the extreme, but nothing like this. This was devastating.

It was just that he'd had all his hopes pinned on it. *Of course I was counting on it,* his inner self replied. *I needed to win! I need a career!* Lotsa luck, his cynical other self retorted.

"You'll succeed. I know you will. We've got lots of confidence in you." Cassie's words positively haunted him. At the moment, he had damned little confidence in himself. What he really needed was a fast ball that could find the plate. His right hand rubbed up and down across his throbbing left elbow, then kneaded the muscles of his forearm and returned to probe the joint for tenderness.

The door lock rattled, and Bucholz tottered into the room. "Shoulda heard Ballard," he anncunced loudly. "In fact, I'm surprised you didn't. On th'other hand, don't reckon you'da wanted to."

Probably not. But he would undoubtedly hear Ballard the next day in any case. He was sure his "owner" wouldn't let his views go unexpressed. "Go to sleep, Buck," he said wearily, and flipped over onto his side, studiously ignoring the thumps and bangs as Bucholz got ready for bed. He wanted sleep, a blessed oblivion where his worries would fade away. He didn't find it, though, until the gray dawn was threading its way through the thin weave of the hotel drapes.

"How's your arm?" Reed asked him first thing in the morning.

"How's your arm?" Ballard demanded at noon, cutting up tiny bites of filet mignon with his knife while his eyes did the same to Brendan across the table.

"How's your arm?" Buck asked him on the bus to the ball park.

"How's your arm?" the reporters wanted to know as Brendan elbowed his way through the throng on his way to the sanctuary of the Mustangs' dressing room. Beleaguered and wondering if he had one more civil reply left in him, he opened the door to his escape when he heard his name called behind him.

Susan pushed her way through the mob of her colleagues to reach his side. She put her hand on his arm, and he held the door for her, ushering her inside before him and closing it firmly on the rest of the magpies chattering outside.

"How are *you*?" she asked gently.

Brendan almost managed a smile. At least someone thought there was more to him than the muscles, joints and tendons hanging from his left shoulder. "Could be better." he said, sighing.

"What happened last night?" Her voice held concern. "Off the record, of course," she added when she saw him stiffen.

"I blew it," he said simply.

"Maybe you're trying too hard."

"I have to try hard!" he snapped, irritated at her mildly reproving tone.

"Why?" She was studying him with her wide gray eyes, seeing, no doubt, the lines of strain and sleeplessness around his own. "Why not just build back up slowly. Wait till next season."

"No." He stuffed his hands into the pockets of his pants and scowled at her. Wait till next season? Give Ballard plenty of time to replace him? Make himself even more expendable than he was? *No, thanks*.

"I suppose it has to do with Cassie Hart," Susan probed.

He traced a line on the cement floor. "What if it does?" he asked belligerently, shooting her a fierce gaze before dropping his eyes again.

Susan rolled her eyes. "Don't sell her short, Bren," was all she said.

Sell her short? He had never in his entire life sold Cassandra Farrell Hart short! On the contrary, it was living up to her that was so damned hard. It was living up to her that he was trying to do right now! Maybe he had been overconfident when he had asked her to marry him. Maybe he really couldn't be worthy of her. *Cut it out,* he commanded himself. If there was one thing he didn't need now it was more negative thoughts.

Two days later he couldn't avoid them. Holt brought him in to pitch again during the fifth inning of a game he couldn't have lost if he had tried. Tom Sanderson had given the Mustangs a nine to nothing lead before pulling a muscle while covering first. Rather than risk injuring his "current best left-hander"—Brendan's teeth grated at those words—Holt had pulled Sanderson out and sent Brendan in to mop up.

"It'll be a good workout for you," he told Brendan, and swatting him on the rear, left him on the mound.

And what a workout it had been. He must have gone a full count with every batter he faced. In the sixth he gave up a single and a home run. In the seventh he walked two, got a double-play ball and was saved by Bucholz's spectacular catch of what in any other ball park would have been a home run. By the eighth his elbow was throbbing, and he tried to place his pitches. It had never worked before. It didn't work this time, either. He gave up three more runs. Holt looked at him from the dugout, shrugged and left him in. Sheer grit got him out alive with the victory intact. His illusions about his pitching career were not.

"We won! Great!" Blanchard, the catcher, shouted at him as he whooped his way toward the dressing room.

"Barely," Bren muttered. His right fingers wrapped his left elbow as if doing so would keep his arm from falling off. Stars shot behind his eyes whenever he went to straighten it out. There was none of the satisfaction of having saved it, only relief that finally the game was over.

Jeremiah Reed plunged his arm into the ice bucket the moment he walked into the locker room. "You didn't have much stuff, did you?" he asked, a hint of sympathy in his normally indifferent tone. "How is it?"

Brendan shuddered at the shock of the ice, then shook his head, weary, disgusted and, above all, depressed. "Bad."

He could scarcely even lift the arm that evening. He went straight back to the hotel and flopped down on the bed, wanting never to have to move again. The phone rang. Five times he let it ring. On the sixth he moved like an eighty-year-old, inching his way across the bed to answer it.

"I just heard you saved the day!" Cassie's voice brightened the room.

Brendan closed his eyes. "Yeah." If you wanted to call it that.

"See? I told you I had confidence in you."

"I did a lousy job," he retorted sharply, the pain in his arm making him wince. He didn't think he could face her optimism now.

"You are improving, aren't you?" she went on. "Isn't that what you wanted?"

He wished he could determine just what it was he was hearing in her voice. Caution? Anxiety? Hope? Or was he still projecting? "I guess so," he said.

"Good. The boys said to tell you they saw the game. I didn't," she apologized. "I was doing surgery this afternoon. Knee replacement."

Competence, he thought glumly. Professional, successful Dr. Cassie Hart. He wished she could give him an elbow replacement right about now. He swallowed. "That must mean you're working hard," he said, trying to inject a note of lightness in his voice.

"Of course. And it doesn't show any signs of letting up. People seem to be breaking bones faster than we can set them." She laughed a moment, but when he obviously didn't join in, she stopped and said seriously, "I miss you, Bren."

Brendan took a deep, shuddering breath and stared unseeing at the hotel-room scene of Paris on the wall opposite the bed. "I miss you, too," he said.

There was a sudden buzzing sound coming through the phone. "Oh, Lord, there goes my beeper," Cassie wailed. "Gotta run. I love you."

"You, too," Brendan answered, but before he'd got the words out, he heard a click and knew that she was gone. Sinking back against the pillows, he dropped the receiver softly back onto the phone and lay cocooned in depression, jealous of her beeper, her career, her life, which went on so smoothly without him when he wasn't there. He loved her with all his heart, and after tonight's game he realized that chances were he had nothing to offer her at all.

Three days later he flew home. The only person he told was Jeremiah Reed. And Reed, he noticed, did nothing to stop him.

"I want further X rays," he told Reed when he called the trainer in his room that morning. "My arm still feels like hell. It's more than just tired, Jer. There's something wrong."

Reed didn't dispute it. "Give me a call as soon as you talk to the doctor," he ordered. "I'll discuss it with Ballard then."

"Fine." Except Brendan had no intention of discussing his arm with Cassie. She might have been the doctor Gene had chosen to deal with his arm, but now that he was off the disabled list, he wasn't going back to her. This time he was seeing Gene. He didn't expect that the receptionist would give him any trouble—Gene was, after all, the doctor he would normally see—but he didn't know exactly how he felt when she told him that of course he could see Dr. Phillips, then added that Dr. Hart had gone to Palo Alto for the day to deliver a talk. He didn't know whether he was relieved or not, but he was not really surprised. Though Cassie hadn't mentioned it, it was just one more indication of how busy, complicated and involved her life was and how very little he could contribute to it. What did she need with a washed-up pitcher on top of all her other responsibilities? "Tell Dr. Phillips I'll be there before five," he told the receptionist.

Five hours later he was in Gene Phillips's office, staring at Gene's long, discouraging face.

"Bone spurs," Gene said, gesturing at the latest set of X rays. "Look here." He pointed. "And the edge of the radial head is flattened."

"But why now?" Brendan demanded. Even though he had guessed things weren't good, it still wasn't easy to hear his worst fears confirmed. Straws were for grasping at, after all.

Gene shrugged. "Degenerative effects that resulted from the injury, most likely. Complicated by stress on the elbow from all this pitching you've been doing."

"But why didn't it hurt at first, then? Why didn't something show up on the Cybex tests?"

"Because the tests were isolated incidents and you

weren't doing as much to it then. The buildup, your comeback actually, is what caused part of the problem. When we look at test results, we're looking at the peak torque. It would be easy to miss the problem if it even showed up at all," Gene explained, hauling out one of Brendan's graphs and showing him the curve with his finger.

"And the prognosis?" Brendan hunched forward in his chair, his fingers laced as he stared hard at Gene across the width of the dark wood desk.

"Not good."

Brendan let out his breath slowly, suddenly aware that he had been holding it. With deliberate care he unlaced his fingers and unfolded his body from the chair, standing up stiffly, feeling fragile, as if one wrong move would crumble him altogether. "I guess that's it, then," he said quietly, offering Gene a handshake. "Thanks."

"Hey, wait a sec." Gene bounced out of his chair and intercepted him at the door. "I'll do what I can for you. Surgery might help. I'll talk to Cassie, and we can—"

"No! No, don't talk to Cassie." He forced himself to say it calmly. "I—" He raked trembling fingers through his hair. "I'll talk to her myself."

Gene patted his shoulder sympathetically. "If that's what you want." He opened the door for Brendan and followed him down the hall to the waiting room. "I'll be waiting to hear from you, then."

"Right," Brendan said. *You'll have a long wait,* he thought as he sagged in the seat of his car and stared unseeing at the steering wheel. So much for confidence, he thought bitterly as he turned the key and the engine roared to life. So much for success. Blinking back the moisture he felt in his eyes, he sighed and backed the car carefully out of the parking space. And so much for love. At least for a while.

IN FOUR MORE DAYS Brendan would be home. Cassie shifted her briefcase stuffed with medical papers from one hand to the other and groped in her purse for her house key. The day had been a harder day than most. She had been even busier than usual, having to fit in an afternoon flight to San Jose, a drive to Palo Alto, a speech to a local orthopedic surgeons' group, a quick meal with the doctor from San Jose who had invited her to speak, then the return flight home. Thank God Gene had agreed to cover for her at the hospital. And double thanks to the Almighty for the arrival the following week of their partner-to-be, a transplant from the Bay Area named Tyler Moran who had been recommended highly and who had been delighted to come. No more delighted than she and Gene were to have him, Cassie thought wearily as she let herself into the cool darkness of the house.

With Tyler Moran established in their practice, she ought to have one more weekend off per month, fewer nights on call, and if people just continued breaking bones at a reasonable rate, a lower patient load overall. And more time for the boys. And Brendan. Even though she scarcely had seen him during the time he was at home, though at the ball park every night, she could still feel the warmth of his arms through the night, still hear him breathing softly and evenly when she ventured to kiss his warm lips and stubbled chin before she slipped away to work.

For eight days now she had had nothing except a rare glimpse of him on television and two brief phone calls, neither particularly memorable and both feats of acting during which she had tried to sound positive and cheerful and confident, buoying up his obviously sinking spirits when she would rather have told him, "Pack it in and come home. It's not going to work. Quit. I love you. That's enough."

But one didn't say that to Brendan. Not when he got that determined, implacable look in his eye or that hard edge to his voice. One just crossed one's fingers and hoped for the best. Right now she wondered what the best could possibly be.

The first thing she noticed was that his running shoes were missing from their station by the door to the patio. Odd. But then maybe Steven or Keith had moved them. Still, having tripped over them for more than a full week now, it didn't seem likely they would have. She reached for the phone to call her mother and let her know she was home so that Raymond could bring the boys home. That was when she saw the note.

She read it twice before she could move from the spot. Then she dashed down the hallway to his room, jerking open the door to stare at the bare mattress, the clean dresser top, the empty closet. "Damn it all, Brendan Peter Craig," she railed aloud as if he could hear her. "You can't do this to me! *You can't!*"

Instead of calling her mother and telling her it was time to bring the boys home, she asked if Elsa and Raymond could keep them for the night.

"Of course, dear," Elsa agreed. "They're just watching the ball game with Raymond. Have you heard from Brendan tonight?"

Have I ever, Cassie thought, her fingers gripping the note, now crumpled beyond saving in her hand. "Yes, I have," she said tightly. "Bye, Mother. I have to run."

She wasn't sure how she knew he would have gone back to his apartment. It just seemed logical, and judging from his state of mind when he wrote the note, Cassie didn't think he was long on imagination right now. He didn't seem to be able to see farther than the end of his nose. Make that *elbow*, she amended, crashing the gears of her Mazda as she zoomed back down the driveway and headed west.

The setting sun cast everything in a vivid orange glow, the sort of peaceful sunset that artists use to evoke calm serenity, acceptance and appreciation of God's handiwork. Cassie didn't notice. She jammed on the brakes of the car, parking it next to his in the narrow driveway, barely registering satisfaction at having been right, after all, before she tore up the steps to his oceanfront apartment like a miniature tornado. Huffing for breath, she banged on the door.

It took a full minute for him to respond, and she was considering kicking it when finally it opened and the love of her life stood before her, bleary-eyed and unshaved, reeking of bourbon and wearing only a pair of disreputable cutoffs low on his hips.

"Damn," he said.

"And a very good evening to you, too." This was the man she had been agonizing over for the past week?

"You got my note." It wasn't a question. He stepped back and let her come into the living room, which she did, brushing past him, striding on until she reached the far wall, then spinning around and confronting him, her hands on her hips and her heart, she knew, in her eyes.

"What do you mean, 'Let's call it off'?"

"I can't marry you now."

"Why not? Or is that supposed to remain a mystery?" She was seething. She knew she sounded hysterical, but what did he expect? After all his "I love yous," a terse note that said, "I need time. Let's call it off. I'll be in touch," did not lend itself to a calm, dignified response. At least not from her. She wanted to shake him. Her heart felt as if it would pound right through her chest.

"Of course it's not a mystery. I can't marry you, because I can't bring anything to our marriage!" He jammed his fists into the pockets of his cutoffs and hunched his shoulders as he glared across the room at her. He sounded as if it were all her fault.

"You don't love me?"

"Of course I love you!"

"Then you're bringing that," she said quietly, more relieved than she could fathom. He loved her. Of course they could work it out. She breathed a bit easier.

"Love isn't enough," he persisted obstinately.

"Of course it is!"

"No." Brendan scowled at her. "Not for me it isn't."

Cassie sighed, hugging her arms to her chest. "Brendan, this is crazy. Less than four weeks ago you asked me to marry you. What's changed?"

"I have. I can't play baseball anymore. I can't pitch!"

"I don't care."

"Well, I do!" His eyes shot fire. She saw hatred in them. And pain. Tons and tons of pain, weighing him down, flattening his spirit.

"Brendan, you can do other things."

"Yeah?" His answer was pure sarcasm. "What? Bake brownies? Sew buttons on shirts? Swell."

"That's useful," she argued, but she knew she was losing ground.

"Sure. And I didn't mind for a time as long as I knew I had another career to go back to. But I don't have that now, Cass. I used to have a future; now I don't. I used to be a success. Now I'm not!" He turned his back to her, staring out the door at the breakers crashing against the wide sandy shore. "You tell me, Cass," he said bleakly. "Now what've I got?"

"Me." She said it hopefully, praying that it would be enough, watching the tense bunching of the muscles in his back, the tautness of his jaw as he slowly turned around to face her again.

"No, Cass. It wouldn't work."

"But why?" She was wailing at him now, wanting to shake him till his teeth rattled, and he just stared at her, his face stubborn and cold.

"Because I need my self-respect."

"Pride," she countered hotly. "It's pride you're talking about, isn't it? Dumb stubborn pride."

"Probably." He didn't seem to mind admitting it. "I do love you, you know," he went on doggedly, apparently deciding she needed a ray of hope. "I don't mean let's call it off forever. I just need some time."

"For what?"

"To be a success again. To find myself something else."

"So let's get married and you can find yourself something else."

He shook his head. "No."

Cassie stared, all her hurt, her disappointment, her disbelief, bubbling up inside her, coming to a boil. "You're serious about this?"

Brendan sucked in a sharp breath. "Yes."

"Well, suit yourself, Brendan Craig," she snapped, anger roiling to the surface as she brushed past him toward the door. "But damn you, you made me a whole, loving, living breathing woman instead of a one-dimensional robot who mends broken bones. I loved you, and I can love another man. Don't expect me to sit on the shelf and wait!" She stumbled down the stairs as the tears began to fall, praying that he would run after her, stop her. But through her weeping eyes she noted, as she slammed the car into reverse and backed swiftly out of his driveway, that Brendan never appeared at all.

Chapter Thirteen

"Scum," Lainie pronounced, adjusting the veil of her wedding gown across her face and peering out at Cassie like a cat behind a lace curtain. "Fink. Dregs of the universe, that's what he is. The world is full of interesting men. Griff's roommate, for instance. I'll introduce you to him at the reception."

In spite of herself, Cassie laughed. It was the first time in nearly two weeks she had felt her face crack into a semblance of a smile, though she had certainly done her share of crying. "No, thanks. I've had enough of interesting men to last me a lifetime."

"But you *need* one," Lainie protested, turning to stare importunately at Cassie, who was fiddling with her yellow rose bouquet.

But not just *any* one. Only Brendan Craig, Cassie thought miserably. And it was obvious that Brendan didn't need her. If he had, he would have turned to her when his pitching career crumbled. He would have wanted her support, her encouragement. Instead, he had chosen to walk away. Maybe he would come back. But right now she was hurting so badly that if he did, she didn't know if she would want him.

He wasn't going to learn that from her, though. She would get through Lainie and Griff's wedding without that happening if it killed her. And it might, too. Why hadn't Griffin had a brother to be his best man? Why hadn't Lainie had a sister to be matron of honor? How were the two of them going to walk through this ceremony together, paired off constantly, smiling for the cameras that would abound? She hadn't seen him since she had left his apartment the day he had walked out of her house, but he had had an ongoing effect on her just the same. She knew for a fact that she looked a wreck. No amount of blusher or artful arrangement of her unruly curls could change that. She had lost five pounds, and her dress, which had previously been only a bit loose, now hung like a potato sack. In an earlier age she probably would have been described as "consumptive." Now she looked merely worn out and, as Lainie said, "ethereal."

"Ready?" One of Lainie's million cousins poked her head in the door to ask.

Lainie laughed. "And raring to go!" She gave Cassie a happy grin that immediately turned sympathetic as she recalled her friend's plight.

Cassie managed a wan smile and gave Lainie a hug, trying not to crush the floor-length Spanish-lace dress. "I'm really happy for you." She meant it; if only her voice hadn't broken on the words.

Lainie squeezed her tightly. "It just worked out," she said softly. "Maybe things will for you and Brendan, too."

Cassie hoped so. Maybe when she saw him again he would be just as he always had been. Maybe the past two weeks would turn into nothing more than a bad dream.

"Let's go!" the cousin exhorted.

They went.

Cassie had been anticipating Lainie and Griff's wedding with almost as much joy as her own. It would be, she had joked to Brendan, "our trial run." But now the solemn beauty of the service, with its softly spoken vows and sweet guitar music, only reminded Cassie of her own empty future and Brendan's "maybe someday" vow. She couldn't bring herself to look at him; she would have dissolved on the spot. How she knew he looked as gaunt and grim as she did was a mystery.

He hardly seemed like the man she had known at all. He was so aloof, so utterly absorbed in the correct performance of his duties as best man. He might as well have been a robot when he escorted her back up the aisle at the ceremony's end. His touch was as cool as steel. "I love you," he had shouted at her just two weeks before, but he was as poker-faced as a palace guard now. He should have been an actor, Cassie thought. She wondered bitterly if she should suggest it to him as a prospective career.

The picture taking was a nightmare. She smiled, posed, preened and, once, at the photographer's request, looked deeply into Brendan's eyes. *Pretend he's Gene,* she told herself. *Or Lem Ballard.* But it wasn't possible, because, for an instant, she saw a flame in his eyes, a hungry longing that proved he was miserable, too.

"Put your arms around her," the photographer commanded Griffin. But for a second Brendan's arms lifted as if to embrace Cassie. Then, as he realized his mistake, a look of stark pain crossed his face, and his hands fell to his sides.

"How've you been?" he asked, his voice rough as they edged their way into the crowded reception hall.

"Busy." It was helping her to stay sane.

His mouth twisted, and he shoved his hands into the elegantly cut black trousers he wore. "It figures."

Cassie itched to slap him. It wasn't *her* fault that her job was demanding! "And you?" she asked, striving for the politeness that would let him know that in her eyes he was simply another wedding guest.

Brendan shrugged, studying the tops of his highly polished shoes.

Cassie sighed. As a reconciliation scene, it wasn't promising. She opened her mouth, determined to try at least once to jolt him out of his stubbornness when a voice at her side interrupted.

"Are you Cassie Hart? Lainie said to bring you some punch and introduce myself. I'm Chase Whitelaw, Griff's former roommate."

Cassie turned to have a glass of punch thrust into her hand and a devastatingly handsome grin dazzle her from an equally handsome, obviously Native American face. Trust Lainie, she thought, matchmaking at her own wedding! She glanced at Brendan to see if he was aware of the obvious purpose of the introduction. His face was inscrutable. He wasn't flying into a jealous rage, but he didn't look particularly welcoming, either. "Thanks. Yes, I'm Cassie," she told Chase. "And this is my fiancé, Brendan Craig."

Chase nodded, though he appeared slightly taken aback by the news. Lainie must have neglected to mention her engagement. "We've met through Griff," he said. "Craig—" he acknowledged Brendan with a thin smile "—I didn't realize you were getting married, too. When?"

"We haven't set a date." Brendan spoke with such a lack of enthusiasm that Cassie was mortified. Why had she ever even mentioned it?

"I see," Chase said. Obviously he didn't at all but was astute enough to sense undercurrents that the bride clearly hadn't warned him about. "Lainie looked lovely today, didn't you think?" He changed the subject adroitly, and Cassie latched on to his choice with such gratitude that she didn't even notice that sometime during the conversation Brendan had left.

Half an hour later, having searched the reception hall from one end to the other, she realized that he hadn't only deserted her; he had vanished altogether. And with him went her hopes that he might have come to his senses at last. She sagged against one of the crowded tables, overwhelmed by noise, the flashing of cameras and a fierce, elemental longing for the man who had left.

"Where's Brendan?" Lainie demanded, waving a cake knife as she darted past.

"Gone."

Lainie scowled. "He's an idiot. How could he leave when he looks at you with his heart in his eyes?"

Cassie shrugged, feeling the return of a familiar pain in her midsection. "He could have me whenever he wanted me," she said in a low voice.

Lainie sighed, shaking her head. "Well," she said, ever practical, "Chase is still here. You needn't wait for Brendan if you don't want."

"I know."

The trouble was, she did want. Even when she had told him she wouldn't wait for him, she had known it was a lie. She only wanted to hurt him as he was so desperately hurting her. But for two weeks she hadn't been able to get him out of her mind. He had turned her into a living, loving, fully adult woman. The trouble was, Brendan was the only man she loved and lived for. Chase Whitelaw might be attractive and fun; but he wasn't Brendan.

Brendan was the one who mattered—the only one who mattered to her. And he was too damned stubborn to see it.

"OW! HELL." Brendan bent to rub his bare toes, which had just connected with the bottom drawer of his dresser. *It's exactly what you deserve, idiot,* he lectured himself, hopping about on one foot as he flung several sweat shirts and pairs of faded jeans into the duffel bag that lay gaping on his bed.

"Punching and kicking inanimate objects is counterproductive," he said aloud in his best Hamilton Craig voice. Well, for once his father was right. But then, what was productive? Stewing around his apartment trying to put his life together like some crazy jigsaw puzzle definitely wasn't. He'd tried that.

For two weeks he had been calling around, checking out possible ideas for a future career—something besides being a bubble-gum salesman or running a restaurant—and he was no nearer satsifaction than he had been when he had walked out of Gene Phillips's office. Farther, if possible, for now he had alienated Cassie, too. He had told himself he was doing all right, that she hadn't meant it when she said she wouldn't wait for him. My God, she loved him, didn't she? But then today—at the wedding. God, talk about torture. She had been so polite, so "porcelain not about to crack," and seeing her had put him into a rare frenzy of need for her. And then there had been Whitelaw.

Brendan sank down on the bed and cradled his head in his hands, the scene at the reception running through his head with the thoroughness of a slow-motion instant replay, just as agonizing the fiftieth time as it had been the first. Until then he had always liked Chase Whitelaw. The scion of a newspaper magnate, a crack investigative reporter in his own right, Chase was witty, entertaining and successful. Exactly the sort of man a woman like Cassie Farrell Hart ought to marry. And she hadn't even looked up when Brendan had walked away.

"Did you want her to run after you?" he asked himself sarcastically. "You walked out on her, after all."

True. But visions of Cassie with Whitelaw provoked him into action. He had spent years of his life trying to impress Cassie Farrell, all to no avail. And he wasn't going to be able to do it now if he stayed in the same city with her where the temptation to give up and simply run to her arms plagued him every hour of the day. And night. He needed a little room. Some breathing space. And some inspiration. A cabin in Oregon, for example. There was the place to get his act together, the place where he had spent the best days of his life.

He finished packing his bag and sorted through his desk, looking for ideas, for direction. Letters from companies that had once asked him to endorse products, letters from schools that had been interested in having him as a coach. He bundled all of them together, then packed his typewriter into its case so he could use it to make inquiries and replies. His eyes lit on a notebook he had tossed on top of his desk. Opening it, he flipped through a few pages. "The Adventures of Fellwell." He smiled wryly. He had been writing them down for the boys. Once he had got back to pitching, he hadn't had the time. Well, now he had nothing but time. Maybe he ought to finish it.

Shrugging, he tossed the notebook on top of the growing pile of things to put in the car. Good old Fell-well. Even he had more of a future than a washed-up major league pitcher who had never grown up.

"SEE THE PAPER this morning?" Gene asked when Cassie dragged into the office late Monday morning just in time for her first appointment.

"The headlines," Cassie said absently. World crises seemed insignificant compared to the everyday chaos of her own life of late. "The Middle East, wasn't it?"

"I meant the sports section." Gene pulled it out from under his arm and folded it open, then tossed it to her before he disappeared into his office. "It's a great shot."

Brendan? Cassie's heart lurched. Yes, there he was, a wooden smile on his face as he stood next to Griffin, who had his arm around Lainie. And there, on the other side of Lainie, stood an equally wooden Cassie Hart. She shut her eyes. Then, gathering her wits from the four winds to which they had scattered, she read the caption about the major league umpire's wedding. Not all of it registered, only the part that read, "Highly renowned orthopedic surgeon Cassandra Hart was matron of honor. Best man was formerly outstanding Mustang pitcher Brendan Craig."

Blinding intuition had never been one of Cassie's prime assets, but she was gifted with it now. "Oh, my God."

Her voice came out as a mere breath, as if someone had knocked the air right out of her. In fact, someone had. Put succinctly, with her "highly renowned" neatly juxtaposed with his "formerly outstanding," she saw in a moment of stark clarity exactly where Brendan was coming from. To have one's "former" success compared so blatantly with one's fiancée's present success had to be devastating. And success, per se, wasn't the whole issue, either. She remembered vividly the grim look on his face as he had turned toward her to tell her that their marriage wouldn't work.

"I need my self-respect," he had said. At the time that had seemed mere foolishness to her. She had wanted him in her life on her terms, as he had been when he was caring for the boys, when he had been no more than an appendage to her own life. He had wanted a career in his own right, and she hadn't understood him at all.

The granola bar she had gobbled on her way from the hospital to the office sat like a lead weight in her stomach as she braced herself with her palms flat on the oak surface of her wide desk and contemplated her reflection in the polished wood. The "highly renowned" surgeon stared back at her miserably before tears clouded her vision and she wiped them determinedly away. "Think, oh, brilliant one," she commanded herself. "Get your brain in gear and decide what you have to do so you don't ruin the rest of your life!"

For it was supremely obvious to her now that it wasn't just Brendan who had to get himself together and make changes. She had some changing to do, too. All along she had been expecting him to mold his life to fit hers. She was a surgeon, after all, a person with a responsible, demanding, all-consuming job! In fact, she realized now that she let herself really think hard about it, her life wasn't one that even she wanted anymore. It was too demanding, too all consuming. It was too much and not enough at the same time. Oregon had shown her that.

After her two weeks with Brendan there, she knew she would never again be wholly satisfied with a treadmill existence where people were no more than charts and fractures and her loved ones no more than responsibilities. Brendan had set her on the road to understanding even before their idyll on the seacoast, but it was there that she had given herself to him completely, trusted him completely, made with him a new way of life. He was more than just an adjunct to her existence, a bit of light relief. He was the center now, the man who gave it meaning.

"God, I'm dumb."

The words echoed around her office, bouncing off the string of diplomas and the rows of thick medical journals, the color-coordinated office furniture and the sterile ivory walls. The realization that she was the one who had to make some changes was, she knew immediately, the hard part. Once she had done it, she was on sure ground again. If there was one thing Cassie Farrell Hart was good at, one thing at which she positively *shone*, it was making and carrying out plans of action, setting goals and accomplishing them.

"Your first appointment is here," Elda buzzed her on the intercom to announce.

"In a minute," Cassie muttered. "Just hang on."

Going around to her desk, she pulled a piece of blank paper out of the top drawer and sat down, tapping a pencil thoughtfully against her front teeth. Then she made a brief note, tapped some more, then scribbled furiously. Thirty minutes later, Elda buzzed again.

"Cassie? Are you there?"

"Coming." She stood up quickly, folded the paper and stuck it in her lab-coat pocket along with all the other tools of her trade. Funny, she'd never noticed it feeling so heavy before. "Elda," she said into the intercom, "tell Gene I'd like to see him at lunch."

It took her a full week to accomplish everything on her list. It wasn't easy, and unlike all her other previous goals, this one was markedly different. It depended ultimately on another person to accomplish it. Everything she did, if Brendan rejected her, she might have done for naught. But even as she felt again the nervous twitter in her stomach and the clammy palms that she wiped on her slacks as she settled herself behind the wheel of her car for the fateful drive to his apartment, she knew it was a move she had to make. What would Brendan say, though, when she told him?

SHE HAD ENVISIONED ten or fifteen different scenarios—everything from his sweeping her into his arms to his shouting a resounding, "No!" and sending her away. She had failed completely to imagine what would happen if he simply wasn't there.

But he wasn't. His silver BMW was nowhere in sight. The drapes were drawn. No one answered the door.

"Now what?" she asked herself as she tapped her foot on the smooth planks of his narrow porch. He might only be gone for the day. But somehow she didn't think so. The apartment looked abandoned. Who would know? Well, Ballard might. He had certainly demanded to know every step Brendan had taken before. But she doubted he would be so diligent a watchdog now. She wasn't even sure he "owned" Brendan anymore. And from everything Gene told her, Brendan was convinced he was washed up as a pitcher. No doubt it wouldn't have been hard to convince Ballard to share that opinion. Who else, then? His father? Not likely. Her mind groped, then sank.

Susan...

It took a fair bit of courage before she could get herself to make that call. She drove home again and stewed, pacing the den as if mileage alone could give her courage. Finally, she picked up the phone. Oddly, once she had, the rest came easily. Susan wasn't an ogre or rival; she was Brendan's friend, exactly what he had been telling her all along.

"Thank God you called," Susan said. "He's in Oregon. Miserable. Get a move on! I'm sure he'll welcome you with open arms."

Cassie wasn't sure at all. She couldn't remember having chased a man in her entire life—not even down a hall, much less seven hundred miles. But then, she reminded herself, this was the new, improved Cassie Hart—one who went out of her way for other people, one who, above all else, loved Brendan Craig. She went.

IT HAD JUST GONE DUSK, and at first Cassie thought the orange glow beyond the last curve up the bumpy gravel road to the cabin was only a sign of the dying sunset. A good romantic setting, she congratulated herself, but all the same she crossed her fingers for luck as she gripped the steering wheel. The car was the same one Brendan had rented when they were there before. She considered that a good omen, but she was grasping for straws, and she knew it. Everything depended on what Brendan said when she confronted him with the changes she had made in her life. Maybe a romantic sunset would help.

But when she came over the rise and spied the cabin ahead, what she saw was not the sunset but a roaring fire. Her headlights caught the silhouette of a man tossing something onto the flames, then stepping back, his hands on his hips, to watch until he became aware of the car and turned to stare into the glare of her light beams.

Cassie's fingers tightened at the sight of him. With every fiber of her being she wanted to stop the car, jump out and run to his arms. But she couldn't. Maybe even now he wouldn't want her. Before anything else, they had to talk. Easing the car to a stop, she opened the door. Brendan still stood by the fire, unmoving in the flickering light, a barely discernible scowl on his face.

"I've got a burning permit," he called as she stepped out.

So he hadn't recognized her in the darkness. She took a deep breath, unable to suppress the smile in her voice. "Good. I hope we're going to need it." She started to walk toward him.

"Cassie?" He sounded stunned. Then he said, "Cassie?" again when she was close enough to be clearly recognizable. Now his voice was wary.

For a week she had rehearsed what she would say, and now, confronting him at a distance of no more than three feet, all sensible thought fled. Even verbal quips deserted her, and she stood twisting her hands in front of her, drinking him in with her eyes, tracing lovingly those rough, unshaved cheeks, the downturned mustache, the taut, firm body that she had come to know so well.

"I—I came to tell you that I've changed my life," she stammered. There, at least it was to the point!

Brendan's eyes shut, and his shoulders seemed to sag. Was that pain she saw on his face? So much for the direct approach. Taking a quick step forward, she touched his arm with nerveless fingers. He flinched.

"You were right," she went on.

"That we shouldn't get married?" His voice was hoarse and cracking. She saw a muscle in his jaw twitch.

"No. That there has to be more to our relationship than you mopping up after me. I love you, Brendan, and any success you find I want us to find together." She took a deep breath. "I know just saying it doesn't make it so. And I wanted to convince you, so I've pulled out. I left."

"What?"

"I quit!" Where was his jubilation, his enthusiasm, damn it? Was he just going to stand there and stare at her, a look of sheer incredulity on his face?

Then, just when she was about to explode, Brendan started to laugh. "You *quit*?" He gripped her arms with both hands, and she could feel the shaking convulse his body. "You honest-to-God quit?"

"Yes." No matter how many scenarios she had come up with, she had never *ever* dreamed of this one! "What's so funny?" she demanded.

"Who's going to support me, then?" he asked, humor still reflected in the deep blue of his eyes.

"What do you mean?" It was Cassie's turn to stare.

He slipped his arm around her shoulders, and she leaned against him instinctively, relishing the warm, hard, familiar feel of him with a sense of having finally come home. "Come here," he said, leading her toward his BMW, which was parked in the clearing by the cabin. The trunk was open, and she saw two obviously stuffed duffel bags and a typewriter case inside. "I was on my way home, Cass. I don't care if I never do more than bake brownies the rest of my life. Living with you is what makes it worthwhile. I tossed all my clever attempts at 'success' on that bonfire. I reckoned to be home by tomorrow afternoon."

Cassie's knees almost buckled beneath her as she assimilated what he was saying. "But you were right," she protested weakly. "All that business about self-respect. That was right! I admit I couldn't see it at the time. But later I realized that I had never really understood what loving meant before. Not the way I ought to have been loving you, I mean. I thought it meant fitting you into my life-style, letting you follow me around and fill up whatever time was left after my job." She was ashamed to think how shallow she had been, embarrassed to even admit it, but she owed it to him. That much at least. "It wasn't until you were gone," she confessed, "that I realized how very much more you were."

Brendan opened his mouth, but she laid her fingers against his lips. "No, don't interrupt me now. This is hard for me, Bren. I don't admit to being shortsighted and unfeeling easily. At least let me get it out."

He nodded, but his arm tightened around her as he leaned against the fender of the car.

"All my life I worked for goals that I thought were everything I ever wanted. And when you came along, you woke me up. I realized there was more to life than that. I fell in love with you, and I could hardly believe it. It was like a bonus, an extra-added attraction I hadn't even bargained on. Another perk, I guess." She wrinkled her nose in self-disgust. "And I couldn't understand how you could just up and walk away. I thought *I* ought to be enough!" She grinned shamefacedly. "Talk about conceit!"

"Cass, you are enough," he insisted, turning her in his arms so that they stood facing each other, knees and thighs touching, their eyes locked.

"No, I'm not." She had at least figured out that much. How they would work things out together, she didn't know. She only knew it was a partnership, a two-person commitment to shared goals, not one person leading and the other tagging along. "What you need is important to me, Bren. Every bit as important as being a surgeon is. It wasn't easy, quitting like that. It's something I've been working toward for most of my life."

"So go back to it, Cass! I learned something, too, this week. There are times when you'll be on top and times when I will, times when you'll be down and times when I will. You were right about the pride bit, Cass. But I know that now. My God, you don't have to quit for me!" He looked genuinely alarmed.

She shook her head, a smile lighting her face. "I have to do it for *me* and for our relationship. You were right months ago when you said we should get another partner. When we came back from Oregon and I got sucked back into the maelstrom again, I knew we had to get busy and find one right now. We found two good prospects. One of them joined us the week you moved out of the house." She saw a flicker of painful recollection cross Brendan's face, and she lifted her hand and touched the rough whiskers of his cheek. "When I finally accepted the idea that you were not the appendage to my life but the heart of it, I got in touch with the other one. He isn't certain he wants to settle in L.A., but he's willing to try it. I've taken a leave of absence to give him time to get established. If it works out, fine. If not..." She shrugged. "I want to go back sometime. If not there, somewhere. I want to be a doctor, Bren. I won't ever leave that behind me. But without you, wherever I go, it isn't where I want to be. So here I am." She spread her hands, offering herself to him. "Do you mind?"

"Mind?" He sounded incredulous. "I can't quite believe it."

"But you'll marry me?" she persisted.

"I'll marry you," he choked out as he wrapped his arms around her, his lips meeting hers with a desperation she recognized only too well, for it matched her own. The bonfire was no more than a candle compared to the flames that raged within her as she pressed against him, needing to be closer. Her hands slipped beneath his windbreaker and slid over the soft wool of his shirt, kneading the muscled span of his back. Brendan molded her length to his as his hungry mouth possessed her. She nibbled at his mustache, tasting woodsmoke, beer and the faintly salty hint of something purely Brendan. Simply being in his arms overwhelmed her, and her knees trembled. Pulling back, Brendan held her up as he drew a long, shaky breath.

"I need a bucket of water to douse this fire," he said.

Cassie snuggled against him. "Which fire?" she teased.

"Guess."

She followed him like his shadow while he carried several buckets from the cabin to the yard, carefully extinguishing the flames and spreading the remaining ashes. Then, on his last trip, she stopped at the car and gathered up both of his duffel bags and lugged them back to the house. "Were you really coming home?"

He was building another fire, in the fireplace this time. She shut the cabin door against the cool autumn breeze off the ocean and went to put the bags down by the couch. "Absolutely. You weren't the only one to see the light, Cass." He straightened up and met her gaze, his own softer and more loving than she ever remembered seeing it. "Seeing you at Griff's wedding damned near did me in. There you were, the woman of my dreams, and I didn't feel I had any right to you.

And Whitelaw..." He shook his head, grimacing at the still-painful memories. "God, Whitelaw."

"Who?"

"Who?" Brendan looked as if he couldn't believe his ears. "You remember. Griff's roommate."

"Oh, him." She had a vague memory of Lainie mentioning the man, of the man himself even. But it was nothing compared to what she remembered about Brendan that day!

"Oh, him?" Brendan rolled his eyes in mock despair. "You mean I worried my guts out over nothing?" He glared at her, his thumbs hooked in his belt loops, making him resemble a gunslinger.

Cassie smiled, sinking back against the scattered pillows on the couch. "What were you worried about?"

"That I'd blown it. That I had been so stupid, telling you that I couldn't marry you until I was successful that you would turn around and jump for the next successful handsome jerk that came along!"

"Thank you very much!" she said dryly, not knowing whether to be incensed or to laugh; he looked so righteous and indignant. But as soon as she said that, he had the grace to grin sheepishly.

"Well, you told me you wouldn't wait," he defended himself.

"I wanted to hurt you the way you were hurting me."

He bowed his head. "You did." He sighed, tracing a pattern on the braid rug with the toe of his sneaker. "After I saw you with Whitelaw, I knew I couldn't just sit there in my apartment and make phone calls, trying out various schemes I didn't really like when all I really wanted to do was run home to you. I thought I needed some space, some perspective. I thought I'd better figure out what I was going to do with my life—and fast! Before Whitelaw or someone else got you!" He shrugged and then rubbed his hand beneath his collar, massaging the tense muscles at the back of his neck. Then he crossed the room and sat down on the couch beside her.

"What made you decide to come home, then?" she prodded gently, laying her hand on his knee.

Brendan's hand covered it with his own. "Fellwell."

"Huh?"

"My detective. You remember?"

Of course she remembered. "I don't see the connection, though," she told him, searching his eyes, seeing the smile in them.

"I was writing up the Fellwell stories for Keith and Steven. And the more I wrote, the more he seemed like a parable for my own life. He was a successful detective in spite of himself, because when he didn't know what the heck to do next, he went home. Mrs. Fellwell loved him," he told her softly as he stretched his other arm along the back of the couch and drew her against him, then leaned toward her and brushed the thick soft bristles of his mustache against Cassie's lips and cheek, teasing, tickling.

"She did, hmm?" Cassie's fingers touched his mustache, toying with it, loving the feel of it as it brushed against her hand and mouth. It was funny, she thought, all the little, endearing things about him she had missed.

"Of course. Gave him all sorts of inspiration. All he needed in his life was someone who believed in him." Brendan swallowed, and his thick, dark eyelashes dropped suddenly, shielding his eyes from view. When he lifted them again, he was smiling. "All I need is you."

"The new, improved me," Cassie corrected, leaning her head against his chest so she could hear the steady, strong beat of his heart. "The one who believes in you."

Brendan laughed; she could feel it. "To match the revised me?" he said. "The one who realizes that partners aren't always on equal footing. Relationships change, I guess. Sometimes you'll be dependent on me; sometimes I'll be dependent on you. The important thing—the part I almost missed out on entirely—is having the relationship at all. That's what matters, Cass." He sighed.

Cassie smiled and snuggled against him. "Aren't we smart, though?" she murmured, then lifted her head and kissed him deeply.

She felt him shiver against her. "Very," he growled as he shifted on the couch so that he could lie back and draw her down on top of him.

"But at the moment," she continued, rubbing her nose gently back and forth against his, "I'd say we were definitely on equal footing."

"How so?" he mumbled.

"Neither one of us is gainfully employed."

Brendan nipped her nose. "On the contrary, my love. At the moment I think we are both very well employed indeed." Their lips met again. The fires snapped and sparked both without and within. "Don't you agree?"

She closed her eyes and hugged him tightly, holding him against her heart. "Oh, yes, Brendan."

How long they remained that way, just holding each other, savoring the gentlest of touches, she wasn't sure. It didn't matter. They had time and love and each other. The rest, Cassie thought, would come. "I love you, Brendan Craig," she said.

He opened his eyes and looked up at her, his expression serious, dark with emotion. "I still have to find a job, Cass."

"*We* have to find jobs, Brendan. *And* rescue my mother from the boys *and* decide where we want to live *and* how we're going to cope."

"You think we can manage it?" He was looking intent, grave, most un-Brendan-like.

"Of course I do," she said, framing his face with her hands, then letting them slide down his neck and across his chest. "I believe in *us*. But," she added, her hands exploring farther, tugging his shirt out of his waistband, tracing the line of his ribs, then arrowing down his abdomen. "I don't think we're quite ready yet."

Brendan groaned and submitted willingly as her hands worked their magic on his body. "Why not?"

"Because," she said, smiling, "I think we need some further hands-on training. Shall I demonstrate?"

Quicksilver sparkled in his eyes as his hands moved in accompaniment to hers. "Please do," he said.

She did.

Readers rave about Harlequin American Romance!

"...the best series of modern romances I have read...great, exciting, stupendous, wonderful."

—S.E., Coweta, Oklahoma*

"...they are absolutely fantastic...going to be a smash hit and hard to keep on the bookshelves."

—P.D., Easton, Pennsylvania

"The American line is great. I've enjoyed every one I've read so far."

—W.M.K., Lansing, Illinois

"...the best stories I have read in a long time."

—R.H., Northport, New York

*Names available on request.